FOR A POINT OF HONOR
THE COMPLETE CASES OF
RIORDAN, VOLUME 2

THE ARGOSY LIBRARY

FOR A POINT OF HONOR

THE COMPLETE CASES OF RIORDAN, VOLUME 2

VICTOR MAXWELL

INTRODUCTION BY
TERRY SANFORD

COVER BY
LEJAREN HILLER

ILLUSTRATED BY
F.M. FOLLETT

POPULAR PUBLICATIONS · 2024

TABLE OF CONTENTS

INTRODUCTION BY
TERRY SANFORD

AS A VORACIOUS reader who once owned a mystery book store, I found myself in a position years ago where I had read almost all of the works by my favorite authors. New authors were filling some of the gap but not quickly enough and I felt like that robot, Johnny Five, in the movie *Short Circuit:* I needed input! If you can't go forward, then why not try backward? I was fortunate to have two world-class pulp magazine collectors living nearby and they guided me into the pulp scene years before the Internet made it so much easier.

I soon discovered *Flynn's, Detective Fiction Weekly,* and its various incarnations. They were very affordable and I began amassing a pile of them. There were a dozen or so authors I soon was reading avidly. One of them was Victor Maxwell, whose Sgt. Riordan tales really impressed me as being intelligently written. Take the subject of interrogation, for instance. Now sweating a subject under a bright light in a darkened room was strictly Hollywood. Beatings from telephone books and rubber hoses did happen in the old days but you won't find that in a Riordan tale. Instead, you find, just as you do today, an investigator lying to a suspect to try to extract a confession and you find the cops concerned that a smart lawyer might shred their case in court. What was so remarkable about this was that these stories were written from 1925 until 1944. Now that is foresight!

A few years ago, I wrote an article for Steve Lewis's on-line *Mystery*File* where I highlighted some of my favorite *Detective Fiction Weekly* authors, including Victor Maxwell. I mentioned that Mr. Maxwell's name was thought to be a pseudonym and no other information about the author was readily available.

A couple of years later, Steve and I were contacted by a nice gentleman named Don Wilde who happened to be the step-grandson of the author known as Victor Maxwell. Mr. Wilde had Googled the pen name and discovered my article. He was excited to see some recognition of his Grandfather and mentioned that he had some ephemera that had belonged to the author. I asked if any of it was for sale. After several conversations, he offered to give it to me! What a bonanza for a Victor Maxwell fan!

Victor Maxwell was indeed a pseudonym. The author's

real name was known but forgotten after so many years had passed. Maxwell Vietor (1880–1950), a long-time newspaper man wrote as Victor Maxwell. Mr. Vietor was born on July 7, 1880 to Edward W. and Agnes C. (McCahey) Vietor. Edward Vietor was a medical doctor and, within a few years, so was his wife. Edward was the founder of the Brooklyn Bird (watcher's) Club, which exists today.

In January of 1882, Dr. Edward Vietor was summoned to a local residence where ten year-old Bessie Thayer had become gravely ill after eating some candy she bought at the neighborhood candy store. Although Dr. Vietor was the third physician to see the girl that day, his was the correct diagnosis: arsenic poisoning! The girl died in his presence.

Dr. Vietor subsequently testified at a Coroner's Inquest where it was resolved to turn the matter over to the police. There is no conclusion to the case that I've been able to find. Is it likely that this became a story that was mentioned from time to time in the Vietor household and fueled the imagination of young Maxwell? Perhaps.

At some point prior to 1910, the Vietors divorced. Dr. Agnes Vietor and Maxwell moved to the Boston area. Maxwell graduated from Phillips Exeter Academy in 1898. He then attended MIT where the records show, "Maxwell Vietor ex. '02 has been granted a leave of absence for one year by the faculty, in order to take up practical railroad work with the Boston and Maine R.R." Like many a college kid before and after him, Max soon realized that manual labor was not a Hispanic gentleman.

During the next ten years, Maxwell moved back to New York and began his newspaper career, first with the *Sun* and then with New York City News, a news distribution service. There was a sojourn to Wilmington, Delaware and there he may have been an "advance man for a show" as he stated once in an autobiographical piece.

By 1910, the Census Bureau shows him back in Boston, residing with his mother and employed by the *Boston Globe*. It was about this time Maxwell married Helena Haworth and the young couple soon moved to the Vancouver, Washington and Portland, Oregon area.

During 1911, Maxwell made a haphazard attempt at keeping a diary. Some of the entries deal with personal matters but many of the pages just bore the letters, "P.P." Later in the diary those initials were spelled out as "Purple Pulp." This was a humorous reference to his newspaper writing as he hadn't yet begun to write for the pulp magazines.

While the Vietors were expecting a child and Max was employed by a Portland newspaper, he continued to seek better opportunities. The diary notes a job offer from a Helena, Montana newspaper which he turned down. He

also took the test and was considered for a position as a
county motorcycle cop but the diary's June 10th entry
reads, in part, "The motorcycle blows up!" The couple

welcomed their daughter, Alice Mildred into their life on August 15, 1911.

In 1915, tragedy struck the Vietor family. Helena's car was discovered parked by a bridge spanning the Columbia River gorge, but Helena was gone! The river flows into the Pacific Ocean from that spot, which was used by many suicidal people over the years. There was no trace of her after that day. Max would never remarry.

The January 20, 1916 issue of *The Popular Magazine* published the first Victor Maxwell story, "The Little Girl Who Got Lost." A second story appeared in the August issue of the same pulp.

Family history tells us that there were times when Max wrote for the pulps full-time and one of those periods may have been in 1917 when eight stories appeared in *The Popular* in an eight-month period.

At some unknown point in his life, Max ran for Sheriff according to him. He won the Democratic nomination but lost the election. He admits to have done some "high class gumshoeing for the state involving Wobblies" which explains a letter found in his effects from the Governor of Oregon, Ben W. Olcutt and dated April 5, 1920. The body of which reads:

"I am in receipt of your report of April 3rd, which I have read with interest. In this connection and in passing I wish to say a good word for the work you have accomplished for the state in the capacity of special agent and for your highly intelligent and understandable report made in that connection."

Reporting must have lured him back as the pulp stories ended until his first appearance in *Detective Fiction Weekly*

(hereinafter: *DFW*) in 1925. He credits his future rela-
tionship with *DFW* to Don Thompson who was a fairly
prolific *DFW* writer who convinced him to give it a try.
And try he did, as that first story became the first of exactly
one hundred appearances in the detective pulps, thanks, in
part, to a novelette that was serialized in three successive
issues of *DFW.*

Max found a home there. All but seven of his detective stories were published by *DFW.* What prompted the inquiry is lost to the ages, but in March of 1931 Max apparently wrote the editor of *DFW* asking if he thought their readers might be tiring of Sgt. Riordan. At this point in time, Max had sold them over fifty stories in five-and-a-half years. Editor Howard V. Bloomfield wrote Max saying that he did not think anyone was tired of Riordan and strongly encouraged Max to continue on or send in even more!

In addition to the detective stories, Max wrote three non-fiction articles for *DFW.* There were a smattering of other stories published in *The Popular, Railroad (&) Railroad Man's Magazine, Short Stories* and *Street & Smith's Complete Magazine.*

With his daughter grown and married, around 1938 Max moved back to the Boston area where his mother resided. He would finish his newspaper career at the *Worcester Telegram—The Evening Gazette.*

His hearing was going and he would be completely deaf in his last few years. He switched from reporting to editing copy and would communicate with his co-workers via handwritten notes. His last pulp story was in the January, 1944 issue of *New Detective Magazine.*

In 1950, increasingly worse back pain was plaguing Max. He went to the Mayo Clinic finally for help. Their diagnosis was inoperable cancer. From the clinic, he returned to the Pacific coast to be with his daughter. Just two weeks prior to his death, there was a heart-breaking exchange of letters between Max and his last employer where he was told that he was not eligible for a pension from them.

He died at a Portland hospital of a heart attack on October 4, 1950, survived by his mother and daughter. His residence, *the farm*, remains in his family to this date.

—Terry Sanford

THE GHOST BURGLAR

He Did His Work in Public Buildings in the Daytime and Without Even Unlocking Doors, and Yet He Was Human

1

A REAL JOB FOR RIORDAN

SERGEANT RIORDAN, SHAVING at home, preparatory to going down to the detective bureau to take charge of affairs for the night relief, was interrupted by the jangling of the telephone.

"Hello," he said, spitting lather from his lips, "this is Riordan."

"I know blame well it is," said the voice that came to him over the wire. "And you got your mouth full of something that sounds like soup. Finish whatever it is, boy, and put on your dress uniform, and meet me in the Mayor's office at four o'clock."

Riordan recognized the voice of Captain of Detectives Brady, his chief.

"Right, sir," he replied. "What are they going to do? Decorate us?"

"They're goin' to try and pin the double cross on us, boy," answered his chief's voice. "The papers have been yellin' so much over this 'ghost burglar' that there's the devil to pay. Doll up and come down for the party. Good-by."

Riordan, while he finished his shaving, and later, while eating what he was pleased to call his breakfast, though it came in the middle of the afternoon, reviewed the advent of the "ghost burglar" in the city. The newspapers were

Parking his car a block away, Riordan made his way—

making front page copy of the series of mysterious prowls that were being made in the business section, and had already dubbed the marauder the "ghost burglar."

And there was reason for the name, for the thief seemed not to mind locked or barred doors, came and went, apparently, when offices were filled with people, and left no traces of his means of entrance or flight. Over a score of "jobs," some of them fairly sizable, were rightfully charged up to "the ghost," while half a hundred lesser prowls, obviously of a different character to professional crook-chasers, were also credited by the press to the same personage.

It was a tough case, Riordan admitted. More than three-quarters of the sleuths in the department had been working in an effort to catch the ghost burglar, but not only had they failed signally, but they had not even obtained any workable clews. It was small wonder that the mayor was taking official cognizance of it.

Still thinking of the case, and the futile efforts that had been made to unravel it, Riordan climbed into his roadster and made his way to the City Hall, where at the appointed

—through the throng until he came to the police lines

hour the mayor's secretary greeted him and waved him toward the inner office.

"Go on in, sergeant," he said, "and meet your friends. You'll find them all there."

He did—and some he would not call his friends. For instance, aside from the chief and Captain Brady, and the sheriff, there was Partridge, manager of the Protective Association. Nobody had ever intimated that Partridge was the friend of any peace officer, and especially were his relations with the detective bureau anything but cordial. Riordan nodded curtly to those he knew, and, after shaking hands with the mayor, found a chair at one side of the room, some little distance from Captain Brady.

He had opportunity then to note that there were several others at the conference that gave it an unusual angle; there were two prominent bankers, one well-known department store owner, and the managers of several of the down town office buildings.

Everybody seemed to be waiting for somebody else, and there was little talk and much smoking. Finally the door opened again, and old Peter Jewett, president of the Home Casualty Company, entered.

"Well," said the mayor, a moment later, "I guess we're all here now, gentlemen. And I guess we all know pretty well what this meeting is for. Perhaps I had better outline our purpose briefly, so we can have a working basis to go on. We are here, gentlemen, at the suggestion of the Building Managers' Association, to see if we cannot arrange some effective cooperation in the hunt for this ghost burglar, who has—er—er—who has, I might say, seemed rather too much of a problem for the police department, single-handed. Isn't that so, chief?"

The titular head of the police force bridled. He chewed his cigar and thrust it up at an angle toward his left eye, which he squinted when the smoke entered it.

"You might say that, Mr. Mayor, if you wanted to," he replied. "But we haven't asked for any help yet. Of course, if the Building Managers' Association wants to run the police force, and you want to let 'em, why that's another thing."

"That isn't the way to talk and get anywhere, chief," spoke up Partridge, of the Protective Association. "The truth of the matter is that this crook has been working in the city now for three weeks and you haven't even got a line on him, have you? I'll admit he's a wonder. Now, it seems to me that if you and your men, and the sheriff and his men, and my men all work together as allies we might make better progress. We'll have more men on the job, anyway."

"That was my idea," said the mayor.

The sheriff stroked his mustache. "I shall be very glad," he said softly, "to do anything that the chief, here, asks. I have always been glad to work with him."

Peter Jewett rose in his place.

"Gentlemen," he said, "we have come to a place where we've got to do something. I was a little late getting here, because I was getting up some figures. This ghost burglar, as the papers call him, in the last three weeks has cost the Home Casualty Company exactly seven thousand, four hundred and six dollars and ninety-eight cents. That is the amount of claims we have paid. He has devoted himself exclusively to high-class offices, where there is either a lot of money or securities about, or where there is gold or platinum or silver.

"I do not doubt the police have done their utmost on the case. I know, personally, that the sheriff has not been idle, though the matter is a city matter and not necessarily in his bailiwick. But the sheriff is a hard-working official, and he has sent out his men on this case repeatedly. And our friend Partridge, here, has had a lot of operatives busy. And all we've got so far is a list of entries and a list of stolen property.

"Now, gentlemen, it is time we did something. It is time we got together and utilized all the forces at our command, and put them under one leader. Incidentally, as an incentive to still greater effort, on behalf of the Home Casualty Company, I will offer a reward of one thousand dollars cash for the capture of this ghost burglar.

"Just as a suggestion, gentlemen, I'd like to move that in this emergency the sheriff be placed in supreme command of all our forces. I'll be glad to turn our special agents over to his direction, and I am sure that Mr. Partridge, here, will do likewise. I think the chief, too—"

The sheriff rose, shaking his head. "I thank you for the

implied compliment, Mr. Jewett," he interrupted, "but I'm not the man to handle this. I will be very glad to assign as many deputies as may be needed, but that's all I can do. It seems to me that the chief, here, is the man to make our *generalissimo.* Am I not right, Mr. Mayor?"

Jewett waved his hands. "I don't care who it is," he said. "But some one man has got to handle this campaign. Otherwise we're just duplicating work."

"What do you think, chief?" asked the city executive.

"I got troubles of my own, your honor. I agree one man ought to handle it. It's detective work—why not Brady, here?"

Brady leaped to his feet. "No, sir, not me," he exclaimed.

Every face turned toward him, with surprise on every feature.

"And why not, captain?" demanded Partridge.

"I'm glad you asked me that, and that it was *you* who asked," snapped Brady. "I won't command any force that's got your men in it. I can't trust 'em to obey orders. We had a sample of that two days ago. I had one of my men stationed in a certain office on a tip. At a certain time he came out of that office, and what happened? Two of your fool dicks in the hall grabbed him as a suspect, and when he tried to show up and prove who he was they yelled for help. Made a fuss in the hall and all that—and if our tip had been any good your fool men spoiled it all, for they made hullabaloo enough to scare away ten ghosts. Anyway, I don't know as I could use any more help than I got."

"Now, Brady," said the mayor, "this isn't the time to start a petty fight. I know you and Partridge—"

"Never mind him and Partridge," interrupted Peter

Jewett. "We all know about that. If Brady says he won't take the job there's no use trying to force it on him: for if he did take it that way he'd not have his heart in it. Sheriff, it looks to me like it was up to you."

The sheriff smiled and in his soft voice said:

"No, Mr. Jewett. There are reasons why I cannot do this. I will do anything else though. But may I suggest that we have a man here who in the past has shown considerable ability—Sergeant Riordan, over there."

Riordan blushed as all eyes turned toward him.

"With all respect for Sergeant Riordan," commented the mayor, "it seems to me that putting a—an officer of but a sergeant's rank—you understand, Riordan, I am speaking merely—"

"Riordan's all right, your honor," broke in Partridge. "We can't stand on a matter of relative rank in this crisis. What we want, as Mr. Jewett said, is some head to this hunt. Give him a couple of days, say, and then if he doesn't make good get rid of him and put somebody else on the job. I'm for Riordan."

"It's no two-day job, and I won't have you give Riordan a black eye with any such scheme as that, Partridge," roared Captain Brady. "If we're going to have a leader for a couple of days, why don't you be the first goat? You've had three weeks at it, and all you've done that's been different from the rest of us is to grab one of my men and spoil his plans?"

Jacob Wentworth, of the Second National Bank, stepped forward from his chair and moved to the center of the room.

"Gentlemen, time is precious," he said. "Airing our differences in this way will not get us anywhere. And, besides, I do not think that we ought to ask either the sheriff or the chief of police to forego all his other duties to handle this case: nor do I even think we ought to ask Captain Brady of the detective bureau to drop all his other work. It seems to me, gentlemen, that the best thing to do would be to detach one man to special duty on this case, and let him pick as many aides as he desires from all the forces represented here.

"Let him form a flying squadron, as it were, and go after this ghost and nothing else. That is the way for us to work. And, gentlemen, I think his honor, the mayor, would be making a wise move if he would detail Sergeant Riordan to this duty, and let Riordan pick as many men as he wants to help him. We all know Riordan, and I think we will all feel that the affair is in trustworthy hands if he is put in charge."

There was a chorus of assent to this, and the mayor, seeing a temporary way out of the embarrassment that was rapidly developing, adopted the suggestion.

"Sergeant Riordan," he said, "you are hereby relieved from regular duty at the detective bureau by my orders. You are to devote yourself to the pursuit and capture of this ghost burglar. I will ask the chief, here, to detail to you whatever men or apparatus you may need. The sheriff, I know, will cooperate with you to any extent you may ask, as will these other gentlemen here. And if you want the fire department or the street cleaning department, all you've got to do is to telephone me. You will report directly to me, Riordan, and pray God you may have luck!"

"How long's he going to have?" asked Partridge.

"I will determine that, Mr. Partridge, as the case progresses," answered the mayor rather sharply.

Riordan stood up and looked at the men assembled in the office.

"Gentlemen," he said, "I'll do what I can. And I'll work hard. I don't know how much help I'll need—I'll let you know later. But I'll ask this much of you. I'll have a man in my office at headquarters all the time I'm not there, and he'll answer the telephone. If any of you hear of any activity of this ghost burglar, or hear of anything that you may think has a bearing on his work, I want you to telephone me or my man, day or night. I'll try and get right on the job. And I want to thank you for giving me this chance."

There was a ripple of applause as he sat down.

A moment later he rose again and made his way toward the door, followed by Captain Brady, and there was a general breaking up of the meeting. Out in the hallway was a flock of reporters, but Brady waved them aside.

"See the mayor, boys," he said. "He'll tell you what it was all about."

2

DARK MOMENTS FOR JIMMY

DOWN IN THE detective bureau Brady shoved Riordan ahead of him into his private office and slammed the door behind him.

"Boy," he said, "before you start on this I want to tell you one thing. You can pick anybody you want to help you out of this department, but don't forget me. You and I have worked on a lot of cases together, and if I can help you on this one all you got to do is to call me, day or night. Get that right in your head first."

"I know that, chief," answered Riordan. "And chances are I'll want you pretty bad. Do you know, they've wished a helluva job on me?"

"Sure they have, boy—but that's what you're a cop for. Now if I was you I'd get out of here for half an hour or so—go take a walk and think it over. While you're out I'll have your desk moved into the sideroom down at the end of the hall, and have you fixed up with two trunk phones, as well as two lines into the switchboard. And when you come back I'll have all the reports on this here ghost waiting for you. Then you can pick your force."

"That's a good idea, chief. I'll do that. I need time to

think this over and get a right start. I'll be back about six
o'clock. You'll put somebody on the night desk?"

"I'll attend to it all, boy—now you go take the air."

Riordan walked over to his own desk, to see that it was
in shape to be moved, and noted a letter lying on top of it.
He picked it up, inspected the drawers to see that they were
all locked, and then stepped over to the window, where he
opened the letter. It was badly written and ran:

SARGENT RIORDAN:

You will remember Jimmy who you pulled out of the river.
I am his mother. Please sargent come and see me as soon as
you can.

MRS. MARY KILVAIN,
226 South Third Street.

Folding the letter, he thrust it in his pocket and left the
office, going to the police garage, where his roadster was
waiting, and, climbing in, was soon rolling down through
the older section of the city. The address on South Third
Street proved to be a little, old-fashioned house set back in
a parched garden, though it was evident efforts had been
made to keep the grass and a few flowers alive. Stepping
from his machine he opened the front gate, walked up a
gravel path to the front door, and knocked. It was opened
immediately by a frail woman, pale of face, and with eyes
red with long weeping.

"Oh, sergeant, 'tis good of you, it is, to come so soon,"
she said. "Come right into the parlor. You'll have to excuse
the looks o' things, sergeant, but I've had so much trouble
I haven't the heart to do my work."

"Why, Mrs. Kilvain, everything looks fine. And what's the trouble?"

She waited until he had taken a seat on the plush sofa, and then, drawing up a rocking chair in front of him, she sat down and sobbed softly.

"You must pardon me, sergeant," she said, after a moment, "but 'tis more than I can bear, it is. Sure, you know?"

"I've been very busy, Mrs. Kilvain. Tell me what the trouble is. Is Jimmy sick?"

"He is that, sergeant. Sick and in jail. They've got him up to the county, and I want you to go see him."

"In jail? Why, what for? I thought he was doing well down at the bank." Riordan's surprise and concern were genuine.

The mother burst into tears again, and it was some moments before she could control herself.

"Ye haven't heard then? Oh, sergeant, they've arrested him as a thief. An' him being found beat up and unconscious, and can't talk yet."

"Who arrested him?"

"The Protective Association men."

"What for?"

"Robbin' the bank, they say. But he never done it, sergeant."

Riordan's face suddenly became hard. His hands clenched on his knees, and then relaxed. His voice was very low when he spoke.

"Tell me all about it—everything, Mrs. Kilvain."

"Ah, God bless you, sergeant. I knew you'd help me. Ye can have all the money I've got in the savings bank,

if you need it. It isn't much, but maybe it'll help. I'll tell
you, sergeant. It was like this. Last Wednesday, it was. It
was Jimmy's sweetheart's birthday—Kathleen Webber;
maybe ye know her? She's the daughter of Mr. Webber, the
butcher on Park Avenue? And a fine girl she is. Well, it was
her birthday. Jimmy had a present for her, you know, and
when he went to work he forgot to take it with him—he
was going to have one of the bank messengers deliver it.

"So about ten o'clock he remembers it. He sends one
of the bank messenger boys here for me to give it to him.
There's been so many robberies lately I didn't know but the
boy was lyin' to me. 'I'll take it to the bank myself,' I says to
him. 'And you can show me the way.' Well, the messenger
was all right. But I wanted to be sure. So I took the present
for Kathleen to the bank myself, the lad going along and
not seeming to mind my mistrusting him, and I gave it to
Jimmy. He said he'd send it to Kathleen's house himself.

"Then I come home. I was doing up the work, sergeant,
when about noon come two men from the Protective Association. I let them in before I knew what they wanted, they
looked like agents or meter men. Once they got in the
house they flashed their stars and said they was going to
search the place. I told them they had no right to do that
without a warrant, but they didn't pay any attention. They
were here for an hour, sergeant, and they turned the place
upside down."

The woman burst into tears again, but presently resumed
her account.

"They didn't find anything, of course. I had asked them
repeatedly what was wrong. As they were leaving they said
I could ask Jimmy. 'And where is Jimmy?' I asked them.

'He's in the county jail,' says one of them, and they went out. It near killed me, sergeant. But I put on my bonnet and took the street car and went to the county jail and asked to see Jimmy.

"At first they wouldn't let me in, but while I was beggin' to be let in the sheriff happened along. There's a grand man, sergeant. He put his arm around me, he did, like he was a son o' mine, and he told me to be brave, that Jimmy was hurt, and he took me up to the top floor, where they've got a hospital all in behind ugly iron bars, and there on a cot was Jimmy.

"He couldn't talk, sergeant. He was just lyin' there, all white and still, with his eyes starin' up at the ceiling. I stayed a little while and then I come home and cried all night. I called up the bank from the store down to the corner, but they wouldn't tell me anything. Next day, sergeant, I went back to the hospital in the jail, and the sheriff let me stay a little while.

"I asked him what was the matter, and he said he guessed there was a mistake somewhere, but it wasn't his case and he couldn't tell me anything. He explained he was only an officer of the law, and that the Protective Association men had brought Jimmy in, and he was their prisoner. Well, sergeant, I've been to the hospital up at the jail every day, and still Jimmy won't talk.

"He's better, and he's stroked my hair when I bent over him, but he either can't talk or he won't. And so last night I wrote to you, sergeant, asking you to come and see me. Because, sergeant, you saved Jimmy's life that day he fell in the river, and you got him that job in the bank, and I know you're a friend of his and that you believe in him. And it's killin' me, sergeant, to have him there in jail like that. You'll go see him, won't you, and find out what's wrong, and help him?"

Riordan put out a hand and placed it on the woman's shoulder.

"I'll go see him, Mrs. Kilvain," he said.

"The sheriff's right; there's been a mistake somewhere. I'll find out about it. You leave it to me, And I'm very glad you called me, Mrs. Kilvain. Now don't cry any more, and you'll hear from me first thing in the morning."

"God bless you, sergeant; you're a fine man."

3

AT SNYDER'S CHOP HOUSE

ONCE OUT OF the house Riordan leaped into his roadster and sped to the county jail. Downstairs there was a light in the sheriff's office, and Riordan found that official at his desk.

"Waiting for you, sergeant," he said. "I thought maybe you'd telephone. What can I do for you?"

Riordan brushed his hand over his forehead.

"My God, sheriff, I'd clean forgotten that," he said. "I—I got something else on. What you got Jimmy Kilvain up in the hospital for?"

"You saved his life, didn't you, sergeant? I remember now. A brave rescue it was—you dived off the bridge and pulled him out of the river. That was a long time ago, wasn't it?"

"What's he in here for?"

The sheriff drew a long breath. Then, in his soft voice, he answered:

"Robbery. Partridge's men got him. At the bank."

"Jimmy never stole a cent—they're crazy."

"Maybe so, sergeant. In fact I don't take much stock in their case myself. But that's the charge."

"But the lad's beat up?"

"They say he's faking."

"What's the doctor say?"

The sheriff paused a long time. Finally he said:

"The doc doesn't know, sergeant. He says there is no lump or mark on the boy's head, yet the case looks like concussion. Or it might be shock. He doesn't think the boy's faking, though. And I don't think so. I've watched him—watched him when his mother was there. A boy couldn't fake when his mother is weeping over him like that, sergeant."

"Tell me the case."

"It's a bad case, sergeant. Looks bad. The boy was signing bank notes on the machine they have, you know-tracing pen. The president and cashier each sign a sheet of notes, you know—with the tracing pen. Of course they're supposed to sign all of them. But you know how it is—they don't. They get some trusted employee to sign the rest of them—trace the signatures off the first ones with that tracing machine. Well, the boy was doing that.

"Somebody came to see him; they don't know at the bank who it was. A woman. The messenger who brought her there has disappeared—frightened that he'd be implicated in the robbery. After the woman was there, the boy called an outside messenger, and they can't trace the call, for there were so many at the bank, coming and going all the time—and sent a package out.

"Later on they found the boy lying on the floor of the room in which he was working on the tracing machine—it's on the third floor of the bank building, and the only entrance is from the corridor in which there's a watchman all the time. It was the watchman who saw the messenger and the woman. The bank notes were gone—all the signed ones—seventy thousand dollars' worth. When they found the boy he was just exactly as he is now upstairs in the hospital.

"You've got to admit it looks bad. Partridge's men brought him here, and the district attorney's office has the complaint. They're going to take the case direct to the grand jury."

Riordan swallowed hard. "It's an outrage," he said. "That was his mother came to see him. The package he sent out was a birthday present to his sweetheart. Can I see the boy?"

"Surely, sergeant. Come with me."

They went up in the elevator and were soon in the barred hospital ward. Jimmy Kilvain was lying motionless on his cot, but his eyes were closed.

"That's the first time his eyes have been closed since they brought him in," said the sheriff.

Riordan placed a hand on the lad's chest, then drew it away.

"He's sleeping," he said. "Best not to waken him. Much obliged, sheriff."

They went down to the jail office again.

"Much obliged, sheriff," Riordan repeated. "About this other business, this ghost hunt, there's nothing you can do to-night, sheriff. Maybe in the morning I'll call you up. Be good to the lad while you've got him here. I'll be going now."

From the county jail Riordan drove to the courthouse, only to find the office of the district attorney closed for the day. So he drove to the district attorney's residence. That official knew him well, and saw him at once.

"What's the bail on that Kilvain case," Riordan asked. "You know, Partridge brought him in from the Merchants' Bank for robbery? He's in the county jail hospital now."

"There hasn't been any set, Riordan."

"Well, set some, I'm in a hurry."

The district attorney laughed. Then, noting Riordan's expression, he sobered.

"Well, suppose we say twenty thousand."

"All right—do you think my place is worth that?"

"You want to go bail, Riordan?"

"You heard me."

"Well—of all things. A cop bailing out a bank robber! Gee, that would tickle the newspapers pink."

"You let it get into the papers, and I'll break your neck. Fix up the papers and I'll sign on the dotted line. And give me a release for him, I want to send him to a real hospital."

An hour later Riordan was back at headquarters. He walked into the police ambulance room, and handed the chauffeur some papers.

"Bill," he said, "go up to the emergency hospital and rout out the best interne they've got, and take him and your bus up to the county jail. Those papers are for the release of a boy named Kilvain they've got in the hospital ward. Pick him up without waking him, and take him out to St. Paul's Hospital, and tell the sister in charge there that he's to have a private room, and I'll stand good for the bill. Now get a wiggle on you if you're a friend of mine."

"Yes, sir—on the way now," said the chauffeur, with a mock salute and a laugh.

Riordan smiled, turned away, and made his way to his new office, just beyond the detective bureau. There he threw off his uniform coat and cap, opened his desk, dragged out and filled his pipe, and lighting it, plunged at once into the pile of reports on the ghost burglar that Captain Brady had seen were prepared for him.

He was still studying the reports when he heard the door of his new office opened. Glancing at his desk clock he saw it was nearly eleven. Throwing down the particular report that was in his hand, he swung his chair around to find Captain Brady standing just within the room, closing the door behind him.

"Well, chief, what's the idea," the younger man asked.

"I dropped in to take you out to lunch."

"It is time for that, isn't it? I've been so busy trying to make something out of this mess I didn't notice how late it was. What are you doing down here?"

"Oh, I was out to the show, and dropped in on the way home. They told me you were here, so I thought I'd come up. Put your man on and come out for a bite."

Riordan laughed. "I haven't picked my staff yet. And the ghost doesn't work at night, any way. There's no use in putting anybody on."

"Boy," said Brady earnestly, "you listen to me. Get a man and put him in here in your place. The ghost may not be working, but you can't tell that the mayor, or the chief, or some of them bankers aren't owling around like me, and may call up. And you told 'em there'd be somebody here all the time. You want to make good. It looks better. I'll get one of our boys to sit in."

"Never mind our boys, chief. I'll get my own man," interrupted Riordan. "Our boys have got enough grief."

He reached for one of the telephones on his desk and

asked for the captain in charge of the first night relief. Getting the connection, he said:

"That you, Daniels? This is Sergeant Riordan. I think you got an order from the chief to-night to let me have what I wanted. Yes. Well, do you happen to still be keeping Joe Fanchetti on reserve? Good, detail him to me, will you? Yes, right now, please. Thanks, good-by."

He hung up and winked at Brady.

"Just a moment, now, chief, and I'll be with you," he said.

Brady sat down to wait. Presently the door opened again, and the swarthy Joe Fanchetti, the department's one Italian member, entered and saluted.

Sergeant Riordan returned the salute and rose from his chair.

"Fanchetti," he said, speaking briskly. "I've been watching you, on and off, for a good many years, and I've reached the conclusion that you're a good cop. The chief has assigned me to some special work, and has let me pick my own men. You're the first one I've picked. I want you to sit here till I come back, and take any telephone calls that may come. Tell anybody that calls that I'm out, and that you're temporarily in charge. While you're waiting, you might read those reports piled up there, and let 'em soak into your head. You're to receive any information that comes in, but you are not to let any go out—not to anybody. Understand?"

"Yes, sergeant."

"Very well. Make yourself at home. Come on, captain, let's go."

Once outside, and in Brady's car, the captain turned to his aid and laughed. "What was the idea?" he asked. "Trying to swell Joe all up?"

"No, chief. Just playing to his temperament. After what I told Joe, he'll think he's the best man on the force, and try to live up to it. As a matter of fact, he *was* the first man I picked. And he'll be good—this stuff is new to him, and he'll do his darnedest to make good. I know the kind he's made of."

"You got a head on you at that, boy. Well, have you mapped out your campaign on this ghost stuff yet?"

"Yep."

"Well, we'll go to Snyder's chophouse and get a box, and have a meal. You can tell me about it there—the place will be so darned noisy with jazz and dancing and shouting this time of night that we'll be just as alone as if we were in the woods."

4

RIORDAN'S GOOD HEAD

BRADY WAS RIGHT about that. Sitting in one of the small boxes in the gallery of Snyder's grill, above the dancing crowds on the main floor, and across the room from the orchestra gallery, the two sleuths were temporarily isolated from the world, except when the busy waiter was putting steaks and fried potatoes and coffee before them. After they had eaten only enough to whet their appetites, Brady looked at the younger man.

"Well, what's the plan of campaign?" he asked.

Riordan smiled. "Waiting," he said. "I'm going to wait till the ghost pulls another job, and then start fresh on him. There isn't a solitary thing in those reports you sent in to work on. They're all the same, and they're all cold."

Brady looked at his aid a long time. Finally he said:

"I don't know but you're right, at that. But you don't want to let the ghost pull more than one job—it won't be healthy. Seems to me, though, that you ought to be able to lay some sort of groundwork from all those reports—I got Partridge's, as well as ours, you noticed."

"I noticed that. But, chief, the reports aren't any good. Every case is just alike. There's nothing stands out. Nothing to get hold of. Every case is typical. The place that was prowled is a closed room, three or more stories from the street, on the outside of a building.

"Somebody had left the room a few moments before, and when they came back the place had been cleaned. The door was locked, or else there were parties in the next room or in the hall, and nobody was seen to enter or leave. But the stuff was gone. No marks, none that were any good. Mark of a footprint on a rug in one place, but not definite.

"Stuff that's stolen turns up regular or else it don't. If it's securities they turn up in from three to five days in Bay City or Meridian; if it's jewelry, the junk turns up about the same time in Bay City or some place farther east. If it's money you can't trace it. And the stuff that turns up you can't trace; if it's securities they were sold through some broker's office or small bank by a stranger of nondescript description. The jewelry breaks in the hock shops. There isn't a single outstanding thing in any of the reports that you can work on.

"So I got to wait till he pulls another job, and then get there myself and start fresh. Maybe I can find something these other birds have overlooked. I'll want you to go with me, of course—but we got to get there right away, before anything's mussed up. And we've got to wait for the job in order to get a chance to catch this guy—if we put a cop or somebody in every building in town, we ain't doing nothing, unless it may be scaring the bird away."

Brady nodded his head. "Yes, boy, you're right. We got to start fresh," he said. "I thought I was going to get in on the last job first—the one in the Empire Trading Company— but by the time I got there two of Partridge's men had been in, and had the place all mussed up and the help scared to death. It was a lunch hour job, and the girl on the gate swore nobody had been in or out. Besides which there were two stenogs who had been eating lunch in the next office, and were certain nobody had got by them. Yet the place was prowled and clean."

"The guy's good, all right," commented Riordan.

"I'll say he's good. Hear you were up to see the sheriff; got anything from him?"

Riordan looked up quickly. "You been trailing me?"

Brady laughed. "No, boy; just happened to hear it. One of the reporters. I been entertaining them damned news hounds all night, to tell the truth, and stalling them off. The mayor or somebody told 'em the conference was about this here ghost bunk; and I had a heck of a time stalling them off you. I told 'em we was all working together, and that you and the sheriff had just been comparing notes. I didn't want 'em bothering you, nor spreading too much news around. What'd the sheriff have to say?"

"I went to him about something else. Little plot of my own."

"And the district attorney, too?"

"You *have* been trailing me!"

"No—but the district attorney called me up and wanted to know if you were still on the force."

Riordan laughed. "He's a sly bird," he said. "And I thought he was my friend. Oh, well—he's got to be careful, I suppose."

"He's a good friend of yours, boy. He wouldn't tell me what you were doing up there, and he said you were the best cop he knew. He just wanted to know if you'd left the force, that was all. I told him the truth; that you were on special duty by the mayor's orders. That seemed to tickle him."

Riordan pushed back his plate and lighted a cigar. "Chief," he asked at length, "did you ever get any report on a seventy thousand dollar job at the Merchants' Bank? Along about last Wednesday it was."

Brady nodded his head. "Saw something on it to-night," he answered. "Didn't pay much attention to it. They got some of the money reported in at Bay City. They had the numbers on the bills broadcast, you know. New paper it was. There was just a line from Bay City saying some of the money had been picked up there coming into the banks from the stores. Why?"

"Oh, nothing much. I just happened to hear of the case to-night, and was curious. The sheriff told me about it. I said I hadn't heard of it, I must have missed the report on it at the time."

"The Merchants' Bank is one of those that doesn't think much of the force," commented Brady. "They turn all their work over to Partridge and his gang. All we ever had on it was that Partridge was pleased to give us, and that was mere mention of it. Lot of the banks, you know, never give us anything for fear the papers will get hold of it."

"What's your idea of the ghost, chief? Give me the low down."

"I'm stumped, boy. I'm like you; I want to get in first on one of his jobs. But I hate to think of sitting back and letting him pull another one, now that they've got you detailed special, to him. It will look bad. But we can't help it, I guess. You'd better tell the mayor what you're going to do—it will ease it over a bit."

Riordan nodded his head, but did not answer. Brady noted that there was a change in his aide's expression—a far-away look in his eyes, as if he was dreaming. The older man watched the younger one for several minutes, and made no move to distract him. Then he saw Riordan's face change again, and he leaned forward.

"Tell poppa," he said. "You got a hunch; let me help."

"Who have you got a drag with that's got a lot of money?" asked Riordan. "I don't mean chicken feed—I mean real piles of kale?"

Brady considered. "Well, boy, there aren't many millionaires on my calling list. But Steve Woodward, of the Underwood Estate, would do most anything for me. And you might say the Underwood Estate had several piles of coin."

Riordan took a deep breath. "Will he take a chance for you, chief?"

"Steve would give me his shirt."

"Well, then, listen. You get to Steve to-morrow and tell him to tell the papers—it will make a good story—that the Underwood Estate is going to audit its books and count its money on, say, a week from Monday. Get him to make it strong—how there's going to be gold and silver and stocks and bonds brought out of the vaults and counted in the estate building somewhere.

"I'll get half a dozen deputy sheriffs with sawed-off shotguns and a platoon of cops, and surround the building and make it look as if it was real, see? Only, of course, it will be all bluff and there won't be any money. Maybe if we tout the thing up big enough this here ghost will read about it and show up. You and I and the best of the boys will be there, and grab anybody who looks suspicious. It's a chance, chief; maybe we can lure the ghost and get him before he pulls the next job."

"I'll do it, boy. Steve will go for it, I know. If he don't I'll lay over him and make him. You got a head on you, boy. I ll not only do that, but I'll tout it up strong with the newspaper boys down at headquarters, and tell 'em how afraid we are this here ghost will butt in and get the coin. I'll lay such a plant that if the ghost has any pride at all he'll try a job."

"Well, you do that, and I'll see what else I can think of. Let's go now—I'll go back to the office and fix it for somebody to relieve Fanchetti when his time is up, and then go home to bed. I'll see you to-morrow, and you can tell me how you've gotten along with Woodward."

The next morning, before going to his office, Riordan drove out to St. Paul's Hospital to see young Kilvain. The sister in charge met him in the hallway, and after greeting him, chided him laughingly:

"And what's the idea, sergeant," she said, "of sending a perfectly well man here, and getting him a private room and a nurse?"

"What do you mean, sister?"

"Why, the Kilvain lad that you had brought in last night. He woke up at seven this morning and wanted to know what it was all about? We told him to wait till after breakfast and somebody'd tell him. He ate like a horse, and the house surgeon says there's nothing the matter with him at all. We're having a hard time keeping him in bed."

"I'll go right up and see if I can explain it. You come along, too, sister."

5

SETTING THE STAGE

THE PATIENT WAS arguing strenuously with his nurse as they entered the private ward. He recognized Riordan at once and appealed to him.

"Say, sergeant, what's the idea of all this? They won't let me get up. How did I get here, anyway?"

Riordan was surprised at the change in the youth's appearance. His pallor was all gone, his eyes were bright and keen, and the healthy flush on his face shone through the stubble of his unshaved cheeks and chin. He appeared to be thoroughly recovered from his semi-coma, or whatever it was that had gripped him while he was in the jail hospital.

"Now rest easy, lad," said Riordan, waving his hands, and then sitting on the side of the bed. "Just hold your horses and brace yourself. You've had an accident—only you don't know it."

"Accident? Why, sergeant, you're crazy. I'm all right. That's what the nurse here told me—but there isn't a hurt or a sore spot on me."

"Do you know what day it is, lad?"

"Sure—let me see, it must be Thursday."

"Guess again. It's Sunday morning—and you've missed church."

"It can't be!"

He looked at the nurse and the sister, and both nodded their heads in confirmation.

"It's Sunday morning, lad," continued Riordan, "and you've been 'out' since Wednesday. Now pull yourself together and tell us what put you out."

Jimmy Kilvain seemed stunned at first, but he forced his mind to realize what Riordan had told him, and shook his head.

"I can't tell you a thing," he said. "It doesn't seem possible. You're not kidding me, Riordan?"

"Not a bit, lad. Now think, what's the last thing you can remember?"

The youth puckered his forehead. "The bank," he said at last. "Yes, I remember going to the bank. The old man said he had something for me to do—he called me to his office—but darned if I can remember what it was! What happened, sergeant: did I fall downstairs? I've often been afraid of that—those metal steps leading up to the galleries are awfully slippery."

"Do you remember signing bank notes?"

"No—not Wednesday. About a year ago I used the tracing machine on some."

"Do you remember somebody slugging you?"

"Slugging me?"

"Yes, hitting you with a blackjack or sandbag, or maybe the butt of a gun?"

"Why, no." He felt of his head and then smiled. "There isn't any bump, sergeant—I guess I wasn't slugged."

"And I guess you were. You've had four days for the bump to go down."

"Why would anybody slug—do you mean the bank was robbed?"

"Seventy thousand dollars' worth."

The youth sank back on his pillow and sighed.

"I can't remember a thing," he said presently. "I wish I could. It might help you—you're working on the case?"

Riordan nodded his head.

The youth suddenly looked up. "My mother, sergeant, does she know?"

"Yes, lad. She's been to see you every day. She'll be here presently. Now I tell you what I want you to do. I want you to stay here and be a good boy till the doctor says you're all right again. Maybe you feel all right now, but you've got to stay here till you get good and strong. And don't think about this robbery—it will all come to you when you're strong again. Just take life easy—that's all. Give me your word, Jimmy, that you'll not ask to leave here till the doctor says you are all right?"

"If you say so, Riordan."

"That's a good boy, Jimmy. It will be all right in the end. Now I've got to leave you and do some work on this case. I'll be in again soon. Good-by."

Out in the hall Riordan drew the sister in charge into a corner.

"Sister, you've got to fix it with the surgeon for me. I want this boy kept here till I give you the word to turn him out. Never mind the bills, they'll all be taken care of. Keep the lad happy, and let his mother be with him all she wants. And don't tell him anything—understand, don't tell him anything—and don't let him get hold of any newspapers. I'll see his mother, and have her help you."

"All right, sergeant. Orders are orders!"

From the hospital Riordan drove to Mrs. Kilvain's and told her the good news about Jimmy, without telling her how it happened he had been transferred from the jail to St. Paul's.

"And I want you to be with him as much of the day as you can," he added. "Keep him amused. Read to him, play with him, anything to keep his mind occupied and to give it a chance to heal. And don't tell him he was arrested. Don't let him know anything about it. I'll see that nobody bothers him or you."

"Ah, God bless you, sergeant, and sure you're an angel in disguise," said Mrs. Kilvain. "First it was you that saved Jimmy's life when he was drowning, and now you're saving him from worse. I'll do just as you say, sergeant, and be thankin' ye every minute of the day."

At headquarters Captain Brady told him Steve Woodward was willing to try the scheme Riordan had suggested the night before, and that the "frame" was already being hatched for the newspapers. Woodward was to make the announcement first, and later Captain Brady was to tell the police reporters how he dreaded the moving and exposing of so much money and wealth while the ghost burglar was still uncaught.

Otherwise there were not many developments. Riordan organized a small staff of aides for his hunt for the ghost, but there was really little that they could do, beyond watchful routine. In fact the week was a dull one, as far as the special search for the mysterious marauder went; though the public found excitement enough in the constantly growing accounts in the press of what was to happen the following Monday when the Underwood Estate counted its cash.

Feature writers tried to outdo each other in describing the processes that would be followed, and the result was that, as each writer had only generalities and his own imagination to work with, the public was fed enough different stories to satisfy it for once. Steve Woodward had even gone a step farther than either Riordan or Brady had hoped, and had persuaded the adjutant general of the State to grant permission for Woodward's company of the National Guard to mobilize on the following Monday and surround the estate building with a cordon of soldiers.

In fact, public interest in the alleged counting of the Underwood Estate wealth was fanned to such a high point that Riordan and Brady began to wonder if they had not overdone the affair, and built up such a condition as would make so many guards necessary that the ghost would be frightened away. However, all plans went ahead.

Daily throughout the week Riordan visited the hospital and chatted with Jimmy Kilvain, but at none of these visits did the youth's mind clear any further than it had on the first day. The hospital physicians interested in the case had brought in a noted alienist to examine him, and this doctor, talking to Riordan afterward, shook his head.

"I do not think we will ever know what happened," he said. "I do not believe the boy was slugged, sergeant. I think he received some great mental shock. I think he realized, at the last minute, that the bank was going to be robbed, and that he could not help it. He is high-strung and of high ideals. When he realized this, something within him broke—that is all. Some part of his mind ceased to function. The shock paralyzed those cells.

"I doubt if they will ever come to life again. Of course, some accidental circumstance may revive them, by another shock—but that would be just a matter of luck. The boy was wrapped up in his work, was the soul of honesty, and when he saw he could not prevent this robbery—why the shock numbed his mind. There are similar cases, you know—the sudden death of a loved one, the receipt of terrible news, the witnessing of some great tragedy—all those things have produced similar blankness or forgetfulness. Otherwise, I believe the boy will recover completely and be his natural self. But I fear, sergeant, that one chapter in his mind is irrevocably closed."

6

A BASKET FULL OF MONEY

ON SUNDAY AFTERNOON—THE day before the ghost trap was to be sprung—Riordan motored out to the hospital just before sunset to call on Jimmy, and to explain that he would be too busy the next day to see him. In the hallway outside the door of the boy's room he was stopped by one of the nurses.

"Just a minute, sergeant," she said. "You know all about revolvers, don't you?"

He laughed. "I've had some experience with them, miss. Why?"

"Well, mine won't work. I wonder if you can fix it for me?"

"I'll try."

"It's one of those little automatics," she said. "I carry it in my handbag when I have to go out on night calls—you can never tell, you know. The trigger won't pull. Here it is, see what you can do with it, will you, and bring it back to me to-morrow?"

Riordan took the tiny gun and put it in his pocket. "I won't be here to-morrow, miss, but I'll send it down to Jimmy's nurse by messenger—if I can't fix it here. If I can, I'll leave it with her."

"Thank you, ever so much."

She went down the hall and Riordan entered his friend's ward. Jimmy greeted him happily, and Mrs. Kilvain, who was also there, flashed him a look of welcome. She had been reading to her son and was glad of the interruption, as her voice was getting tired. The sergeant chatted with Jimmy for some little time, and then, at the youth's request, took a chair beside the bed, while his mother took up her book again.

"I want you to hear this story, sergeant," said the patient. "I think you'll like it."

But Riordan didn't. He had too much else on his mind to care for any story just then. However, he wanted to please his young friend, so he sat still while the mother resumed her reading. Presently he idly put one hand in his pocket and his fingers closed about the nurse's automatic. He took it out and quietly pushed his chair over toward the window, to get a stronger light, and raised the tiny weapon to examine it.

Taking the clip of shells out and putting them in his pocket for safety, he worked with the little gun several minutes before he discovered that the "safety" lever was jammed. To remedy this was a matter of but a second or so, and after freeing it and bending it so it would not jam again, he cocked the gun to test the trigger action.

As the mechanism clicked there came a hoarse shriek from Jimmy's bed, followed by a scream from his mother. Riordan, jumping up, rushed over to the bed and found the boy lying pale and rigid, his eyes staring at the window and an expression of the utmost horror on his face. Mrs. Kilvain was wringing her hands beside him, and moaning.

Riordan had no more than noted these details when the
door of the ward was opened and the room nurse, attracted
by the shriek and scream, rushed in, followed by one of the
sisters, who, at a sign from the nurse, at once dashed out to
call the house doctor.

During the swift confusion that followed Riordan stood
with a puzzled frown on his face, doing his utmost to
comfort Mrs. Kilvain, and wondering what had happened.
Presently the horrifying thought occurred to him that
there had been a shell in the weapon he was examining,
and that when he pulled the trigger it had exploded; but
instant examination showed him this had not occurred;
in fact, the clip was in his pocket, so such a tragedy was
impossible. He sighed with relief, however, and then told
Mrs. Kilvain about it.

"No, sergeant," she said, "it wasn't that. You couldn't
make a mistake like that. Jimmy's just had a relapse, I guess.
And he seemed to be so well, too. I was looking at him
when it happened—his eyes were on my face as I was reading. Then they shifted toward the window, and he shouted
out and went pale and his eyes took on that terrible stare.
Oh, sergeant, what shall I do?"

The doctor came over from the bed. "He'll be all right
now," he said. "Just a shock. It happens sometimes in these
cases. Something must have reminded him of his experience. I've given him an opiate, and he's relaxed and gone to
sleep, and when he wakes up again he'll be all right. Curious, though—I wonder what it could have been?"

"Can I stay till he wakes up, doctor?" pleaded Mrs.
Kilvain.

"Yes—it would be better if you did. Sit just as you were, by his bed, so when he opens his eyes he'll see you."

Riordan patted her on the back. "The best medicine for him, little lady," he said. "When he sees you he'll be all right. I'll try and drop in to-morrow, though I shall be pretty busy."

In the hallway he happened to meet the nurse who had given him the automatic, and he returned it to her, explaining how the safety catch had become bent and jammed. She thanked him warmly, and he left the hospital, going to headquarters to check up for the last time on the next day's program of ghost baiting.

As it had been worked out, the supposed counting of the wealth of the Underwood Estate was to begin at ten in the morning. Half an hour before that time Steve Woodward's militia company was to deploy about the building, and uniformed policemen were to be posted in the entrance lobby and the hallways. At ten o'clock one of the police patrols, supposedly containing a small fortune brought from down town bank vaults, was to roll up to the estate building, guarded by six deputy sheriffs with sawed-off shotguns, and employees of the Underwood Estate would take from the patrol bulky packages and boxes and carry them up to the fourth floor of the building, where Steve Woodward's offices were.

The packages would be put inside the office and there, according to the program, trusted clerks would be supposed to check over the money and securities. After an hour the packages were again to be carried downstairs to the waiting patrol and taken away, presumably back to the bank vaults. If this performance failed to bring the ghost burglar into evidence, an hour later it was to be repeated, the patrol and the dummy packages returning as if with a second load of securities.

While uniformed guards were to be as thick as bees about a hive on the street floor of the estate building, scrupulous care was to be taken to leave the hallways of the other floors apparently unprotected, to invite the ghost by seeming carelessness; though at strategic points behind doors and transoms detectives were to be stationed, ready to pounce out upon any mysterious-looking stranger. Thus the trap was to be set.

To control the crowd that was sure to be on hand in the street below, and to keep them moving, extra motor cycle men and traffic police were to be posted. The idea was to keep people moving, so the ghost would have plenty of chance to get into the building from the passing throngs.

With every detail settled, Riordan left one of his assistants in charge and went home for the night, hoping something tangible would come of the preparations; but as the time drew near actually far less confident of the success of the scheme than he had been when it first occurred to him.

The next morning, as luck would have it, for the first time in months Riordan overslept, and did not waken until almost eight o'clock. By the time he had shaved and dressed and bolted his breakfast it was a quarter to nine. He telephoned Captain Brady and was assured that everything was going as planned, and that already a curious crowd was milling around the estate building.

"All right, chief, I'll meet you there at ten o'clock, in the lobby," he said. "I got to go somewhere first."

And hurrying out to his car, he sped to the hospital.

Jimmy Kilvain, the sister in charge told him, had completely recovered again. He had awakened from the opiate-produced sleep the night before, about eleven, had smiled at his mother and dozed off again. Mrs. Kilvain had then gone home, much relieved. The morning report was that Jimmy showed no recollection of his second seizure, and had awakened at the usual time and at once asked for his breakfast. Riordan went up to his ward for a few moments, found the youngster enjoying poached eggs and toast, and waiting for his mother to come.

Riordan chatted with him a few moments, explained that he had a big case on, and promised to come back later in the day. Then he drove down toward the estate building. The militiamen were already in place before it, and the street was a seething mass of curious folk, kept moving by the traffic men. Parking his car a block from it, Riordan made his way through the throng until he came to the police lines. A patrolman nodded to him and let him through, saying jokingly as he did so:

"Better go up and get grand stand seats for the show, sergeant, like them fellers."

He pointed up. Riordan, raising his eyes, saw a group of window-washers working on the sixth floor of the estate building and looking down at the crowds below.

He laughed. "They've got one thing in their favor to-day," he said. "If one of 'em breaks a strap and falls he'll land on the heads of the crowd instead of the pavement."

Then he entered the lobby of the building. Captain Brady came forward from the cigar stand, where he was leaning on the counter, and drew his aide over to a corner behind the elevator grillework.

"Say, you young fool," the older man said, "Partridge is looking for you with two guns. Of course he's got to make a fuss to-day, of all days. He's found out you bailed out one of his prisoners, and he's crazy. I told him he was a liar, but he's gunning for you and going to raise hell. What's the idea, anyway?"

Riordan's face clouded. "Why," he said, "Partridge got him wrong. I guess I got a license to bail—"

He stopped talking, looked blankly at Brady a moment, then tensed.

"Think fast, chief," he said, speaking under apparent strain. "Where can I get a bushel basket full of stage money?"

"You gone nuts, too," said Brady. "What's biting you now?"

"Where can I get it?"

Riordan was insistent.

"Globe Theater, next block," answered Brady. "Bill Trevis, the doorman, will let you into the property room. What's the idea?"

7

THE GHOST BURGLAR

RIORDAN WAS GONE without answering. Ten minutes later he was back, with a bulky paper parcel under his arm. He rushed into one of the elevators and, as the door closed behind him, found himself confronting Partridge, black of countenance and trembling with rage. They both got out at the fourth floor, Partridge following the detective sergeant from the car.

"Say, you, I'll have you broke for this," he shouted. "I'll go to the mayor and the commissioners. Bailing out one of my prisoners, and a bank robber at that. You're a fine—"

Riordan's left fist swung out, hit Partridge with a resounding blow on the side of the jaw, and the Protective Association man dropped in a heap. The hallway happened to be empty, and the elevator had risen out of sight. Riordan hesitated a moment, then reached down, grabbed the inert Partridge by his coat collar, and dragged him along the hall to Steve Woodward's office, against the door of which he kicked. Emmet, one of the police detectives, opened the door a crack, recognized Riordan and swung the portal wide.

"Take this lummox and get him out of here," said Riordan. "Is Drake with you?"

"Yes, sir."

"Well, the two of you take Partridge here and get him out through the back way, if this building has a back way. Get him in a taxicab and drive out in the park with him. Keep him there. If he gets too noisy take him down to my office and lock him up and stay with him till I get there. I haven't got time to monkey with him now."

"Yes, sir."

Dropping the limp form of Partridge to the floor like a sack of flour, Riordan pushed on into Woodward's inner office, the third of the Underwood Estate suite. There he ripped open the parcel he carried and a shower of stage money fell over the carpet.

"Ah," laughed Woodward, "the Underwood fortune. I didn't know it was so much. What's the idea, Riordan?"

Riordan looked quickly around the office, at the window, at a small closet opening off one side, at the doors leading out of it, one to the hallway and two to adjoining offices.

"The idea, Mr. Woodward, is this: I want this office of yours for the next hour—maybe an hour and a half. You've been such a good sport so far, and helped us, I hope you'll let me make just a little more trouble. And in the next room I'd like to have you detail a couple of nice young men to count this stuff."

"Count it?"

"That's what I said. I mean have a couple of them sit at a table and act as if they were counting it. Run it through their fingers and stack it up in piles, and make notes from time to time on a paper or in a book beside them. It won't be a very interesting job, but it will help a lot."

Steve Woodward smiled. "Riordan, I believe you've

either got a real idea or else you're crazy. I'll take a chance.
You can have this office, and I'll put two of our clerks in
the next one, playing at counting that stuff. I'm a game guy,
Riordan—maybe Brady told you that. If all this monkey
business results in your men catching the ghost burglar I'll
be a hero with the estate. If it doesn't result in a pinch—
most likely I'll lose my job."

"I hope you won't lose your job, Mr. Woodward. If you
do, you and me will go fishing, for I think I'm in the same
boat."

"Well, let's get busy. I'll help you carry that trash into
the next office."

"Not all of it, Mr. Woodward. I want some of it here.
And one thing more—I want you to instruct everybody
here that no matter—"

"I have," interrupted the representative of the Underwood Estate. "I've told 'em already. I've told them to go on
with their work—those that aren't engaged in this game—
and that no matter what happens they're to keep on with
their work."

"Fine—that's what I was going to say."

They took most of the stage money into the next office,
and Woodward and Riordan superintended the placing of
two clerks at a table with it and saw them begin to "count"
this unexpected addition to the "treasure." Then they went
back to Woodward's office. Riordan scooped up what was
left of the stage money from the floor, arranged it in neat
stacks on Woodward's glass-topped table, and then smiled.

"Now, please, Mr. Woodward," he said, "I want you to
leave this room—and stay out till I call you or till a squad
of harnessed bulls—I mean uniformed men—come in

and want me. I'll try not to muss your place up any. You can amuse yourself, meanwhile, watching the play going on outside."

Woodward extended his hand, and Riordan grasped it. Neither man said anything, but they looked each other in the eye. Then Woodward went out, closing the door behind him. As soon as he had departed Riordan made another survey of the room, rearranged the piles of stage money on the table moved a chair back as if somebody had just risen from it, and then walked over to the closet at one side of the room, and stepped within, leaving the door ajar about two inches.

From his concealed position he could hear the murmur that rose from the crowd outside as the patrol wagon, filled with bogus packages of treasure, drew up to the building; and later he heard tramping in the hallway outside and the slamming of a door, which told him that the supposed wealth had arrived for its "counting."

After that he heard nothing save the half-hushed noises of voices in the outer office, the faint clicking of a type-writer somewhere, and the far-away rumble of street traffic four stories below. He stood motionless in the closet, his eyes glued on the glass-topped desk in the room outside, upon which rested the several packages of stage money.

He was not excited, he was not particularly hopeful that the ghost burglar would appear. He just waited. He had laid the best trap he could conceive, and beyond that it was all in the day's work. He was used to waiting, and to make it less tedious he forced his mind to be a blank; and so stood there, watchful but devoid of thought. For a long time he waited, and then he heard sudden laughter come from the next office, where the two Underwood Estate clerks were "counting" that stage money over and over and placing it in stacks. Then all was still.

Without making a sound, and scarcely moving, he raised his right hand and drew his automatic from his shoulder holster and held it in front of him. His breath came regularly, slowly. His eyes remained fixed upon the glass table-top in the office beyond the crack of the open door. Suddenly he saw a shadow flash across the table; then it flashed back again. Then there was no sign of movement.

Followed a dull thud and the sound of dripping water, and the shadow flashed across the table again—across and back and then up and down. There was another soft thud, again the sound of dripping water, and again the dance of shadows on the table. Then, for a second, the shadows vanished; to reappear again, dancing this time more rapidly. Then they stopped entirely, to be followed by a slow-moving and darker shadow some moments later—one that started at one side of the table and moved gradually across to the other. For a moment it hovered over the table, then disappeared in a twinkling.

Riordan's eyes, fixed on the piles of stage money, saw nothing more for several seconds, and then a long, lean, swarthy hand came into his line of vision and closed over one of the piles.

Noiselessly Riordan pushed the closet door open and raised his automatic.

"Don't move," he said.

The hand clutched at the pile of stage money and remained motionless. Riordan's gaze traveled back over the wrist and up a hairy, bare arm till it came to the rolled-up sleeve of a flannel shirt. Then he widened the focus of his eyes, and took in the whole figure.

8

THE PROSECUTING WITNESS

A TALL, THIN, sinewy man was standing before him, clad in overalls and flannel shirt, a heavy leather belt about his waist, from which dangled two short ropes with hooks on the ends of them. Over the man's shoulder was a damp, stained, piece of chamois skin. On the back of his head was a little cap, from underneath which black, curly hair protruded like a fringe. The man's face was drawn with agony, its paleness acccentuated by the bulging veins on the side of his neck, which almost throbbed with the terrific beating of his heart, as his black, beady eyes gazed at the muzzle of Riordan's automatic, pointed straight at his heaving chest.

Behind him the window was open, and on the ledge outside was a bucket containing water and a sponge. Resting beside it was a squeegee.

"Mind, now, don't you move an inch," repeated Riordan, stepping from the closet and kicking the door shut behind him, without moving his eyes from the intruder's. He stepped forward to the desk, sat down slowly in the chair he had moved back when baiting his trap, and rested his right elbow on the glass top, the automatic still pointing unerringly and steadily at his opponent's heart.

His left hand reached out and gathered in a desk phone, pulled it toward him, and lifted the receiver from the hook.

"Gimme police headquarters quick," he said, without moving his eyes from his man. The phone clicked several times, and then purred slightly.

"Hello, that you Foley? This is Sergeant Riordan. Hustle them reserves out of the back room and into a wagon and send 'em down to the estate building. Yes, and now listen. When they get here they'll see a gang of window washers working on the outside of the building somewhere—maybe on the fourth floor. You tell 'em I want all of those birds gathered in and cuffed up tight. I don't want any of them to get away. Get me? After you get 'em all nabbed, come on into Steve Woodward's private office. Got that right, now? All right, make it snappy."

He hung up.

The man standing tense before him opened his mouth.

"There's no use of that," he said. "Them other guys is on the level for all I know."

"I figured that myself, friend," answered Riordan. "But I'm not going to take any chances. I'll find out. Keep still now, I'm beginning to get nervous."

For several minutes neither man moved. Then the screech of the siren on the patrol sounded below, and the sound of the clanging gong floated up to the pair through the window. The man's head turned ever so slightly.

"One more move," said Riordan levelly, "and this thing goes off. Never mind how far away you are from the window—you can't make it in a jump. If you really want to commit suicide just make a swing at me."

The man became motionless again.

From the street outside came shouts as the crowd below vented its pent-up feelings, trying to figure what all the excitement was about. Then came a series of protestations from nearer the window as other window-washers were dragged protestingly from their precarious perches. Then the noises died down, only to grow louder and different as the tramp of feet sounded in the outer office and the door was abruptly thrown open.

Ahead of the bluecoats came Captain Brady; behind them crowded in Steve Woodward and half a dozen detectives. But they all paused inside the door and looked silently at the tableau of the two men in the center of the room.

"Fasten on to this bird, some of you," said Riordan, "my arm's cramped. Take the whole gang down to headquarters and put 'em through."

The window-washer, still gripping a pile of the bogus money, was jerked away. Riordan shoved his automatic back in his holster.

"Much obliged, Mr. Woodward," he said. "You might tell those two boys of yours in there to stop counting that stuff now. I guess our show's been a success.

"Chief, have a couple of the boys take that stuff back to the theater for me, will you? I've got to go see a man, and then I'll be back at my office—I guess by that time they'll have these window-washers pretty well sorted out."

Brady stepped forward and slapped his aide on the back.

"Good boy," he said. "Take all the time you need."

An hour later Riordan had considerable difficulty getting into headquarters without being observed by newspapermen and photographers. But he knew the ways of the old building, and presently reached the inner office of the detective bureau. The mayor was there, sitting at Captain Brady's desk; old Peter Jewett was there. Captain Brady was walking up and down with a broad smile on his face. The moment Riordan entered he turned toward him gleefully.

"I guess you got him, boy," he exclaimed. "We've had the Bertillon gang working on him, and he's got a record a mile long. Here and on the other side. Jake Renaldi, he is, made his first bust in Naples and been going good ever since. The rest of the window-washers seem to be clear—they just worked for this Renaldi guy. He's the 'City Window Washing Company, Jacob Reynolds, manager.' Has the contract to clean windows on most of the office buildings in town—and every one that's been tapped by this ghost burglar was employing him. I got some of the boys out now checking up on dates of the robberies with his gang's window-washing."

Riordan smiled. "That's a good idea, chief, but you needn't bother," he said.

"But we got to make a strong case, boy," persisted Brady. "This guy's got a lot of money and will fight—"

Let him fight. I got a witness that will identify him."

Brady dropped into a chair.

"You got a what?"

"Got a man he robbed that will identify him. Got a fellow who will tell how he opened the window on one of his jobs, climbed in, pulled a gun and stuck him up. Positively."

Brady leaned back in his chair and winked at the mayor.

"What did I tell you, your honor," he said, slapping his thigh. "Ain't the boy good?"

How'd you do it, man," demanded Peter Jewett. "Tell us, and we can work up the case afterward. Remember there's a thousand dollars reward in it for you."

Riordan smiled slowly. "Partridge give me the tip," he said. "Maybe he ought to get the reward—let's have him in here."

Brady opened the door and bellowed out into the main office:

"Hey, one of you run down to Sergeant Riordan's office down the hall and tell Emmet and Drake to drag what they got in here with 'em."

A moment later the two detectives entered, almost literally obeying Brady's order. Partridge was writhing between them, and he had a large swelling on one side of his jaw. At sight of Riordan he broke out into a string of profanity.

"I'll get you for this, you blankety-blank blank," he shouted. "Mr. Mayor, I want to prefer charges—"

"Shut up," growled Brady, "or I'll make you. You'll get your chance later. Listen to Riordan."

"Partridge," said the sergeant, "you recall Jimmy Kilvain, that you took out of the Merchants' Bank and locked up on a burglary charge? How'd you like to have him sue you for about twenty-five thousand for false arrest?"

"On what grounds would he sue," surlily demanded the Protective Association's man.

"I just told you—false arrest. You not only picked him up without any evidence at all, but you held him when you knew that the stolen bank notes that were taken from him were being unloaded two hundred miles away, up the line. I've got your reports to show it."

"That don't prove anything. He sent a package out of the bank."

"Yes, and he can prove what was in it. And *you* can't."

Partridge was rapidly growing less belligerent.

"Well," he demanded.

"I knew all about the Kilvain case," said Riordan, "but I didn't hook it up with this ghost business till this morning, when you got fresh with me down at the Estate Building, You reminded me of it, and gave me the winning tip, but you didn't know it."

"You're welcome to whatever I gave you, sergeant."

"Thanks, and you're welcome to what I gave you, too. I'll let you know later whether Jimmy will sue you or not—it will all depend on how quickly you quash that complaint against him, and on whether you see that he immediately gets his old job back at the bank."

"You and Partridge can fight it out later," interrupted old Peter Jewett. "What we want to know is how you pulled this thing?"

"It was the simplest thing, sir," said Riordan. "That is, it was simple when I got it straightened out. You see, I framed this 'money counting' stunt down at the Estate Building just as a trap—with Captain Brady's help. I figured it would be too good a chance for this ghost burglar to miss. But when we framed it I figured we'd have to trust to luck to 'make him' and grab him. Just as we were ready to start this morning I noticed a window-washing gang working on the building, but didn't think anything of it—you see 'em all over town, you know.

"Then Partridge here got fresh with me about this Kilvain case. And Jimmy's a friend of mine, sir. I had him up at the hospital. Well, when Partridge got gay with me it came into my mind all at once—Jimmy, the doctor said, had been shocked by realizing his helplessness when he was robbed, by realizing the disgrace that was coming to him. Up at the hospital last night I was standing at the window looking at a toy gun one of the nurses had and he looked up from his bed and saw me—and at once went out of his head again.

"Well, when Partridge tackled me this morning that flashed back into my mind—and I also thought of those window-washers, and it all came to me. This ghost burglar was covering up as a window-washer and prowling whatever happened to look good to him. *He* had robbed Jimmy, and scared and terrified him out of his wits, up on the third floor of the bank, when he was signing bank notes.

"It was a simple thing—his getting in that way—he was just a sort of glorified second-story man, with a ready-made alibi if he happened to get into an office that was occupied; he'd say he came in to wash the inside of the window. Well, I saw it all—and I ran out and got some stage money, laid it out for him to see, and waited out of sight.

"After it was over I went out to the hospital and told Jimmy—and then, when it was explained to him, his mind opened up, the terror of the thing left him, and he remembered it all. Why, he even described this bird for me. He's going to be my prosecuting witness."

A JEWELER'S REPUTATION

Riordan Plays a Hunch, While Brady
Helps, and Frenchy Chaumond
Takes the First Prize Away

1

THE RUBIES FROM SIAM

"YES," SAID CAPTAIN of Detectives Brady, tossing his uniform cap upon his desk and facing his aide, Sergeant Riordan—"yes, the mayor was going to make you a lieutenant and raise your salary, and all that; and then the budget committee got hold of it, and now you got as much chance as a jack rabbit has to catch an airplane.

"Why, some of those idiots down at the budget meeting asked me why we couldn't run a 'bum-wise' town and cut the police force in half. They said if we passed the word round that we wouldn't bother crooks here as long as they laid off, we wouldn't need so many dicks. I told 'em plenty."

"I'll bet you told 'em, chief," said Riordan.

"I did that, my boy. I looked some of those fine gents right in the eye, and I said: 'That's a fine idea. The only trouble with it is that there's just as much honor among thieves and safe blowers as there is among business men—and, agreement or no agreement, if any of 'em sees a chance to pull a good job and get ahead of the other fellow, he'll do it.

" 'Running a bum-wise town isn't any economy, 'cause you got to watch 'em just the same, and besides that you're simply harboring a lot of bad actors that will put one over on you if they can. And you'll also make all the neighboring towns sore.'"

"Did they believe you, chief?"

"Well—they didn't cut the police budget any. But they didn't vote to raise it any, either."

One of the men from the outer office opened the door and passed a card to Captain Brady. The head of the detective bureau looked at it, shot a glance at Riordan, and signaled the man to show the caller in. There entered a plainly successful business man, more than ordinarily well dressed, plump and well fed, and wearing two large diamond rings, and a stickpin in his tie that must have appraised at several hundred dollars.

Captain Brady placed a chair for him.

"Be seated, Mr. Westcott. This is my right-hand man, Sergeant Riordan. Riordan, this is Mr. Westcott, of West-cott & Morse, the jewelry firm. What seems to be the trouble, Mr. Westcott?"

The visitor hesitated, and looked at Riordan as if he was waiting for him to depart. But Brady's man, at a signal from his chief, drew up another chair, sat down, and leaned forward attentively. Captain Brady produced a cigar from his pocket and slowly lighted it. Riordan, as the silence continued, did the same thing. Mr. Westcott, seeing how the land lay, cleared his throat.

"I don't know just what's the trouble, captain," he said. "Perhaps not very much, perhaps a great deal."

"What's Partridge, of the Protective Agency, think?" Brady asked.

"Partridge is a fool—that's why I've come to you," West-

"So zat is why!" he exclaimed. "Well, tell
me, my frien', is zis woman here?"

cott expostulated. "He— But how did you know I'd had
the matter up with Partridge?"

"You pay a hundred dollars a year for his agency's
services, don't you? And you try to get your money's worth?"

"Yes—but I don't get it." Westcott's lips compressed
into a thin, straight line. "Partridge himself said he couldn't
help me unless I do— Oh, he's a fool!"

Brady smiled dryly.

"I wouldn't say he was absolutely a fool, Mr. Westcott.
He's pretty good at his line. The trouble is, you people seem
to expect too much of him sometimes."

Westcott strummed on his knees with his fingers. Brady
and Riordan smoked, apparently contentedly.

"Well, I'll tell you about it," the jeweler said finally. "But
I don't want you to give it to the papers. You'll see why
presently. Young Mrs. Danzig—she was Muriel Desborough, you know—had a ruby necklace. Her mother bought
it for her about five years ago—bought it from me. Siam

rubies they were: not pigeon-bloods, but first class stones. I picked them myself.

"Well, last week she wanted the thing changed, captain, and brought it in. She happened to give it to me. Wanted it lengthened, she did. No more rubies—I rather fancy she can't afford them—but wanted me to put in some bangles and things.

"This morning she called for the necklace. She asked for me at once, and before I had a chance to get the thing she told me she was a little short of money, and would I be kind enough to charge it? It wasn't very much—merely a matter of some sixty dollars or so—and they're good people, you know. I said, 'Certainly,' and went upstairs to the shop to get the necklace.

"Captain, somebody had substituted reconstructed rubies for the original stones. I went downstairs and made an excuse to her—told her we hadn't got the work completed as yet. Asked her to let us send it out to her, promising to try and have it ready by to-morrow.

"She was very nice about it, fortunately. Then, as soon as I got rid of her, I went back upstairs.

"Everybody who had anything to do with that necklace swore it was just as they received it. I called Partridge— personally—told him to hurry over. He said it was a very simple thing. Said she'd had the stones changed herself. I told him that was impossible, because she had given me the necklace, and I would have noted the change.

"He laughed at me; said I was probably in a hurry; said young Danzig was up against it, and probably had framed the whole thing, and would accuse me of substituting the reconstructed gems, and demand—"

"Never mind what Partridge said," interrupted Brady. "Are you sure you got the original stones when she brought in the necklace? Could there have been a substitution before she brought it to you?"

Westcott shook his head. "No, captain. In the first place, you know, I sold the original necklace. I selected the rubies for it. Then we don't—we don't deal in the cheaper jewelry, you know. If the necklace, when she brought it back, had been composed of reconstructed stones I would have noticed it instantly. We don't handle that kind of stuff at all. No, the substitution was made after it reached our store—while it was in our keeping."

"What's your system?"

"Very simple. In a case like this the salesman who receives the object to be altered or repaired makes an entry in one of our record books. In this case I made the record myself. Then the jewel, or whatever it is, is turned over by the salesman to the head of the repair department with orders as to what is to be done. The head of the repair department writes out the order and gives the salesman a carbon copy—that is his receipt—the salesman's receipt. I got such an order on this necklace.

"The head of the repair department then intrusts the jewel to one of the workmen, who signs the order blank. When the repair is completed he turns the object back to the head of the department, who marks on the order blank the time and date of its return, and then places it in the strong room, to await its being called for or sent out. The jewel is not released until the original salesman or the shipping clerk signs for it. In that way we have an absolute check on every article that is brought to us."

"You have checked up on this necklace, of course?"

"Most certainly. The head of the repair department remembered it particularly, because I had brought it to him myself. When the necklace had been altered and returned to him he is sure it had the original Siam rubies—that there had been no substitution. In fact, he noticed the change in it practically at the same time I did, when he took it from the strong room and gave it to me for delivery. The necklace must have been withdrawn from our strong room and another one substituted for it."

Brady blew a cloud of smoke into the air. "And what worries you, Mr. Westcott," he said, "isn't the necklace, for which you could easily substitute more genuine rubies, but it's the possibility that other jewels have been tampered with, and that your house may have unwittingly sent out phony stuff to your customers. Isn't that it?"

Westcott gave a sigh of relief.

"The very thing, captain—and I didn't have to mention it to you. Why, Partridge couldn't see that, even after I told him. This ruby necklace is nothing—relatively. I will select other stones for it to-morrow. But the big thing is, captain, the reputation of our house.

I must find out if there has been a replacement in some other work—if we have sent out, in return for good jewels, cheap and spurious ones. I must find that out, even if I have to bargain with the—with the thief who has done this thing. Of course, I want to find the guilty party; but most of all, I want to protect our customers and clients, and keep the good name of Westcott & Morse. I am glad you have seen that."

"That's the simplest thing of all to see, Mr. Westcott.

And of course there will be nothing of this in the newspa-pers. I want to assure you that we are just as discreet—even more so—than Partridge or any of the other agencies. We tell the reporters what is proper for them to have, but noth-ing else. Who has access to your strong room?"

"Only two people, aside from myself, captain—the head of the repair department and his assistant. Mr. Morse, you know, simply has an interest in the firm financially—he practically never comes to the store."

"Who are these two people—your repair man and his helper?"

2

THE MARKED NECKLACE

MR. WESTCOTT HESITATED some minutes, as if he were either weighing something in his mind or else searching his memory for the details asked. Finally he seemed to pull himself together, and, leaning forward in his chair, said:

"I don't suspect either of them, captain. I don't want to do them an injustice. I do not want to give you the impression that either of them might—"

"Don't worry about that, Mr. Westcott," interrupted Captain Brady. "I don't suspect anybody myself, just now. But it is necessary that I have certain information to commence work on. And I want to know about these two men. From what you have told me already, I think this matter will prove difficult enough without your making it any more difficult."

"I am afraid so, captain. I shall be glad to give you all the information I possess—I simply did not want to seem to direct suspicion at anybody unjustly. Well, the head of the repair department is Daniel Buxton. He has been with the firm for eighteen years. An excellent man—married, and the father of two children. He owns his own home out on Waverly Heights; is a deacon in the Waverly Heights church.

"I have never found the slightest irregularity in any of his work. He has a slight interest in the firm—Mr. Morse and I thought best to give it to him after he had been with us ten years."

"And the other man—the man who is his assistant?"

"His brother, captain. Considerably younger, but an excellent man. He has been with us for nine years. Mr. Buxton—Daniel, that is—came to me himself about engaging him and gave me his personal guarantee that he would be responsible for him. The younger brother— Harry is his name—has always seemed devoted to the firm's interests and to his work. Incidentally he is a very clever artisan himself, and, when we are rushed, helps out with the repair work."

"You say the older brother gave you his personal guarantee—you mean the youngest one is not bonded?"

"Er—no, captain, he is not bonded. Daniel Buxton's bond is for ten thousand dollars, however, and Daniel would be responsible, under an agreement between us—"

"Why isn't he bonded? Are there any other of your employees who aren't bonded?"

"No, captain. Harry is the only one."

"Why?"

"I was hoping you wouldn't ask that."

"Why?"

"Well, captain, I see I shall have to tell you. Harry, in his youth, was somewhat unfortunate. In brief, he served two years in an Eastern penitentiary for theft. He wasn't really responsible. But the sentence and his own realization of his misdeed were lessons to him. At his brother's suggestion he came West to start life over again; and I am positive he has reformed thoroughly. I would trust him with anything. Of course, with his penitentiary record, he naturally couldn't get a bond. But I have always found him thoroughly trustworthy. He lives with his older brother, has no bad habits, lives regularly, and has only the best of friends.

"I have never regretted giving him this chance to redeem himself. As far as this ruby necklace is concerned, you may count Harry out of it, because he has been home with an attack of influenza for the past ten days. So he could have had nothing to do with it."

"Thank you for being so frank, Mr. Westcott," said Captain Brady. "It will save us a possible unpleasant surprise in the case later. Well, we will do what we can for you—just what, I can't say now. But I'll keep in touch with you, and I want you to let me know instantly if you notice anything irregular."

"I will do that, captain. Anything else?"

"Yes. I want you to take Riordan, here, back to the store with you, and show him around. Particularly I want him to see your strong room and all the details of your repair department. And if while he is at the store he makes any special request of you, I hope you will grant it. He will have to be the eyes for me on this case."

"Very well, captain."

After Westcott and Riordan had left Brady's office, the head of the detective bureau sat thinking for several minutes. Then he reached for his telephone and called the Protective Agency, asking for Partridge personally. When he got that worthy he said:

"Pat? This is Captain Brady, down at headquarters. What's the ruction between you and old man Westcott?"

"Oh!" answered Partridge. "He's been to see you, has he?"

"Uh-huh. Spoke very highly of you, but said you didn't want to handle the case. What's the idea?"

"Did he tell you about that ex-con he's got working for him?"

"Uh-huh."

"Well, that's all there is to it, isn't it? I told him when I first found out about that fellow that he'd be sorry some day he had him round. Looks like now he ought to be sorry. But he wouldn't listen to me. So I told him to pack his troubles to somebody else."

"What did he tell you the rocks were worth?"

"He didn't say."

"How'd he tell you they were lifted?"

"He didn't seem to know."

"Did he tell you anything at all?"

"Not a whole lot. As soon as he got started I began to cuss him out about this here ex-con, and he got sore and left."

"Thanks. Good-by."

Pushing back the phone, Brady made some notations on a pad, tore the sheet off, and placed it in his pocket, and then turned to the mass of routine reports that were always being piled endlessly in the metal basket before him.

SERGEANT RIORDAN, MEANWHILE, had accompanied Westcott to the big jewelry store that enjoyed the cream of the city's trade, as well as much outside business. They went at once to Westcott's office, where the jeweler left his coat and hat, and then they began a casual tour of the establishment, the proprietor pointing out the different departments as if merely showing the store to a visiting friend, and occasionally stopping to exhibit some particularly fine piece of art or bit of jewelry to his companion. In this way Riordan's inspection attracted no special notice, for he was in plain clothes, and gradually they made their way all about the place, finally reaching the repair department.

Westcott introduced Riordan to Daniel Buxton, who acknowledged the greetings perfunctorily, and then the two passed inside the grilled railing that shut this department off from the rest of the store, and entered the workroom beyond, where various valuables were being altered or repaired or manufactured.

After making the rounds of the tables and benches at which the artisans were working, they paused at a desk near the door where the records were kept, the jeweler explaining the system again to Riordan. And then they turned to the strong room, with its rows and tiers of numbered cases and drawers. Coming out, Riordan paused to examine the locking mechanism on the heavy steel door of the room, and then, as they made their way into the body of the store again, he nodded to Buxton, but did not pause to speak.

"Anything else, sergeant?" asked Westcott.

"No, I think not, sir—not now at least. Unless—you might show me that necklace."

"I have it in my office."

They returned to the jeweler's own room, and there Westcott opened his desk, and, unlocking an inner drawer, drew forth a tissue-wrapped parcel which he handed to Riordan.

The detective sergeant unrolled it and let the mass of gleaming stones and metallic bangles rest in the palm of his hand.

"So they're phony?" he said, looking at them.

"I suppose you'd call them that," answered Westcott. "As a matter of fact, they are valuable enough—they are the best of reconstructed stones. But they are nothing like the original stones I selected for it."

Riordan let the necklace run from one hand to the other, looking at it.

"Get me a real ruby, will you, Mr. Westcott, and let me compare them?"

"Certainly, sergeant. I will return in a moment."

He left the office, and Riordan dropped into a chair, weighing the necklace in his hand and examining it closely. While he was doing this the door opened and he looked up, expecting to see Westcott returning; but rose instantly to his feet as he noted that the newcomer was a woman and not the jeweler.

"Oh, pardon me," she said. "I thought Mr. Westcott—"

"He will be back in a moment," said Riordan. "He just stepped out to get me something."

She smiled.

"One of the clerks said he was up here. I'll wait outside." And withdrawing, she closed the door behind her.

Riordan blinked, looked down at the necklace in his hand, then hastily stepped over to the window at the far end of the office. Placing the necklace on the sill, he drew a heavy diamond ring from his finger, and then picked up the necklace again, sorted out the fifth ruby from the grip end of the clasp, and, holding it against his chest, drew one of the points of the diamond across its largest facet, exerting all the pressure that he could. A faint scratch on the facet rewarded his efforts.

Then he replaced the ring on his finger, and when West-cott reentered the room, was sitting in the same chair he had occupied when the jeweler left. Westcott went to his desk, placed a small leather wallet before him, and, opening it, beckoned Riordan over.

"These are real Siam rubies," he said, pointing to the gleaming red stones that lay exposed in the wallet. "Compare those in the necklace with them, and you will see the difference. You will note that the color of these is darker. Perhaps you can also see a difference in the way the light shines through them."

Riordan compared one of the stones from the wallet with those in the necklace, holding both to the light, feeling of them, studying them.

Then he smiled.

"Yes," he said. "There's a difference. But I guess you have to be an expert to tell them apart. I'm much obliged, Mr. Westcott."

He placed both the uncut stone and the necklace on the jeweler's desk and turned toward the door.

"You'll hear from the captain," he said. "Thank you very much for showing me around. And we'll do what we can for you. Good day."

Walking out, he did not even glance at the woman who was waiting outside.

He hurried from the store.

3

RIORDAN HAS AN IDEA

BUT HE DID not return at once to police headquarters. Instead, he swung toward the lower part of the city, and presently entered a small and not overly prepossessing jewelry shop on one of the side streets. The proprietor, known to many and various people as "Frenchy" Chaumond, was sitting in the rear of the store reading the afternoon paper. He looked up, laid the paper aside, but did not rise.

"Hello, sergeant—and now what?" he said by way of greeting.

Riordan dragged forward another chair and sat down. From his pocket he produced two cigars, passed one silently to the proprietor, and lighted the other one himself.

"Frenchy, I want you to uncork. I gotta get some information."

"Surely, sergeant. You know I am always ver-ee glad to help you or Capi-taine Brady. What is zee mattaire?"

"Nothing—yet. Who's got the biggest pile of ice in town?"

The Frenchman cocked his head on one side and regarded his visitor. Then he slowly lighted the cigar Riordan had tendered him, and, holding it between his thumb and the first three fingers, smoked at it slowly.

"You mean diamonds?" he said at length.

"Got me the first time."

"Well, I do not exactly know, sergeant. It might be Mis' Wallace, or it might be Mis' Gerrold, or it might be this Mis' Kendall from New York, who is zee guest of General Pelton and his wife."

When Frenchy spoke slowly and thoughtfully his diction was good; when he spoke hurriedly, it was filled with odd accents.

"That's the bird I'm thinking of—I couldn't recall the name. How much ice has she got?"

Frenchy waved his hands expressively.

"It depends," he said, "on how much she bring wiz her. In New York she have so much diamonds zat even zee Treasury Dee-partment do not know how much. Las' I hear from Antwerp, she ins' had spec'ly cut and matched enough diamonds to make a rope from her neck to her knees and back again."

"What's the idea?"

The Frenchman's hands again filled the air, and he laughed. "Zee idea? My friend, zee idea is vani-tee. Her deares' friend, so they say, has a rope of pearls zee same size. So Mis' Kendall she orders zee rope of diamonds."

"What'd they be worth?"

"You mean, what would zey be worth to steal? Well, my friend, cut up again, zey would be worth anywhere—oh, I do not know. Maybe two hundred thousand—maybe not so much as zat."

Riordan pushed back his hat.

"Can you find out if she's got 'em with her?"

"Maybe—in two, three days. I will call you up."

"All right, Frenchy—do that. Now, what are rubies worth?"

"To steal?"

"Got the idea again. You're smart."

"Zey are worth nozzings."

"Huh?"

"No. Nobody who knows anything—anything at all—would steal zee rubies. Pigeon blood, extra large, maybe yes—but ver-ee hard to dispose of. They are too well known, the big ones. Recut, zey are not worth it. Look—you see zat ruby ring there in zee case? It is worth fiftee dollar that way. Stolen, you could not sell it for twenty. Recut, it would be worth nozzings. Reconstructed, would bring more. No, my friend, nobody who knows anything will—what you call it—monkey?—yes, zat is it. Nobody who is wise will monkey wiz rubies."

"But they're worth a lot of money?"

"Yes—but I tell you zey are not lucky. And zee big ones, zee really big ones—everybody knows them."

"How about these rubies Mrs. Muriel. Danzig has—got a necklace of 'em?"

"Yes, I know. Westcott he sell them. Siam, zey are. Two thousan' dollars he charge Mis' Desborough for them. Nice stones—but if a thief bring them here, an' I was in zat business, I would not give him two hundred for all. I could not sell them for four hundred."

"Well, I'll be darned."

"Has somebody stole them, sergeant?"

"No—nothing like that at all. I just happened to know

about them. Much obliged. You find out, Frenchy, if Mrs. Kendall has that rope of ice, and let me know. Don't tell nobody but me, either."

Riordan left abruptly, and bent his steps toward headquarters. Captain Brady was waiting for him, though he had his coat on and was ready to go.

"Well, boy, took you a long time. What did you see?"

"Not a darned thing, chief. Westcott's place is still just as air-tight as it was last time we looked it over—during the yegg scare two years ago. Everything's wired and barred, and there's watchmen's boxes all over the place, inside and out."

"The Buxton party—you see him?"

"The old one—yes. Sour old skinflint. I betcha he makes his wayward brother's life a burden. What are you going to do?"

"Wait. In the meantime I got a coupla the boys checking up on the help. I called up the bookkeeper and had him send over a pay roll list. Told him not to say anything to anybody about it, that we were just making our annual check before the winter sets in. Jim Taggert's the bookkeeper—you know him. Think's he's foxy. Sent me everybody's name and address but his own."

4

RIORDAN TURNS JOKESMITH

DURING THE WEEK that followed Captain Brady and Sergeant Riordan met only late in the afternoon, when the latter came on duty to relieve the former. And they did not always meet then; several times Riordan simply found a scrawled note on his desk, containing a memorandum of the more important "hang-over" matters to which Brady desired to call his attention. Both of them were busy—on their routine duties, and extra ones—self-imposed.

When Riordan came down to take up his tasks on Saturday, however, he found Captain Brady waiting for him, and in no hurry apparently to depart. The elder man looked at his younger aide for quite a time and then smiled.

"What's the matter, boy? You look kind o' peaked. You ain't gone back to your bad habits, have you, and started playing poker again with that night owl bunch in the garage?"

Riordan shook his head. "No, chief. Just off my feed, I guess. For that matter, you haven't been any too sociable the past week. Been busy on something?"

This persiflage, of course, was mere sparring between the two, who knew each other's moods and ways in all detail.

"I've been a little busy," admitted Brady. "Too bad it's a

one-man job, too. You might have helped me if you hadn't been so occupied with the detail work I left you."

"You mean the Westcott thing?" Riordan said innocently.

"Uh-huh. He was in Wednesday with another report. This time it was an emerald brooch. The biggest stone, he said, had been lifted and a substitute put in. This ex-con of his is back on the job, too."

"You watching that ex-con, are you?"

"Now, don't you get sarcastic, young man. You bet I'm watching young Buxton. When them rubies was lifted he wasn't as sick as he was supposed to be. I been checking on him. He wasn't so sick but what he could go automobile riding with that saintly older brother of his 'most every day. Brother tells the neighbors he's taking him out to get a breath of air."

Riordan raised his eyebrows.

"What did old Westcott do about those rubies?" he asked.

"Replaced 'em with good stones—practically gave Mrs. Danzig a new necklace—and pocketed the loss. Had to uphold the honor of the house, you know. Done the same thing with this emerald. By gad, you got to admire the old codger. He's game, anyway."

Riordan made no comment, and Brady eyed him intently.

Finally he said: "Well, boy, I've told you what I've been doing. Now it's your turn."

"My turn?"

"Uh-huh."

"Why, chief, I just been plugging along—"

"I see a letter from the New York Detective bureau. It came by air mail and was addressed to 'Sergeant Matthew Riordan, in Charge Detective Headquarters' here. How come them birds 'way back there to get you on their mailing list?"

"If you're so curious, why didn't you open it?"

"I don't open nobody's mail—that is, nobody but a prisoner's, and not often his."

Riordan swung round to his desk, opened a drawer, and drew forth a large envelope.

"There it is," he said. "Look it over."

Brady took the extended container, glanced again at the address, and then opened it, drawing out a photograph, mounted on cardboard. It was the picture of a rather prepossessing woman, tastefully gowned, and with her hair piled on her head in a fashion of some years back. He turned it over and read the "booking" on the back—a lengthy series of names and aliases, certain notations that referred to an official record or records, and at the bottom, Bertillon measurements and fingerprint information. The head of the detective bureau studied it silently, then looked in the envelope again, found nothing else, and returned the picture to its container, tossing it back to Riordan.

"Where's the rest of it?" he asked.

"That's all they sent."

"The darned fools! You'd think a bunch as smart as those New York dicks would send the record too!"

"I didn't ask 'em for any records. I just wired 'em to rush me the photograph. They did what I asked."

Brady seemed startled at the simplicity of this. He reached for the envelope, and again studied the picture and the notations upon its reverse side. Then he tossed it over to Riordan's desk.

"I pass, boy," he said. "It doesn't mean anything at all to me. And I guess I'm getting fossilized, too. What's your interest in Belle Fontaine, alias all those names? And what's her line? Or isn't it any of my business?"

"I just got a hunch, chief. I didn't want to bother you with it, knowing you had troubles enough of your own. Maybe if it works out a little later I'll ask your help. Just now it isn't working out so good."

"Stay with it, boy. My experience has been your hunches are usually pretty good. And any time I can do anything— you know you only got to ask me."

"All right—I'll ask you now. Gimme the low down, real inside on Frenchy Chaumond."

Frenchy's as straight as they make 'em."

"So I supposed, or you and he wouldn't be friends. But what's he doing running a little jewelry shop down in that end o' town? Come on, now, chief—I got to know."

"Listen, boy, if you've spotted something in Frenchy's place that isn't all right, it's because he doesn't know it's wrong. You—"

"I'm not worrying about anything in Frenchy's place," interrupted Riordan. "But I got to know who he really is. I've been buzzing round quietly, trying to find out, and I can't. He knows something that maybe it's all right for him to know, and that maybe it isn't. Before I play ball with him I've got to know the low down on him, so I can know how strong to go. Now come across."

Brady took a deep breath, looked over his shoulder at

the office door, and then hitched his chair over beside Riordan's.

"I promised never to tell anybody, boy," he said. "I gave my word to a—to a certain party. When Frenchy first came here and opened up that shop I was leery of him. It looked too much like a fence, see? I went down and had a talk with him, and he wouldn't tell me anything. Well, I was going to lean on him and make him either come clean or get out of town, when this certain party came to me and told me to lay off. He told me who Frenchy was. He showed me a letter from the French ambassador, back at Washington. That's all I can tell you, boy, except this—if you want to play ball with that frog, it's all right. He'll play fair."

"He sure knows an awful lot."

"I'll tell the world he knows a lot, boy. If you or me knew half as much as he knows, we'd never work another minute."

"Thanks, chief. I guess you've told me enough. Want to take a walk with me before the stores close?"

Brady snapped to his feet, threw on his coat, slammed his desk shut, and opened the door, calling out to the outer room:

"Hey, you, Willis, come and sit in here. Riordan and me have some business to attend to."

Riordan had put the photograph away and locked the drawer containing it, and was beside his chief almost as the order was shouted.

Together they left the building and headed toward the retail district, but a block before they came to it Riordan turned down a side street and presently pushed Brady into the doorway of a great warehouse occupied by several wholesale firms.

"We just got time to catch Danzig before he goes home," he said. You introduce me and then play me up strong."

If Brady was surprised, he gave no sign. Once in Danzig's office he introduced his aide and urged Danzig to do whatever he asked, as the matter was important.

Then he let Riordan do the talking.

"Mr. Danzig," said the sergeant, "this is going to sound funny, but it really isn't. I want to know if you'll take the captain and me home with you and let us have a look at your wife's jewels. She's out to the country club, I happen to know, and so won't be in the way. Understand, there's nothing at all the matter with Mrs. Danzig's jewels, and they're all there, as far as I know. But I've got a tip that somebody's planning a bit of hocus-pocus, and I want to spoil it."

Danzig laughed. "Why, surely, sergeant. I'll give you the jewels, if you want. Anything Brady, here, says is all right with me. What's the idea—somebody planning to rob Muriel?"

"Nothing like that, Mr. Danzig. But there's a woman here who picks up an odd living copying jewels that prominent people wear. That's all right. Only I understand that she's promised one of her clients to make a copy of Mrs. Danzig's ruby necklace, and I don't think she's going to deliver the goods. I want to get a look at that necklace, that's all, so when I see the copy I can see whether she's obtaining money under false pretenses or not. Naturally I don't want Mrs. Danzig to know anything about it, because she might talk. And this thing mustn't get nosed around."

"I understand perfectly," said Danzig. "Glad you came to me. Come on, let's go. My car's downstairs."

On the way to Danzig's house Riordan proved himself a perfectly inexhaustible fount of funny stories, and both Danzig and Brady roared with laughter throughout the trip.

Riordan was still telling side-splitting anecdotes as they alighted from the automobile and entered the dwelling, and only ceased when Danzig left to ascend to the second floor, where his wife's boudoir was. He returned in a moment with a jewel case, and, placing it on a table, drew out the ruby necklace.

Riordan reached for it, spread it out between his two hands, and exclaimed to Brady:

"Beautiful thing, isn't it? The combination of bangles and gems sets the stones off better, don't you think?"

Brady went into ecstasies over it, too, following his aide's lead, and fingered the necklace admiringly. As the two officers drew it through their hands, Riordan backed around so the light came over his shoulder, and quickly grasped the fifth stone from the grip side of the clasp, turning it over and over, examining its facets carefully. Then he returned it to Danzig.

"Ever so much obliged, Mr. Danzig. I am sure this woman couldn't copy that. In fact, she'd be a fool to try. But they will do it, you know. We're a hundred times obliged to you—now slip it back before the missus comes, and don't tell her we've been playing with her toys."

Danzig took the gems, replaced them in the case, and left the two sleuths alone. Brady shot a searching glance at Riordan, but the latter only grinned and shook his head.

And the moment Danzig returned to the room Riordan had another funny story to tell. After its climax had brought on another burst of hilarity he nudged Brady, and the two made their departure.

5

FRENCHY'S SECRET

AS THEY WALKED rapidly down the street to the car line, Riordan sighed.

"That was some work," he said. "You know, chief, I've been darned near a week getting those stories on tap, so I could reel 'em off. If I'd had to tell one more I'd have been stumped. I shot the whole works."

"I've seen a lot of fool stunts," growled Brady, "but you got 'em all beat. If you'd told me what you wanted I'd have put you in a padded cell. But you got me in there so sudden I just had to play up to you. Have you gone nuts?"

"I had to push you right into it, chief, for I knew you'd balk if I told you first. You did fine. You helped a lot. You—"

"Sure I did. Do yuh think I wanted Danzig to know I had a lunatic on my staff? What was the idea of all them stories, in the first place? And that yarn you told him about a woman—"

Riordan laughed. "To fuddle him. I couldn't tell him what I really wanted, chief. And I knew if I kept him laughing he'd get all mixed up and never be able to figure what it was all about. By the time his wife gets home he'll be scared to tell her a blame thing, because he'll know he can't explain anything. Gee! The way you looked at me when I pulled that line about a woman copying that necklace, I thought you were going to spoil it."

"Well, what do we do next—go jump in the river?"

"Take the car back to headquarters, chief. Here she comes—hop on."

They both swung on to a passing trolley, and all the way down town Brady was mum. Riordan had a twinkle in his eye, but made no effort to explain the joke. At headquarters Brady motioned Willis out of the office, and then shut the door and locked it.

"Now," he said savagely, "you tell me what you're up to, or I'll take a paste at you."

Riordan burst out laughing.

"Go ahead and paste," he said. "You know you wouldn't hurt me. If it makes you feel any better, take a swing."

He held his jaw forward as if waiting for the blow.

Brady slammed into a chair, shaking his head.

"It's no use, I got to humor you," he said. "Tell papa where it hurts."

Riordan sat down in his chair and looked at his chief with seriousness in his eyes.

"Last week," he said, "when you sent me down to West-cott's to look the place over, I asked him to let me see the phony bracelet that the bad man had substituted for Mrs. Danzig's rubies. He showed it to me. I asked him to show me a real ruby to compare with the fake ones, and he went out of the room and got a wallet full of 'em.

"While he was out I got a hunch, and I took off my diamond and scratched one of the phony stones—the fifth one from the grip end of the necklace. Well, up there at

Danzig's just now I looked at that stone—you saw me doing it—and that scratch is still there."

Brady leaned forward in his chair. "So he give her back the phony stones!" he exclaimed slowly. "Give her the bum rocks—after making that play here about the reputation of his house. The old crook!"

Riordan shook his head. "Nothing like that at all, chief."

"But you said you found the scratch on the ruby—the same one?"

"Uh-huh."

"Then he gave her back the phony ones. You've proved it."

"There never were any phony ones!"

"What?"

"I say there never were any phony stones. There never was any replacement. It's all bunk."

Captain Brady tipped his chair away back, looked at Riordan, and then at the ceiling. Then he reached for a cigar, lighted it, and blew great clouds of smoke upward, watching them curl and twist.

"Say it over again—and say it slow, boy."

"There never were any phony stones in the case, chief. Westcott invented the whole thing. He got the necklace to alter. Mark you, he got it himself. He turned it in to Buxton to be altered, and initialed the record himself. And he got it out of the strong room himself and receipted for it. Then he came down here and told us that fine yarn about the mysterious substitution of reconstructed rubies for the real thing. And said how he was going to replace the fraudulent stones with good ones, at his own expense, to protect the honor of the firm.

"And two or three days later he sends the necklace out to Danzig's, and tells you how he has put good stones in it and pocketed the loss. And then pulls another one about an emerald being substituted the same way. You didn't see any phony emerald, did you?"

"No, but by God, I will! We'll go right down there now—"

"Easy, chief, easy. We won't go near him—not yet. Let him think we've swallowed it, bait, line, and sinker. Let him play us. He's laying an air-tight plant—can't you see? He's framing something—and making himself good first for an alibi. He's the one man we don't want to be suspicious.

"And you've got to admit he's good. We've taken his word for it. I've seen a necklace which he said was phony, and Mrs. Danzig has got one that's good. He can claim he replaced the stones—"

"The hell he can! How about the mark you put on 'em?"

"He doesn't know anything about that mark. That's all we've got on him so far. We can't afford to get him suspicious. We have got to go easy and wait."

Brady nodded his head. "Yes, I can see that. Boy, you're clever. What gave you the hunch? I never suspected a thing—only that ex-con he's got working for him. What is the next thing?"

"The next thing is for you to go out to dinner and give me a chance to clear up the routine work here. Then you get hold of Frenchy Chaumond and be back here with him about nine o'clock. Don't tell anything. Go on, chief—get out and eat, and give me a chance to clear up this mess of reports."

CAPTAIN BRADY AND Frenchy Chaumond reached the

inner office of the detective bureau promptly as the chimes in the city hall were booming out nine. Riordan turned to greet them with a smile. While Chaumond was finding a chair Brady slipped the catch on the lock upon the door so they would not be disturbed and then came over and stood by his aide's desk.

"I been telling Frenchy what a bright lad you are," he said. "I figured it would save time if I mapped out the preliminaries for you. Because I suppose you want us here to spring something on this Westcott case, don't you?"

"Sergeant, you're a deep one," interjected Frenchy. I am almost beginning to suspect why you came to me last week and asked about zee diamonds of Mis' Kendall. You remembaire I tol' you she had zem wiz her?"

"Yes, Frenchy, and I remember you wouldn't tell me how you found out, either."

Chaumond showed his teeth in a smile.

"Frenchy's got ways of finding out things, boy," explained Brady. "Now what you got to shoot at us?"

Riordan looked at his chief.

"You'd better sit down," he said.

Brady moved from the desk and pulled his own chair over beside the one Frenchy was occupying.

"Now I'm all set," he declared. "Let's go."

Riordan swung round to his desk a moment and extracted from the inner drawer the photograph he had received by air mail from New York. Taking it from its envelope, he extended it to Chaumond without saying anything.

The Frenchman took it, looking at Riordan in a puzzled way, and then glanced down at the picture. It had a strange effect upon him. First he turned deathly pale, then he flushed red and began to tremble violently, seeming to be barely able to hold the photograph steadily enough in his hands to focus his eyes upon it. Gradually he forced himself to a better control, though his effort was plainly noticeable to the two sleuths who watched him.

Finally he raised his eyes to Riordan's and spoke.

"Nom de Dieu!" he exclaimed. "So zat is why you ask me about diamonds! Tell me, my frien', is zis woman here?"

"You know her, do you?" asked Riordan, ignoring the other's question.

Chaumond looked back at the photograph, and again his hands trembled. Then he leaned toward Riordan and said huskily: "My frien', it ees time I tell you something. The capitaine here, he knows it. Listen. Long time ago zis woman here"— he tapped the photograph with a nervous finger—"was in Paris. So was zee Czarina of Russia. So was I. I was a secret agent of zee Surety. I was tol' to make zee acquaintance of zis woman an' watch her. Humph. Zey did not tell me enough.

"I make her acquaintance. She make me fall in love with her. She make me, I say. She is *vraiment un diable*—she is a devil. She steal some of zee Czarina's jewels. And she get away. Me—zey blame me. Zey say I let her get away, that I love her. *Mon Dieu!* I *did* love her! But I did not know! For a long time I did not believe.

"Well, I will be brief. I lose my place. But I have friends, and finally zey get me work wiz what you call zee customs service. And there I find out about zis woman—and see what a fool she make of me. I promise to find her, to arrest her. But nevaire do I do it. Always she is gone when I get there.

"In time I live down the shame of what she did to me, and I get promoted. They send me here, as a secret agent, to keep an eye on many things, mostly smugglers. Not in your city, sergeant, but on French ships that on your west coast may have things on board from the Orient, from the French colonies, that they would smuggle to the mother country. Nevaire mind how I work—my little store what you call 'covers' me. I meet funny people there—the capitaine here can tell you.

"But all zee time I have promised to find zis woman here and take her back to France for what she did. You are my frien'; the capitaine is my frien'; if you know where zis woman is—and I know you do—you will take me to her?"

"So you want 'the Big Russian Blonde,' do you?" Riordan laughed. "Well, I thought maybe you could tell me about her. Maybe I want her, too."

"I have zee first claim—"

"Not till I get done with her," interrupted Riordan. "I tell you what I'll do, Frenchy. You help me in this, and when the pinch comes, if I can do it, I'll throw you onto the woman. I'm not so certain I want her, anyway. But I got an idea that through her I can get somebody I *do* want. Now, will you agree to keep your hands off till I give you the word—and in the meantime help us?"

"My frien', I agree. I swear on my soul—on the soul of my poor dead mother! I will do anything—yes, I will murder—if you will let me get zat woman."

"Well, I don't think it will be a homicide case. Let's shake hands on it."

6

RIORDAN STAKES ALL

RIORDAN EXTENDED HIS big hand, and, in spite of its strength, the Frenchman nearly crushed it in his fervid grip.

"Suppose you let me in on this, boy," said Brady. "What's all this stuff about a Russian blonde? That the jane whose picture you showed me? How'd you get onto it?"

Riordan laughed.

"You remember, three years ago, chief, when you sent me back to New York to get Billy Huffmann on extradition? Well, while I was down at headquarters there one day some of the boys showed me round. They were all lit up at that time over a big jewel robbery there, and they said it was the work of a woman known as the Big Russian Blonde.

"They showed me pictures of her, and told me a good deal about her work. She was some clever. And they didn't get her, though she's wanted for half a dozen known jobs and a lot more that she's just suspected of.

"Well, not so long ago I saw a woman in town here who looked like her, so I wired for the picture to freshen up my memory."

"She is following those Kendall diamonds," interjected Frenchy.

"I wouldn't be surprised at all," admitted Riordan. "In fact, I'm framing it so she can get 'em."

Chaumond jumped to his feet.

"No, no, no!" he cried excitedly. "No, you mus' not! If she get 'em, she is gone like that—pouf! No, you mus' not make any what you call 'frame' like zat."

Brady pulled the man back into his chair.

"Keep your shirt on, Frenchy," he said. "This is Riordan's case. Damn, I thought it was mine when it started, but the boy's taken it clear out of my hands. All you and I can do is to play up to him."

"But, capitaine, I know zis woman. She is a devil, I tell you. Eef she get those diamonds, eet ees good night."

"Maybe yes, and maybe no. Leave it to Riordan."

The Frenchman shrugged his shoulders.

"I think you are both zee big fools," he said.

"I don't doubt it at all, Frenchy. But we like it. As for me, I only wish I was as big a fool as Riordan. You figure, boy, that this Russian Blonde has got to Westcott and charmed him to swipe the diamonds you're talking about for her?"

"Something like that, chief. To tell the truth, I'm a bit ashamed of myself—what with all I've been doing since you sent me down to Westcott's that day when he was up here belching about the Danzig necklace.

"I've been out with ladies' maids and chambermaids and butlers and millionaires and everythin'—and keepin' it all from you, chief, because I didn't dare tip my hand for fear you'd think I was crazy—like you did up at Danzig's house. But here's what I've found out:

"Westcott has been very attentive to this Russian Blonde for—for some time. He's a widower, you know, and she seems to have hit him hard. They've had one or two fights, too—lovers' spats, you might say. Evidently there was some argument between them. Understand, I didn't get this all at once—I been picking it up gradual.

"Well, they finally seem to have come to an understanding. And it was right after they come to this era of good terms, as you might call it, that Westcott comes down here and tells us this yarn about the rubies in that necklace bein' substituted. I never did like that from the first—somehow, when he told us about it I couldn't swallow it. And after I looked over his store and that strong room I liked it less than ever. And when I saw this blond party—well, that was why I played that trick of scratching the stone in that necklace."

"Where did you see zis blonde?" asked Frenchy, intentness in his tone.

"Never you mind where I saw her or when I saw her. You keep off, see? Remember what you promised. And if I find you snoopin' round Westcott's, I'll brain you. Get that in your head solid. I don't want this Russian woman to see you till the blow-off comes—then you can do as you please."

"You see the sense of that, don't you, Frenchy?" asked Brady.

"Yes, capitaine, but it is ver-ee hard. But I will do as Sergeant Riordan says. I have promised."

"Where's all these diamonds, anyway?" asked Brady.

"Mrs. Kendall, wife of the New York railroad man, is out here visiting the Peltons, chief. Frenchy, here, come through with the information that she had a coupla yards of ice with her, all on a string. Old General Pelton's going to bust the string for me, and then have the ice sent down to Westcott's to be restrung."

"You been to see General Pelton and put that up to him?" exclaimed Brady.

Riordan looked a bit sheepishly.

"Sure," he said brazenly. "I'm a cop, ain't I? Sworn to protect the citizenry, and all that stuff? And Pelton is a good sport. He treated me real white. When I explained the play to him he was real excited about it. Thinks it's a sort of a lark."

"But, good heavens, Pelton's Morse's brother-in-law, and Morse is Westcott's financial backer and partner!"

"I know. Maybe that's why he took such an interest in it."

Brady shook his head.

"I'm getting old," he said. "Boy, that's all there is to it. I'm getting old."

"And where, sergeant, does the blonde come in?" asked Frenchy, who had been following the conversation eagerly.

"Never mind, Frenchy. Don't let your thoughts stray to that Russian jane. The less you know about her, the better. You'll get your chance when this thing breaks. Before then, what you don't know won't hurt you, and it won't put any temptation in your way."

Chaumond smiled grimly. "You are so clever, sergeant," he said. "You theenk of ever-ee little thing."

"You bet your life I try to. If I bingle this thing I'm sure going to get in bad."

"When does the big thing come off?" asked Brady.

"Monday some time. It starts Monday morning about ten. We got to wait, after that, 'till it happens. Frenchy, can you manage to be here at ten Monday morning?"

Chaumond laughed loudly.

"Be here at ten!" he exclaimed. "Listen. Ten thousand wild cannibals could not keep me out of here. I will be here on zee dot."

"That's all for you, then. Now beat it. Brady and I have got to make some medicine. And keep your mouth shut and your shirt on. You'll get your chance Monday."

Chaumond rose and grasped Riordan's hand again, giving it a frantic grip again, and then turned toward the door with tears in his eyes.

Brady got up and let him out, then locked the door again and came back to his chair.

"Now you know who and what the frog is, boy," he said. "And maybe you see why I couldn't tell you this afternoon. What do you want me to do Monday?"

"A whole lot, chief. I'm going to give you my resignation Monday morning, and if this thing flivvers I want you to keep it and have me pinched. There'll be charges enough against me, all right. If it don't flivver, you can burn the resignation up. That's—"

"Never mind talking silly, boy. I'm the man who's responsible for this department, not you. Whatever you do, you're doing under my orders. Now tell me what you want."

Riordan looked deep into Brady's eyes, but said nothing for a moment; but he was telling his chief what he thought of him. They didn't need to talk to understand each other sometimes.

"Well, chief, I'll tell you," he said at length. "I didn't tell you any of this before, because it wasn't ripe. I didn't want to start you on a bum trail. But I guess after what Frenchy

Chaumond told us it's right enough—taken along with
what I've picked up.

"Monday morning General Pelton is going to ask Mrs.
Kendall to let him see her famous diamond necklace. She's
packing it out here, like a darned fool, to wear at the Char-
ity Ball at San Francisco, which is where she's bound. Of
course she'll let him see it, and while he's looking at it
he's going to bust it—bust the catch, if he can, but bust it
anyway.

"He'll apologize and be awfully sorry, and offer to have it
fixed right away, and he'll take it down to Westcott himself.
Then he'll telephone from his office for Mrs. Kendall to
send her maid down to get it, at whatever time Westcott
says it will be fixed.

"All we got to do is to fill Westcott's place full of
classy-looking dicks, have a strong-arm squad at the back
door and the side door, and be at the front door ourselves
to see who and what comes out. I got an idea we'll get
something."

Brady looked blankly at his aide.

"Yeah," he said. "And where does this Russian Blonde
come in?"

"Oh, I forgot to tell you—she's working as Mrs. Kendall's maid."

Brady gave a start. "You mean to tell me Westcott's been
running around with a lady's maid?"

"Yes, but he doesn't know it. She dolls up something
nice, she does, when she goes out."

"Well, what's to prevent her runnin' off with the
diamonds when they're fixed—just like Frenchy warned
you?"

"Two or three things. Frenchy, for one; you and me for a couple of others. And Burley, of the motorcycle squad, will be driving Mrs. Pelton's car. Her own chauffeur took sick just about a week ago, and recommended Burley very strong. In fact, he said Burley was his brother. To tell you the whole truth, General Pelton and I fixed that little thing up between us to sort of safeguard the rocks."

"I begin to see what you're driving at, boy. You've been pretty busy while I was fussin' round that ex-convict, haven't you?"

Riordan grinned sheepishly. "Maybe, chief. Can you fix it up so the dicks will be round, careless like, Monday? We're going to need 'most all of the outside men."

"You leave that to me. There won't be any loopholes at all on the outside."

7

THE TRAP IS SPRUNG

MONDAY MORNING AT ten found the detective bureau strangely deserted. A uniformed sergeant from downstairs was sitting at the desk in the outer room as Captain Brady, Sergeant Riordan, and Frenchy Chaumond walked out. There were no coats in the lockers where the sleuths usually left their personal belongings; there were no waiting men sitting at the tables in the back room, playing cards, or arguing, or poring over the "picture books."

Brady, his aide, and Frenchy made their way downstairs to the police garage and climbed into one of the large touring cars. The driver, in plain clothes, let in the clutch as soon as the doors slammed, and, without any orders, drove rapidly off, bringing the car to a halt in a vacant parking space directly across the street from Westcott & Morse's large jewelry store. A uniformed policeman moved away from the vacant spot at the curb as the police car rolled up.

"I have two tickets from here to Paris," said Frenchy Chaumond as the car stopped. "One reads in my name, and the other is for 'his wife, an insane person.' And I have lots and lots of money for expenses."

"Good," said Brady. "I hope you get to use them."

"I will. I have sold my jewelry business already. A man

named Osborne—I think you will find him all right, capitaine."

"Can the chatter—there's Pelton's car," said Riordan.

The three watchers saw General Pelton's runabout drive
up to Westcott & Morse's, and the general alighted and
hurried inside. Five minutes later he came out, stepped
into his machine, and drove away. The trio in the police car
sat and waited—five, ten, fifteen, twenty minutes. Then,
without warning, a passer-by paused, stuck his head in
the car, and said:

"He says to tell you, cap'n, that the maid's to call for
'em at eleven o'clock." The man withdrew his head and
walked away.

"Who was that?" asked Frenchy.

"Ennis, one of my men," answered Brady. "He was in
Pelton's office, waiting. Well, we only got forty minutes
to wait."

Chaumond, sitting between Brady and Riordan in
the rear of the big touring car, drew forth a cigarette and
lighted it, puffing at it nervously. Captain Brady closed
his eyes and sat like a man dozing. Riordan, leaning back
in the outer corner, looked vacantly at the passing traffic.
Chaumond threw the cigarette away, half smoked, folded
his arms, and sank his head upon his chest.

Thus they waited.

Eleven o'clock chimed out from the city hall, the ringing
notes floating over the city. Brady opened his eyes, yawned,
stretched, and rose from his seat.

"See you boys later," he said, opening the door and stepping from the car to disappear at once in the passing down
town crowd.

"Where is he going?" asked Chaumond.

"To keep a date. Shut up," answered Riordan.

"I will shut up, sergeant—but, oh, it ees so hard to wait."

Riordan made no reply.

Fifteen minutes later a big sedan rolled up to the entrance of Westcott & Morse's, and a woman got out and hurried inside the store. Riordan poked the driver of the touring car in the back, and the man at once started the engine and tooled the car up to the next corner, where he turned it completely around and started back down the block, driving slowly. As he circled around, the traffic cop at the intersection swung his semaphore to "Stop," and no other cars were allowed to come in the block from the same direction.

The police car rolled up to just behind the sedan parked in front of the jewelers, and stopped, its engine still running. Riordan opened the door beside him and stepped out.

"You sit in the car, Frenchy, till the driver tells you what to do," he said, and dodged around the rear of the machine.

Chaumond was surprised. He looked around. Immediately he was impressed with the fact that there was a sort of waiting silence in the air. Puzzled, he sought the explanation, and then noted that for some time the traffic signs at either end of the block had been set at "Stop," cutting off the usual stream of travel.

At the corner ahead, he could see autos and trucks were being diverted down the cross street, while three street cars stood in a line on the track, the motorman of the first one exchanging compliments with the traffic cop on post.

Then he felt the police car in which he was seated give a little jerk, and noted it was moving forward behind a sedan which had pulled out from the curb in front of the jewelry store. Through the rear window of the sedan he could see that it was occupied by a woman and a man.

The sedan turned to the right at the corner, and the police car followed it. It continued along the cross street for three blocks, then turned to the right again, with the police car still in its wake. Another block, and it turned to the right again, kept this course for five blocks, still with the police car close in its wake, and then again it turned to the right.

Frenchy wished Brady or Riordan would appear, wished they had told him what it was all about, and when his chance was to come.

Then he heard the subdued purring of a siren barely turned on behind him, and a second later a motorcycle policeman passed the car in which he was riding. A second and third motorcycle policeman followed and all three passed the sedan ahead.

And then a peculiar thing happened. The sedan suddenly turned sharply in toward the curb and crashed into an iron pole that supported a street light bracket. Frenchy saw the three motorcycle men leap from their machines and leave them lying in the street and surround the sedan at once. The chauffeur of the police car drew up alongside the sedan and stopped. Turning to Frenchy, he said:

"Better move over, young feller—we are going to have company."

Chaumond, bewildered, moved over, and even as he did so the door of the tonneau of the touring car was opened, the door of the sedan opened alongside of it, and the man in the forward car was jerked out by one of the motorcycle men and tossed unceremoniously into the police machine. There followed some commotion in the sedan, and just as a crowd of idlers began gathering, two of the motorcycle men emerged from the closed car, carrying a woman between them, and piled in on top of Frenchy and his unexpected companion.

At the same minute the police car shot ahead, its siren screeching out a warning, and hurtled around the next corner. But Frenchy saw no further details—his eyes were fixed upon the face of the woman between the two policemen, and she was staring wildly at him.

They still were looking piercingly into each other's eyes when they were led into Captain Brady's office at headquarters, the woman held firmly by her captors. The man brought with her slumped into a chair in a corner and sat, a miserable-looking heap, silent and rocking his body slowly back and forth.

For a long time nobody said anything. The woman was the first to speak.

"Let go of me," she said, jerking her arms. "What's this mean?"

"Keep quiet," said Frenchy.

The policeman still retained her arms.

"Are you in charge here?" demanded the woman. "If so, what is the meaning of this? Let me telephone General Pelton."

"Keep quiet, I tell you."

And so they waited—for how long Frenchy knew not. At last, however, footstep's sounded outside, the door was thrown open, and Captain Brady and Sergeant Riordan entered, with two men. Behind them came two of the detectives. The last one closed the door and locked it. Brady pulled up chairs, and the two men who had come in with him sat down. Riordan took his own chair, Brady remained standing.

"Well," said one of the men, "what is the meaning of this, Captain Brady?"

"Darned if I quite know, Mr. Westcott," answered the head of the detective bureau. "Maybe General Pelton, here, can tell us."

The other man turned to Riordan.

"Sergeant," he said, "I took a necklace down to Mr. Westcott to be repaired this morning. When I went to call for it, the man in the repair department said it had already been delivered. I am informed it has not reached my home."

Riordan looked at Westcott. "Know anything about it?"

Westcott shook his head. "I gave it to one of my trusted employees to deliver," he said. "Harry Buxton. Mrs. Pelton's maid called for it, and I sent Buxton with it—with her."

"That him, over in the corner?" Riordan pointed to the man sitting rocking back and forth.

Westcott turned his head and started slightly.

"Yes, that's the man. Buxton, what have you done with that necklace?"

The man came forward, reached in his pocket, and handed Westcott a package done up in velvet and tissue paper, Westcott took it and held it toward General Pelton.

"Here is the necklace, general. I am at a loss to understand what this is all about."

General Pelton opened the package, and a shower of

brilliant stones cascaded over his hand, held together by a fine silver thread. He looked at the bauble closely, then said:

"This isn't the necklace—any fool could see these are glass."

The woman drew in her breath with a sucking sound.

"Frisk that bird," snapped Riordan.

The two detectives stepped forward. Westcott struggled fiercely, but only for a moment. One of the officers held him in a grip that paralyzed him, while the other ran an exploring hand over his person. Presently he drew forth, from inside the jeweler's vest, a flat package, which he handed to Riordan, who in turn gave it to Captain Brady.

The head of the detective bureau ripped it open, and suddenly his hands seemed to be bathed in a flood of sparkling, leaping fire, as strands of diamonds slipped over his big fingers. He passed the mass of gems to General Pelton, who carefully counted them and then slipped them into his overcoat pocket.

"Now," said Riordan, what were you doing going through the gate at the depot for the Overland Limited?"

"Fool!" exclaimed the woman bitterly.

Westcott stammered, then pulled himself together.

"I will not say anything till I have seen my attorney," he said.

"Take him upstairs and lock him up," commanded Brady. "Let him send for all the attorneys in town, if he wants to."

The two detectives led the jeweler away.

"Well, folks," spoke up Riordan, "I guess we're through. You can go now—all of you."

The two motorcycle men let go their hold of the woman's

arms, but Frenchy stepped to her side and gripped one of her wrists.

"What's this mean?" she said. "The captain said I could go."

"Sure," laughed Riordan. "We've got nothing on you. We might have had, but your friend crossed you up. You didn't think he had it in him, did you, Belle? I didn't either, at first. On your way, girly, and don't come back!"

"Make this man let go of me, then."

"He's no man of mine, Belle. You go outside with him and see if you can argue him out of it."

Chaumond jerked her wrist. "Please, *madame*," he said gently, "you will come with me, and I will explain. It is ver-ee droll, yes."

THE HOLE IN THE CHIMNEY

*Sergeant Riordan Gets On the Trail of
an "Inside" Crook, Protects the Little
Fellow, and Gets "The Man Higher Up"*

1

AN EXPLOSION AT MIDNIGHT

"YES, SIR," OPINED Detective Halloran, "the Interurban Company is backed by the Overland Pacific Railway, and I'm ag'in' their getting any franchise on Union Avenue, or any common-user rights over the traction company's tracks. Why, if the city lets 'em in, first thing you know they'll run steam trains down past the city hall, and make us look like a hick town with choo-choo cars on Main Street."

"You're crazy," replied Detective Sergeant Riordan, tipping back in his chair and eying the clock, whose hands were gripped about the figure "II," as if they hated to part from it. "In the first place, it don't matter who's backing this new road; they got a right to run their tracks through the city.

"In the second place, there's an ordinance against operating steam trains in the street. Of course, it would be better for the traction company to give 'em common-user rights, because otherwise there'll be four lines of track on Union Avenue."

"Yes, and that would be fine, wouldn't it? With the Interurban cars on the outside, shutting off the traction

Ten minutes later half a dozen reporters stood in the vault—

company; so if you or me wanted to ride home we'd have to dodge these big new cars—"

The jingling of the telephone interrupted him. Riordan reached for the receiver and growled a "hello" into the mouthpiece. Then he pulled himself closer to his desk, listened intently to the words coming over the wire, and with a curt, "All right, I'll be right up," pushed the instrument away.

"Go get your coat and gun," he said to Halloran, "and if there's any dicks in the back room, tell 'em to heel up, and then herd 'em down to the garage. I'll be waiting for you."

He slipped on his own holster, examined his automatic to see that it was in service order, and then drew on a heavy mackinaw, reached for a soft cap and hurried downstairs. In the garage he found Halloran, Ebbitt and Nickerson already seated in his car. Jumping in he started the engine, slipped the gears into mesh and drove out onto the street.

At a speed that showed his companions he was bent on business and not pleasure, he turned corners until he reached Union Avenue, and then kicking on the siren

—while the electric fans swept the smoke back in the strong room

button, he let the big car out. Keeping his eyes on the street ahead of him, he shouted out of the corner of his mouth to the men in the tonneau:

"Fire department alarm office up in the city hall phoned they heard something like a blast. Thought it might be a safe job."

"There ain't no safes up there worth cracking," Ebbitt shouted back. "Nothin' but little shops up there. O' course, some stranger in the city, or some cheap yegg, might take a chance on them; but no good man would."

Fifty miles an hour, however, was no speed at which to carry on a conversational argument, and the detectives were silent until Riordan brought his machine to a shrieking stop beside the city hall.

"You, Ebbitt and Nickerson," he said, "take a scout around-two, three blocks each way. Halloran, you come with me."

He pushed down into the basement entryway of the city hall, and into fire alarm headquarters, known technically as the telegraph room. Electrical devices in glass cases were all about the chamber, while at a switchboard at one side sat two men. Riordan threw back his mackinaw and flashed his shield.

"You the guy that phoned?" he demanded.

One of the operators left his stool and came forward.

"Yes," he answered. "Sounded over in that direction—to the north. Wasn't much of a noise—sort of a smothered bump, if you know what I mean. Bill, here, said he felt a jar, but didn't hear anything. Thought you'd like to know. You sure got here quick."

"Can you get into the city hall from here?" asked Riordan.

"Sure, that door there—leads into the basement lobby at the foot of the stairs by the elevators. Make a noise so you'll wake the watchman up."

Riordan nodded to Halloran, and the two hurried through the indicated door, found their way around the elevator cages, and to the stairs.

"City treasurer's office, on the second floor," said Riordan. "It's the only good thing that I know of in this neighborhood. Better get your gat out, but don't shoot; it might be the watchman."

The two detectives climbed the dimly lighted stairs to the main floor, their eyes examined all the shadowy nooks of the hallway, crossed the lobby to the other side without seeing any sign of life, and then moved on up the second flight of stairs. As they reached the landing of the floor above there came the sharp sound of a door banging, somewhere down the hallway.

Riordan reached out and grasped Halloran's arm, shoved

the big detective behind one of the pillars and whispered in his ear:

"You stand here and peel your eyes. I know where the light switches are, and I'm going to flood this place with light."

He moved away in the shadows. Halloran heard him padding about for a moment, then lost all sense of sound, and a second later the second floor lobby and the radiating halls were brilliantly illuminated as Riordan found the switches and snapped them on, one after another. Halloran blinked, then surveyed all the territory within his range of vision. Riordan, from the opposite side of the lobby, was doing the same thing.

"Well," he said, after his survey was completed, "let's go."

He led the way down one of the halls, and very presently came to the city treasurer's office. The door was shut and locked. Peering in through its upper glass panels, both detectives breathed easier as they saw the safe doors in the far corner apparently undisturbed.

"Well, that's that," said Riordan. "Now for that door that slammed."

He stepped out into the middle of the hallway, and shouted:

"Oh, watchman—watchman—police calling. At the treasurer's office."

"Coming," answered a distant voice.

"You go meet him," whispered Riordan to Halloran. "Just on a chance, you know, that it isn't the watchman."

Halloran moved silently along, close to the wall, and turned a corner.

Riordan heard a sharp interchange of voices, and then

Halloran came into sight again, a short, gray-haired man in his shirt sleeves walking beside him. Riordan flashed his shield as the two came up.

"You the watchman?"

"No, sir. Watchman's sick to-night. I'm Joe Collins, sir, working for him."

"Hear a noise here a little while ago?"

"Yes, sir, that was me. I slammed a door down at the health office. They've got a window open there, and the draft—"

"I don't mean that. I mean before that—ten minutes before that. Something like an explosion?"

"No, sir, didn't hear nothin', sir."

"Open this door."

"Yes, sir."

The man produced a bunch of keys and unlocked the treasurer's office. Riordan pushed in first, Halloran and Collins following.

"Turn on the lights," said Halloran.

Collins turned to the wall switch, and flooded the room with brilliance. Riordan passed through a swinging gate at the counter and made his way to the steel doors of the vault. He tested the handles thoroughly, but they would not budge, and everything seemed tight.

"All right here," he said. "Let's take a look round at the other offices. You lead the way, Collins."

They inspected all the department offices on the second floor, made similar rounds on the third floor, then returned to the ground floor. Nowhere did there appear to be anything amiss.

"What did you say you heard, sir?" asked Collins, as they stood in the main lobby.

"I didn't hear anything," answered Riordan. "Party in the neighborhood here said he heard a noise. It was probably outside. But I wanted to be sure of this dump first. Let us out the main door, will you, and we'll say good night."

Collins opened the main entrance, nodded to his callers and locked the door behind them. Riordan and Halloran went down the steps, and then walked back and forth for a block or more on several of the streets radiating from the municipal building. They noted nothing suspicious, and returning to the automobile, found Ebbitt and Nickerson awaiting them.

"Not a thing in sight, sergeant," said the former of the two. "All shop doors fast, and lights burning over the safes in that little jeweler's shop, and the furrier's on Jefferson Street. Not a soul in the alleys either."

"Well, I guess we've done all we could; climb in and we'll mosey back."

As Riordan started his car, a uniformed patrolman came running toward them. The detective sergeant stopped the machine and waited for him to come up.

"Well?" he asked.

"Oh, it's you, is it, sergeant," replied the man. "I didn't recognize you."

"The boys in the fire telegraph room said they heard something like a box being blown—twenty or thirty minutes ago. Hear anything?"

"Not a thing, sir."

"We couldn't find anything; maybe it was a blast over in

the quarries. On a quiet night like this that carries a long way sometimes. Did you hear us coming up?"

"Yes, sir. I heard the siren. I was down at the other end of my beat, and run pretty near all the way up. I thought it was a fire."

Riordan laughed. "Don't run next time, officer," he said. "Call in from the nearest box; it may save your breath. Good night."

He slipped the gears into mesh and headed for head-quarters.

2

"CITY HALL'S ON FIRE!"

CAPTAIN OF DETECTIVES Brady, in his office next morning, smiled as he read Sergeant Riordan's report of his investigations. Riordan was a good man, one that could be relied upon.

"That's the boy," Brady said to himself.

"First thing he thinks of is the treasurer's office. Nine men out of ten would never have gone into the city hall at all—they'd have figured the watchman there would keep anybody out. But not Riordan; that boy doesn't take any chances."

He went through the rest of the reports, but there was none of a safe-cracking, either near the city hall nor anywhere else in the city. He looked at the clock; it was a few minutes to nine. All stores and business houses were open, and if there had been a "box job" it would have been discovered and reported. Well, he wouldn't have that to worry about.

"Fire at the city hall, captain," said the doorman, thrusting his head into the room.

Brady leaped from his desk, grasped his hat and joined the stampeding crew of sleuths running downstairs to the garage. A patrol wagon filled with reserves was just pulling out, and Brady tooled his own car into its wake, waving to as many of his men as could to pile on.

Two blocks from headquarters he passed the patrol, and three blocks farther on he was enjoying a neck and neck race up Union Avenue with Battalion Chief Duane. He beat the fire department officer to the city hall by half a block, the sleuths that accompanied him tumbling off from the running board to help establish fire lines a block from the building.

Following two lines of hose already laid into the structure, Brady made his way up the stairs to the second floor, and around to the City Auditor's office, from the door of which smoke was lazily pouring. Diving in, he found four firemen standing in the doorway of the vault, from which denser clouds of smoke were belching, each pair of them holding an idle nozzle, though the hose was throbbing and writhing in their hands from the pressure of the water within.

An engine company captain came out of the vault, wiping perspiration from his smoky face.

"Job for you, cap," he said, recognizing Brady. "Hold your breath and come on in and take a look."

Brady followed him into the vault, his chest bursting and his eyes running tears.

The fireman turned a flash light on the rear wall of the vault, and from a roughly squared hole in the brick, heavy smoke was pouring like a murky serpent. Brady looked as long and as well as he could, and then turned and went out to the relatively clearer atmosphere of the office.

"Get them lines of hose out of here," ordered the fire captain. "Shut the door and open the windows."

As the hosemen moved back, Battalion Chief Duane came in.

"Better get a chemical," he said.

The fire captain saluted, but shook his head. "No use, chief; no fire. Hole in the chimney, that's all."

The city auditor pushed forward. "The records," he asked, "are they burned?"

"Nothing's burned; don't worry. Get back till we get this truck cleared up. Get them electric fans from over the other side of the room, and bring 'em here."

Ten minutes later Battalion Chief Duane, Captain Brady, Auditor Pangbourne and half a dozen reporters stood in the vault. Three electric fans at its door were blowing a stream of air into the strong room that was sweeping the smoke back. An electric light, hanging from the ceiling of the chamber, revealed a gaping hole, nearly square, in the rear wall. Into this hole the smoke was being blown, and through it could be seen the shifting but dense vapor in the chimney beyond.

"Now that you boys have had a look," said Brady, "suppose you get out of here for a minute or two and let the chief and me see what we've got. You can come in later and photograph the place, if you want to."

The reporters reluctantly withdrew, one of them buttonholing the auditor and taking him with him. Brady and Duane both stepped close to the rear wall of the vault, and examined the strange opening. It was about a foot wide and ten inches across where it pierced the vault, and it sloped out toward the chimney, being half as large again where it entered the flue on the farther side of the vault wall, which was approximately a foot thick.

In each corner of the hole was the plainly marked, semi-cylindrical course of a drill. Between the corners, on the top and bottom, were the marks of three other drilled holes, and on either side were evidences of two other drillings. The half cylinder of the middle hole on the bottom was angular instead of rounded.

"I've seen a lot of things since I been a fireman," said Duane, "but this is the limit."

"What you make of it?" asked Brady.

"Simple as your nose on your face, captain. Somebody drilled those fourteen holes through the wall, and then put a bar in the lower middle one, pried on it, and broke the whole prism loose and shoved it into the chimney. But what for?"

"Drilled from this side, wasn't it, and pushed through?"

"Sure—you can tell that from the marks. Look, here you can see where it scraped in going out. But what's the idea?"

"How long, chief, do you reckon it would take to drill those holes?"

"Darned if I know, cap. Quite awhile. A power drill, now, would probably go through that wall—it's rotten brick—in half an hour. That would be seven hours. A hand drill—that would take maybe two hours for a single hole; that would be four hours more than a day, if a fellow worked steady at it."

"It don't look like a power drill to me," said Brady. "The back ends of the holes would be chipped out more where a power drilled would push through. Looks like hand drilling."

"But why?" demanded Duane.

"That's what I've got to find out."

Captain Brady turned and surveyed the inside of the vault, its shelves and filing cabinets. After looking around carefully he poked a finger at a shelf, gingerly, and drew it with a little laugh.

"Soot," he said. "Soot everywhere, an eighth to a quarter of an inch thick. Not a mark. If there were a million finger-prints here you couldn't find one of 'em, buried under all that soot. Well, let's get out of this. I don't envy Pangbourne his job of cleaning up."

They left the vault, to be surrounded by the reporters.

"Go on in, boys, and help yourselves," said Captain Brady. "And listen, I want photographs of that hole. You fellows with cameras and flash lights, take a couple of extra shots for me. Get me a couple of good close-ups. Charge 'em to the department—and rush 'em down to my office as soon as you get 'em printed. I got to talk to Pangbourne a minute."

As the reporters and camera men swarmed into the vault, Captain Brady led the auditor across the main office and into his private room, shutting the door behind him.

"You got to clean that stuff all up, Pangbourne," he said. And while you're getting the soot off it, I want you to check it over. Send me a list of anything that's missing. Better get the engineer's office to block that hole up for you—I don't want the hole any more, and besides, the boys will give me photos of it. But I want you to check all your stuff, and as soon as you get done call me up and tell me what's missing. Get that?"

"Yes, captain."

"Good, now tell me what you know about it."

"It's a mystery to me, captain. There was nothing in the

vault, in the first place, but city records. I don't think any of them have any value in particular to anybody—certainly not enough value to steal. You can get copies of all of them if you want. In fact—"

"Never mind that, Pangbourne. Tell me when you first discovered this."

"Why, this morning, captain. I got to my office a little after nine. Lowry, my chief deputy, who usually opens the vault, was delayed in getting down—there was a jam on the street car lines. So I opened the vault myself.

"As I swung the door back there was a great burst of smoke, and, of course, I thought the records were on fire. So I rushed to the telephone and notified the department. You got here almost as soon as the firemen, I believe; so you know as much as I do about the rest of it."

"Who shut the vault last night?"

"I happened to have shut it, captain. I was putting away the assessment rolls for the Euclid Avenue sewer; the city clerk sent them in about five o'clock, and I happened to take them over the counter myself. We were all through for the day; so I put them away and closed the vault myself."

"Smell any smoke then?"

"None at all, captain."

See any hole?"

"No, of course not, captain."

"Could you have seen one if there'd been one?"

"What do you mean?"

"Was the rear wall covered?"

"Er—come to think of it, captain, there was a filing case against that back wall. Files L and M were back there. But, of course, if the hole had been there—"

"Filing cases hard to move?"

"No, they are mounted on castors. You see, we have to pull them out from the vault sometimes when we are looking for certain records."

"Had that particular case out recently?"

"No, I don't think we have."

"Ever smell smoke in the vault, that you can remember?"

"No, captain."

"Who's got the combination beside you and Lowry?"

"Miss Nelson, my confidential clerk."

Captain Brady considered. Then he asked:

"This Nelson woman, and Lowry—know 'em well, do you?"

Pangbourne smiled. "They've been with me for the three terms that I've been auditor. In fact, my whole force has been with me, captain. I've carried them all along, and the city has never increased my appropriation so I could hire any additional clerks."

"You don't mistrust any of them?"

"Of course not, captain,"

"All right, Pangbourne. You check that stuff as you clean it up, and let me know what's missing."

Assuring the inquisitive reporters that he didn't know a thing more than they did, and was deeply mystified, Captain Brady made his way to the basement and hunted up the chief engineer of the heating department. From that worthy he learned that the fires under the boilers were banked at night, but were never out, and that they were fired up for the day's pressure about five in the morning. At six in the evening they were banked. The engineer was much mystified over the occurrence, of which he had heard various reports.

"Tell you what you do," said Brady. "To-night you pull your fires and have somebody crawl into the base of that chimney. I want those bricks and anything else you may find there. You can do that?"

"Oh, yes, sir."

"All right, have it done. I'll be in my office at headquarters about eight o'clock, and I want you to bring what you find down—or have it sent down."

3

WHERE WAS RIORDAN?

LONG TOWARD FOUR o'clock in the afternoon, when Sergeant Riordan was due to appear and take charge of the detective bureau for the first night relief, Captain Brady frequently smiled to himself. He rather fancied the expression he would see on his aide's face when he reported; and he wondered what he would have to say about the affair of the city hall.

Then the afternoon newspapers gave Brady cause for secret mirth, too; for the news hounds seemed to have settled upon the theory that yeggs, possibly amateurs, had attempted to drill in the vault of the City Treasurer's office, and had by mistake got into the auditor's strong room.

It was not beyond reportorial imagination to explain how the burglars had lowered themselves down the chimney after the fires had been banked, and had worked unmolested and unseen.

One reporter suggested oxygen-masks to overcome the peril of fumes from the banked fires below; another suggested a sort of diver's helmet, with an air hose operated from the roof of the city hall. They all intimated that, however it was done, it was bungled.

Four o'clock came, but not the usually prompt Riordan.

Captain Brady busied himself with reports from the day crew, just going off shift—particularly those reports upon employees of the auditor's office, which he had detailed two of his men to furnish. But the reports showed nothing of interest. None of the clerks appeared to be pressed for money, none had been living beyond his means, nor had any been keeping noticeably late or irregular hours.

The report of a detective who had questioned the night janitor, who had charge of the crew that cleaned the city hall each evening, contained nothing of interest either. The janitor had seen no strangers about the building up until half past ten, the hour at which he had gone home; nor had any of his aides reported any unusual rubbish from the auditor's office.

At half past four Mr. Pangbourne dropped in to report that his force had cleaned up all the files and checked the records, and that nothing appeared to be missing or disturbed. He was inclined to credit the theory advanced in the press, that the hole in the vault had been drilled by yeggs seeking entry to the treasurer's office; and Captain Brady did not argue with him.

Five o'clock showed no trace of Riordan. Captain Brady telephoned his house, but got no response. He began to feel vaguely uneasy. Not because he was worrying over Riordan's welfare, but because he felt his aide was not playing fair with him.

Undoubtedly, he decided, Riordan had some clew on which he was working; but Brady felt that he should have reported first. Perhaps some of Riordan's previous triumphs rankled a trifle in the captain's mind; it is never pleasant for an older man to see his younger aide outstripping him.

At half past five Captain Brady called Phillips in from the outer room and put him in charge while he went out to dinner, first telephoning his wife he would not be home. He ate slowly, considering what he should say to Riordan when he returned; and after finishing his meal he even killed more time by taking a brief walk through the business section. Finally, having philosophically decided to let Riordan work in his own way—if that was the explanation of his absence—he turned back toward headquarters, arriving there somewhat before eight.

Phillips turned a package over to him, and stood by as Captain Brady opened it. Within the burlap and paper which he unwrapped were several broken and partly calcined bricks, two one-inch 'farmer' drills, and a hand ratchet, the tools bearing evidence of having been in some very hot place.

"The guy that brang these in," said Phillips, "wasn't very talkative. He said you'd know what they were, and to tell you he also had seen some wood ashes in the same place, but that they all sifted loose when he tried to pick them up. He said to tell you it looked as if a two-by-four had been thrown down after the tools."

"Good stuff," commented Brady. "This is the junk they drilled into the auditor's vault with, up at the city hall."

"You mean to tell me, captain, that them fellows worked from inside that chimney? I don't hardly believe it."

"Neither do I, Phillips. But this is the stuff they drilled that back wall with. When they got through, they threw it down the chimney. These are the bricks they plugged out—what's left of them."

"Tell you what it might have been, captain. You know

the treasurer's office is right back of the auditor's. Some guys might have drilled there, thinking they'd cut through to the treasurer's vault—not knowing about the chimney being between the vaults."

"That's possible, Phillips."

"Well, if that was it, it was an inside job, captain—somebody who knew the combination on the auditor's vault and who could get in there nights."

"That's reasonable, too."

Phillips looked at Brady and smiled. "You don't think much of that, eh, captain?"

"Not a whole heck of a lot, Phillips. But at that you might feed it to the reporters. We've got to keep those birds fed up on some new ideas, or they'll be pestering us to death; and that's a good line. You feed it to 'em—tell 'em you figured it out yourself.

"Here, you take all this junk out into the outer office and let the reporters see it, and give 'em that theory of yours. I don't care how strong you make it. At that it might be the right dope.

"Think it over, after you've told the boys, and if you can figure anybody in that auditor's office gang who's got guts enough to try a stunt like that, put a couple of the boys on him."

Phillips, not greatly encouraged, gathered up the "evidence" and left Brady's office for his own desk in the outer room. The captain, alone, glanced over the few reports that had come in while he was out, then again read the reports his men had given him of their work earlier in the day when checking over the employees of the auditor's office.

Then he leaned back in his chair, closed his eyes, and tried to visualize the scene at the auditor's office when he had reached it in the morning, recalling to his mind the expression on each person's face, and his or her actions during the excitement. Conning over these pictures that flashed before his closed eyes, he shook his head. There was nothing, as far as he could see, to support Phillips's theory, attractive though it was, as an easy solution. This introspection took perhaps some thirty minutes, and then he opened his eyes.

Over in his accustomed chair at his own desk was Sergeant Riordan, apparently going over his own reports.

"Sneaked in on me, did you?" commented Brady not unkindly.

Riordan turned around. "No, chief. I came in as usual, only about four hours late. Thought you were asleep. Didn't want to waken you, because I knew I had a calling-down coming."

"What made you late? Why didn't you telephone? Where you been?" Brady's voice was harsh, but his eyes had a twinkle in them.

"I'll tell you, chief. I've been fighting—"

"You don't look that happy, boy," interrupted Brady, smiling broadly.

"Don't kid me, chief. It's tough enough as it is. I've been fighting myself. When I got up this afternoon and saw the papers, and realized what I'd let slip through my fingers! There I was up in the city hall last night, not a hundred feet away from where this thing was pulled—and didn't even get a smell of it. I guess you've got me listed for a sap already, haven't you? And I was beginning to think I was good.

"I wasn't going to show at all, chief. I was just going to send you my star and go away somewhere. I been wandering around the streets ever since four o'clock trying to get up nerve enough even to do that. Then I decided I'd better come in here and take my medicine. You'd better have me sent up on charges."

Brady regarded his aide curiously, the smile fading from his face, and deep concern taking its place. Then he spoke:

"Listen, boy—you forget it. You did more than I'd have done last night. I wouldn't have thought of the treasurer's office even. I'd have gone round the neighborhood looking for the job if I'd been tipped the same as you were.

"Why, this morning when I came down and found that report of yours telling how you boys had gone up there and drilled that neighborhood and the city hall as well, I was proud of you. As for your getting the men that did this thing—they were out of the building before you got there. I'm satisfied the last thing they did was to push that stuff down the chimney; and it was that, falling, that the boys in the fire telegraph office heard. No, son, you haven't got a thing to be ashamed of.

"And as far as falling down goes, I don't know any more about this case than you do. But that's a secret between you and me. Now snap out of it, and forget all this fool stuff about quitting or getting put up on charges. We'll both of us be on charges if we don't get somewhere on this pronto. I've got Phillips stalling the reporters now, so as to give us more time."

Riordan cheered up at that, and, drawing his chair over

to Brady's desk, went over, with his chief, all the reports available on the strange occurrence. Then the two officers talked the matter over, discussing it from every angle.

They got the calcined bricks and the drills and ratchet in from the outer office and examined them, but to no avail. The bricks were so badly burned the material crumbled as they handled it, and there were no marks of possible identification on the tools.

The only conclusion they were agreed upon at the end of their consultation was that the hole had been bored from within the vault into the chimney; that it had probably taken a total of at least twenty-one hours to accomplish the thing, and probably more; and that the man or men who did it had braced the ratchet against a two-by-four, which in turn was set against the filing cabinets, as they worked within the vault, the combination to which they must have known. But why it was done—

"It don't stand to reason, chief," Riordan summed it up, "that anybody wise enough to pull that job would be so foolish as not to know where that chimney came up. And it don't stand to reason that any sane man would spend twenty hours or more breaking and entering into a chimney. He couldn't hope to spoil the records, for they were all in metal cabinets; and anyway, there aren't any records there worth spoiling. And Pangbourne says that none are missing."

"All of which is true," agreed Brady; "but, boy, you got to admit also that somebody put in a lot of work there, and no sane man works like that for nothing. Now we got to find out what for—and find it out before the novelty of the thing wears off and the papers start kidding us about it."

4

A WOMAN WITH A QUEER STORY

PHILLIPS OPENED THE door from the outer office. "Captain," he said, "there's a woman out here who wants to see you. She won't talk to nobody but you, she says."

Brady motioned for the caller to be shown in. A young woman, twenty or thereabout, plainly but neatly dressed, entered. She looked inquiringly from one to the other of the officers.

"I am Captain Brady, miss. What can I do for you? This is my sergeant. You may feel perfectly free to speak before him."

Riordan shoved a chair forward for her, and moved his own chair back toward his desk, where he sat down again.

The visitor hesitated a moment, apparently choosing her words, and then, throwing her head back as if she were at last determined to do something, she said:

"I am Miss Mabel Turner, captain. I live with my uncle, Charles Turner, 3839 Foster Road. You probably know him, captain?"

Captain Brady nodded.

"Well, captain, I am very much alarmed about him. He did not come home last night, and he has not been home all day, and up to the time I left the house he had not been home this evening."

"You should report that case downstairs, Miss Turner, at the desk. They handle the missing persons."

"I know that, captain. But I feel that there is something in my uncle's absence that should have your attention."

Captain Brady raised his eyebrows. "Why mine?"

"Because I have read a great deal about you in the papers, captain, and I do not think my uncle's disappearance is—is of the usual kind."

"What do you mean by 'usual kind,' Miss Turner?"

"Well, I don't think he has met with foul play, or that he is dead, or anything like that."

Brady hitched forward in his chair.

"Tell me all about your uncle," he said kindly.

The girl seemed much relieved.

"I thought you'd understand," she said. "Well, my uncle, as you know, is quite old—seventy-two. Up until about three weeks ago he was the same as always. Since then he has been getting more and more—more and more excited, if I may use the word.

"I mean by that that he has been getting worked up over something. I do not know what it is. I have tried to question him, but have found out nothing. He still acted as before in the main things; he got up at the same time, stayed around the house through the day, and went to his lodge in the evening at the same time, and came home at the same time; but there was a tenseness about his face and his actions that showed he was laboring under some increasing strain.

"It has been getting steadily worse—and now he has not

been home for more than twenty-four hours. I think he is afraid of something, and is hiding somewhere."

"Have you called up his lodge?"

"No—you see, I don't know what lodge he has gone to."

Brady looked at Riordan, flashing him a signal.

"What lodge does he belong to?" asked the sergeant, leaning forward.

"I don't even know that. It's funny, but I don't. You see, his going to lodge has been such a matter of fact occurrence all these years that I've never asked him. He just says, after supper, 'Well, Mabel, guess I'll go over to lodge,' and then goes out. That's about half past seven, perhaps a little before. He gets home at eleven. I'm usually in bed then, but I hear him when he comes in."

"And what time does he usually get up in the morning?" asked Riordan.

"About ten. Of course, I'm only home Sundays and holidays and during my vacation. I get up at half past seven, leave breakfast for him, and go to the office. But I know he gets up about ten. He gets a cold lunch, and reads or works about the house or yard during the day, or gossips with some other retired men in the neighborhood. I get home a little after four, and get dinner—or sometimes we go out to dinner. Then in the evening he goes to lodge."

"And you work where?" interjected Brady.

"I'm a stenographer in Mr. Saunderson's office at the traction company."

"Oh, yes—I might have remembered that. I think I've seen you up there. Well, Miss Turner, just what do you mean when you say your uncle has seemed excited recently?"

"Just that, captain. Like a small boy before Christmas time, you know. Eyes unusually bright, movements quicker than usual. A bit testy, then immediately anxious to make amends. Preoccupied at other times, and starting slightly when he finds my eyes upon him."

"Maybe he's worried over money matters," suggested Riordan.

"I think not," the girl answered. "My uncle is pretty well-to-do, you know; and we spend very little. He has a good deal of property, and it is all rented. I keep books for him on that end of his business, so I know."

"Well, Miss Turner, just what is it you want me to do?" asked Brady.

"Why, find my uncle. You know all the hotels and lodging houses, don't you? And you can get information from them? I think he is staying in hiding at some hotel or place in this city. I have a feeling that he is hiding."

"Why?"

"I don't know; I just have that feeling."

Brady considered. "That isn't enough," he said finally. "You haven't told me all; you haven't told me the one incident that might be the key to the whole thing. You are keeping something back."

"No, I'm not, captain."

"My dear Miss Turner, if you want me to help you, you've got to help me. I've been in this business a great many years, and I think I have learned in that time certain signs. I think you are quite correct—that your uncle is in hiding somewhere. Now, what unusual thing has he done recently that has made you extra keen, that you have noticed this excitement of which you speak?"

"Why, there is nothing, captain. Don't you suppose that after living with my uncle since I was twelve years old, I know him pretty well, and would notice anything out of the ordinary—"

Captain Brady shook his head.

"I am sorry, Miss Turner," he said, interrupting her. "But there is nothing I can do. You'll have to report this case downstairs at the desk, in the regular way. Riordan, take her down to the desk and see that she gives Mulcahy, or whoever's on, all the information he thinks that is necessary."

He turned back to his desk. Riordan rose, opened the door, and beckoned to the young woman to follow him. She hesitated a moment, then followed him from the room.

It was twenty minutes before Riordan returned, alone. Captain Brady had his hat and coat on and was ready to go home.

"Well?" he asked.

"I took her down to the drill room," said the sergeant, grinning. "Now we got two fool cases, instead of one. I told her you were busy as the dickens on this city hall job, and so you were short with her. Then I sympathized with her and blarneyed her, and told her I'd look after her uncle for her—and what was it all about, anyway?

"Finally she came through. Said he was all worked up over this fight between the traction company and the Interurban Company for common-user rights on Union Avenue. He hasn't been himself since it started, she said.

"Naturally, with her working for the traction company, his sympathies are with the old concern. Said he was working on a plan to help them. Got her to bring the franchise home from the office one night, so he could study over it.

"She did it to humor him. He sat up all night copying it, she said, so she could take it back the next morning when she went to work. That's what he's bugs about.

"She didn't want to tell you, she said, because she didn't think you'd approve of her slipping the franchise home and back again. Said you looked too strict, and that anyway that wouldn't help in finding her uncle.

"I told her not to worry; that I'd start a still hunt for him. I'll put a couple of the boys buzzing the hotels and lodging houses to-night, and probably locate the old bird."

Brady laughed shortly. "Hop to it," he said. "I'm going home. Call me if anything breaks—and forget all that stuff you were fighting early this evening, boy. You did just right last night."

5

"DON'T TIP YOUR HAND!"

SERGEANT RIORDAN, SITTING in the Rainbow Café at a little after ten, eating his usual lunch, suddenly choked over his coffee, put his cup down with a bang and, rising from the table, dashed out, throwing a silver dollar to the cashier as he went past her cage. Several guests of the café laughed at the incident, others looked up in astonishment, which increased as they heard the sudden roaring of the open exhaust of Riordan's car as he started it from its place before the café and sped down the street. One of the waiters went out on the sidewalk and looked after him, thinking to see the cause of the officer's sudden departure; but all he could note was the flickering of the tail light on Riordan's car as it flashed around the first corner.

The next person to see Riordan was City Auditor Pangbourne, who was roused from his first peaceful moments of slumber by the jangling of his doorbell and a pounding on his front door. Hastening to see what the trouble was, he opened the door and was nearly trampled by the impatient Riordan.

"Get your clothes on quick—just throw 'em on—and come with me," said the officer. "Don't stop to ask questions; I'll tell you in the car. Now, for Heaven's sake, get a move on you!"

Three minutes later Pangbourne was lurching against Riordan as the detective sergeant sent his car swinging down the street.

"We're going to your office, Pangbourne," the driver shouted. "I got to know something right away. Had to get you, and so I came out to your house. I may have a bum hunch, at that, but I've got to find out. Just thought of it— in connection with that hole in the vault. Listen, did you check over everything you got in that place?"

"Yes, sergeant."

"Everything—sure?"

"Well, now, sergeant, not every individual paper. We couldn't do that, you know—there are thousands of them. But we— Look out, man, you'll tip us over if you drive so fast around the corners."

"Don't worry; this bus won't tip over. What were you saying about not checking everything?"

"We couldn't check each paper, sergeant. That would take days. But as we cleaned up each set of files, we went over them rapidly. If they didn't show any sign of having been disturbed recently, we let it go at that. If the papers looked mussed up, we checked four or five documents where they were mussed. Nothing appeared to be missing. What have you found out?"

"I ain't found it out yet. That's what I came after you for—to find out. Now, you'd better hang onto something; I got a straight stretch here, and I'm going to let the old bus out a bit."

Riordan kicked open the siren and "let her out." Pangbourne was busy "hanging on" until the big roadster came to a grating stop beside the city hall. The auditor had a key to the front door, and he opened it to admit them, just as Collins, the man working for the watchman, came forward.

Riordan showed his shield.

"It's all right, Collins," he said. "Me and the auditor, here, want to go to his office a moment."

"Step right in the elevator, gents, and I'll take you up," responded the man, and they were whisked to the second floor. Collins accompanied them to the office, turning on the lights as they went. In the auditor's rooms he waited in the outside chamber, while Riordan and Pangbourne went into the inner office.

"Now I'll tell you what I want you to do," said the detective sergeant. "You go to the vault and get the files that have the franchise of the traction company inside. Don't open 'em, but bring 'em here. See?"

"Yes, sergeant. That will be Case B in File F."

"All right, Pangbourne; bring Case B in here, please. And don't tell that watchman nothing, but ask him to stick around and watch the vault while you leave it open. Maybe I'll want to talk to him later."

Pangbourne stepped outside, and Riordan watched him through the glass partition, saw him speak to the watchman and then work for a moment at the combination of the vault, swing the doors open, and step within.

He returned in a moment with the case he had sought and placed it on his desk.

"Now find that franchise—I want to see it," said Riordan.

Pangbourne opened the case, ran his fingers over the

inclosed envelopes, and then suddenly looked at the outside of the case again. Then he took the envelopes all out and sorted them on his desk. His face paled.

"The franchise isn't here, sergeant," he said weakly.

Riordan grinned, but not unpleasantly. He licked his lips with his tongue.

"I didn't figure it would be," he said.

Pangbourne sat down, a helpless look in his eyes.

"There now, don't you go to taking it hard," said Riordan. "Buck up. Put that stuff back in the case, and put the case back in the vault, and lock it, and then come in here and bring that watchman with you. I want you to hear this."

The auditor listlessly placed the files back in the case, sighed, and took the cabinet out to the vault, Riordan watching through the partition.

After he had closed and locked the big steel doors, he returned to his office, followed by the watchman. Pangbourne sat down, but the other man remained standing, regarding Riordan expectantly. Finally he said:

"You wanted to ask me something, sergeant?"

"Yeah. What time you come to work?"

"Half past ten, sir."

"How long you been working? How long has the watchman been sick?"

"Oh, it's two weeks to-morrow, sir. Mr. Swett—he's the regular watchman—he had his appendix cut out at the hospital. I work for him whenever he lays off. I used to be watchman here, under the other mayor. When the new mayor come in, I was let out. You know how it is."

"You know all about the robbery of that vault, don't you?"

The watchman laughed. "I read the papers, sergeant."

"That all you know about it?"

"Yes, sergeant. You didn't tell me why you was in here the other night, you know. I hadn't heard anything, as I told you then."

"And you didn't see anybody round here?"

"No, sir."

"Well, suppose you tell us just what you did that night. Start with when you came in—everything you can remember."

The watchman drew a chair forward and sat down. For a moment he considered, and then he said:

"Well, sergeant, I got here a little before half past ten, like I always do. I went to the cloakroom downstairs and put on my jumper and overalls, and then I come up to the door and let the janitor crew out. Then I locked up, and started round the building, turning off the lights, like I always do.

"Up on the top floor the door leading to the stairway to the roof was open, and the trapdoor at the top was also open. I thought maybe somebody was working on the roof, and I went up there. There was nobody there. I went all around the roof—I thought maybe there was some metalworker fixing the skylights—but there was no sign of anybody.

"I came back down, closing the trapdoor and closing the door at the bottom of the stairs. I supposed maybe there'd been a fire alarm, and that maybe one of the janitors had gone up on the roof to look around. We used to do that when I was here before, if there was a big fire.

"Then I came down to the second floor, and I felt a draft. I went to see where it come from, and it was the health bureau. They'd left a window open. I went in there and closed the window, and while I was in there the door slammed. Scared me, and for a few moments I didn't move.

"Then I figured out what it was, and come out, and seen the lights down the hall was turned on. That seemed funny, for I knew I'd turned them off when I went up. I was standing there, trying to figure it out, when I heard you shout, saying you was police. I come down the hall then, and met that officer who was with you."

Riordan considered this awhile.

"And all that time," he finally asked, "you didn't hear anything that sounded like an explosion or something dropping?"

"No, sir, I didn't hear a thing—not until I heard you call."

"Let me look at your hands."

The watchman extended his palms, and Riordan inspected them silently.

"What do you know about the janitor's crew, Collins?" the detective sergeant finally asked. "Any of 'em late in getting out?"

"N-n-no, sir, not specially," the man answered slowly.

"What do you mean by that?"

"Well, sergeant, there's old Uncle Turner. That's what I mean. He's a bit slow sometimes. Sometimes I find him asleep down outside the mayor's office. He's pretty old, and don't do much more than hang on the pay roll, you might say."

"I know the man, sergeant," spoke up Pangbourne. "He's one of the pensioners. Used to work for Rufus Ward when Rufe was city clerk in the old days. Then Calhoun took him on. He got so he didn't do anything, and Calhoun let

him go. But Ward put up a holler, and they gave him a job
as assistant janitor. All he does is polish the brass railing
about the secretary's desk outside the mayor's office, and
clean a few spittoons. He's a harmless old fool."

"That's him, sir," corroborated Collins. "I wish I had his
drag, and could hold my job, no matter who was mayor.
Well, sometimes I've found him lying on the bench down
there at the mayor's door, and I wake him up and send
him home."

"Found him there during the two weeks you've been
back on the job?" asked Riordan.

"Once, sir. But lots of times in the old days when I was
the regular watchman."

"What day was it you found him there?"

"The night before you and that other officer bust in
here, sir."

"Did you notice him the night I was here—last night?"

"No, sir. I didn't see him at all that night. He didn't check
out with the rest."

Did you ask about him?"

"No. I didn't think anything of it."

Riordan sat quietly for a few minutes, and then rose.
"Well," he said, "I guess that's all we can do to-night. Let's
go."

He drove Pangbourne home. The auditor was much
excited about the disappearance of the franchise. Riordan
let him talk about it till they reached his residence, and
then he said:

"Now, listen to me, Pangbourne. You forget about that
franchise, see? I mean it. I don't want you to mention it to
anybody—not unless somebody calls for it, and that isn't

likely. Just act as usual, and don't tip your hand, or you may make it harder for us to get it back.

"You see, I already figured it was gone; so you can know we were working on it. Keep still about it, and don't worry. Don't look for it in any of the other files. Either me or Brady'll call you up in a day or so, and let you know what's doing. I'm much obliged to you for letting me rouse you and coming down to the office—now good night to you, and pleasant dreams. And don't you worry at all."

6

CHARLIE MAKES A FRIEND

WHEN DETECTIVE SERGEANT Riordan got back to headquarters he half expected to find Captain Brady waiting for him, but the inner office was vacant, and Brady's desk was still closed.

Riordan smiled to himself, and, forgetting for the time being both the missing franchise and the missing Charles Turner, plunged into the routine work of the evening, which had been much neglected. He was just cleaning up the odds and ends at the time his official shift ended when Detective Halloran dropped in to see how chances were for a ride homeward in Riordan's car.

"You in a hurry, Mike?" the sergeant asked.

Halloran shook his head, and, dropping into a chair, produced a cigar, at the same time offering one to Riordan.

"The only time I'm in a hurry, sergeant," he said, "is when you or Cap'n Brady is on me tail. I been in this police game too long to hurry very much—that is, you know, except when there's something doing."

Riordan laughed. "Guess you have, Halloran," he answered. "Why, if I remember right, you were in plain clothes when I was a probationer. And I'm no spring chicken myself."

Halloran nodded his head. "An' I been in plain clothes ever since," he muttered. "Nobody's ever offered me gold braid, and I've managed to keep out of the other kind of uniform. Oh, well, I guess I'm lucky at that."

Riordan paid no attention to Halloran's reference to his lack of advancement. It was something generally avoided.

I got a good one to-night, Mike," he said, to change the subject. "Old Charlie Turner's disappeared. His niece was in here, wanting him looked up."

Halloran cocked one eye at the sergeant. "Many's the time I've steered old Charlie home," he said, "an' his niece was never worried. She knows the old boy has got to have his drink every so often. If she was in here, there's something beside the usual bun on. The girl don't scare easy."

"Yeah." Riordan's tone was non-committal.

"Yeah is right, sergeant. And if you want a line on old Charlie, and can't find one anywhere else, give Old Rufe Ward a ring. That is, if you know him well enough."

Detective Sergeant Riordan was interested. Rufus Ward was one of the old school politicians, a former city clerk and State senator, and now presumed to be senior member of the law firm of Ward, Hotchkiss, Delaney, and Smith, though it was generally understood that Ward knew mighty little law. He knew a great many other things, however, and was still somewhat of a power in city politics.

"Charlie's a friend of Rufus, is he?" he hazarded.

"Well, now, I wouldn't go so far as to say that. But I'll bet this much, that old Charlie don't turn round unless Rufe says he can. In the old days when Rufe was city clerk, Charlie was his 'man Friday.' Rufe was the brains, Charlie was the hands. Them two has a good deal on each other, they have. That's why Rufe keeps Charlie on the city pay roll even yet. He wants to have him where he can see him."

"His niece didn't say anything about his working," said Riordan.

"His niece don't know it. There ain't many people know it. Charlie don't boast of it none, and Rufe is close-mouthed. But I know it—and two or three others know it. Charlie's one of the night janitors down at the City Hall. He don't do much; polishes brass, and cuspidors and just enough else to keep on the pay roll."

"Humph, he can't get over sixty dollars a month for that! What's he want to work for? He's got property."

"What's anybody want to work for? To keep the time passing. And, then, Charlie's been on the city pay roll so long, it wouldn't seem natural to him not to be getting his regular handout. Every night you'll find him up at the City Hall, except Sunday's and holidays, or his two weeks off. Tells that girl of his he's gone to lodge. An' about every other pay day he used to liquor up. Now that things are dry, he don't do it so often."

Riordan rose from his chair. "Well," he said, "maybe I'll go up to Rufus Ward's to-morrow and look for him, like you said. Right now I'm going home. Come on, and I'll give you a lift as far as the boulevard."

After dropping Halloran near his home, Riordan drove out into the newer section of the city, taking pains to pass Rufus Ward's castlelike residence, which was set back in spacious grounds. He regarded it carefully, drove around the block and looked it over again, and then drove slowly out to Foster Road, slowing his car down in front of No. 3839, finally deciding to stop.

The house, Charlie Turner's, was dark. Riordan sounded the horn of his car briefly, and the jarring notes shattered the stillness of the night. Nothing happened, and after a few minutes he sounded the horn again.

He saw a second story curtain move, but nothing else. Climbing from his car, he walked to the door of Turner's house and pushed the bell. There was no response, and after waiting a few moments he pushed the bell again. Still there was no response. Waiting for a few moments, Riordan took a pin from his coat lapel, pushed the bell button, and, wedging the pin in beside it, stepped back.

Several minutes elapsed, with no developments, though Riordan knew the bell within must be ringing frantically and steadily. Then suddenly the front door was jerked open, and a very irate little man, swinging a clublike cane, appeared, making a threatening motion with the stick, which stopped in mid-air. Riordan was glad he had stepped back a goodly distance from the door.

"What's the matter, ye wakin' decent folks at this hour of the night?" the householder demanded, looking first at Riordan and then at the bell.

"I'm looking for Charlie Turner," said Riordan.

"It's a fine time of night to be lookin'. What you want of him?"

"I'm an old friend of his."

The householder peered into the night at his caller, then reached for the bell button, found the pin, and jerked it out with a curse.

"You're no friend of Charlie Turner's," he said. "Gwan away now, or I'll call the police."

Riordan turned back his coat, and his gleaming shield reflected a flash of light from somewhere.

"Go ahead and call 'em. I'm the first one to answer. Don't you know me yet, Charlie?"

The little man peered again. "Come in closer," he said. "But not too close, or I'll swing on ye. There—'tis a police star ye have, all right. What's your name?"

Riordan laughed. "What's me name. That's a good one, Charlie. And me, in the old days, often taking you home when you couldn't find the way yourself. You was glad enough to call me friend then. And slip me something every now and then. That was when I was a harnessed bull on your beat. Now because I'm in plain clothes you don't know me."

The little man considered. "You ain't Jimmy Doyle," he said at length.

"Jimmy Doyle wasn't the only cop on your beat. Back, before that time. You remember."

The householder peered again at Riordan, and shook his head.

"I don't remember," he said. "But let it go at that. Suppose I do know ye. What ye want here at this time of the night?"

Riordan lowered his voice and pointed upstairs with his finger. "She might hear," he said.

The little man turned his head and looked back within the house. Then he slowly pulled the door to behind him, and took a step forward, still keeping his heavy stick ready for action, however. "Well?" he demanded.

Riordan bent forward. "Listen, Charlie," he said confidentially. "I'm a friend of yours, see? An old, old friend. And another friend of yours, who's also a friend of mine, told me to come see you and tell you something. He says for me to tell you just two words—that you'll understand. The two words are these: 'Be careful.' Get me, Charlie?"

The little man looked up at Riordan, who towered over him. In the dark he could not make out the detective sergeant's features as plainly as he wished. But he slowly nodded his head.

"All right," he said.

"All right, Charlie," answered Riordan. "Now, let's shake hands, just to show you appreciate what an old friend has done for you."

Slowly the little man extended his left hand.

Riordan laughed. "No, Charlie, not the left hand. Friends don't give each other the left hand. Shake hands like you was a real friend."

The little man hesitated, then transferred his stick to his left hand, and extended his right. Riordan gripped it heartily, and gave it a fervent shake. "That's the boy, Charlie," he said. "And remember what I told you. Now, good night."

He turned hastily, made his way to his car, and climbed in, driving off without once looking back while the little man stood, puzzled, watching his departure.

7

A CALL ON A BIG MAN

DESPITE HIS LATE hours, Sergeant Riordan rose fairly early the next day, explained to his mother that he had some extra business to attend to, and left his home in the middle of the morning. His first call was at the offices of the traction company, where he sent in word that he would like to see Miss Mabel Turner.

The girl came out to an anteroom, and before Riordan could explain his business, began to apologize.

"I'm so sorry, sergeant," she said, "to have bothered you last night. Uncle came home shortly after I got back from headquarters building, where you were so kind to me. I was so relieved. And I meant to call you right up and ask you not to look for him, but I was busy, first, getting him a bite to eat, and after that I forgot it. I do hope you didn't go to any effort—"

Riordan was all smiles. "I'm very glad he came home, Miss Turner. I was calling to ask if he had. The boys couldn't locate him last night, and before I looked further to-day I thought I'd ask you. Now we won't have to bother. Call on us any time, miss; that's what we're there for."

He bowed his way out before the girl could offer her thanks or express further regrets.

From the traction company building he drove to the office structure that housed the temporary headquarters of the Interurban Company, the rival line that was bidding for the city's business. He told the clerk at the hall desk that he wanted to see the general manager, showing a glimpse of his shield as he made his request. After the briefest possible wait he was ushered into an inner office.

"I'm Detective Sergeant Riordan," he said. "I want to see the king pin—the man in general charge."

"I guess you're looking at him, sergeant. I'm George Lownsdale in person, as they say in the movies," answered a genially stout man seated behind a large, flat-topped desk. "What can I do for you?"

Riordan dropped into a chair, took out his wallet, and drew from it his formal commission, which he passed across to Lownsdale.

"Just to show you I'm on the level," he said.

Lownsdale looked the paper over, and passed it back.

"Now, Mr. Lownsdale, I got a hard job ahead of me," said Riordan, smiling, "I want to ask you something about your business, and I haven't got much right to do it. But I've got to have your help. Understand, I'm not coming to you to snoop around, or anything like that; but in order to clear up a case I've got on I've got to know something. And I figure the best way is to ask you right out and out."

Lownsdale looked sharply at his caller for a moment, and then nodded his head.

"What I want to know," continued Riordan, "is this: Has anybody here come to you lately and volunteered to help you in your fight for trackage rights in the city?"

"That's a pretty broad question, sergeant."

"I know it is, sir. Now I want you to get me right. I'm coming here on my own. I don't represent anybody. I'm working on a larceny case. What was stolen might be valuable to you in this fight of yours. I know you had nothing to do with stealing it, and wouldn't stand for that sort of a play, anyhow. But there's people in this city who might try and sell this something to you, or dicker with you over it. That's why I'm asking you."

Lownsdale looked steadily into Riordan's eyes for a long time. Finally he said:

"Sergeant, you look like you meant what you said. You look like a straight shooter. Now I'll tell you something. The company I represent really doesn't care whether we get these trackage rights that the newspapers are hollering about, or not. If we can't get tracks on one street, we can get them on another.

"The Interurban line is merely passing through your city, and it doesn't make a whole lot of difference to us whether we pass through on Jefferson Street, or on Front, or on Rodney Avenue. So we aren't making any deals with anybody."

Riordan smiled momentarily. "That's all right," he said, "and I believe you. But it doesn't help me any. I'm not worrying about you; I'm worrying about somebody else. What I want to know is, has anybody been to see you lately to make you some kind of a proposition?"

"Several people have been to see me."

"Any of 'em lawyers?"

The Interurban Company's general manager shrugged his shoulders. For several minutes the two men looked at each other, and then Riordan spoke again.

"Listen, Mr. Lownsdale, I'll lay my cards on the table. The franchise of the traction company has been stolen. It has been offered to you. I don't know who offered it, but I know that one of four men made the offer.

"Now, since we know it's been stolen, it wouldn't do you any good to accept the offer; for you'd just be compounding a felony. It will save us a good deal of bother, and three of the four men a lot of embarrassment, if you'll tell me the name of the man who made the offer."

"How'd you like to be one of our special agents, sergeant?"

"Nope, not me. I'm working for the city."

"I'll pay you five hundred dollars a month, and any reasonable expenses."

"I've got a good job, thanks."

"I meant five hundred dollars a week."

"I'm sitting pretty, just as I am, thanks."

Lownsdale studied his caller some more.

"Sergeant," he said at length, "I guess you're on the level. I am, too. I don't buy franchises. My company doesn't do business that way. We don't have to.

"And I don't mind telling you that if you'd accepted the offer I just made you, I'd have gone right to the mayor and turned you in. Now listen: Nobody has offered to sell us a franchise. Up until a moment ago I didn't know one had been stolen. But if that's the way the case lies, I'm as anxious as you are to nail the guilty party.

"There was a man in to see me yesterday with a proposition. He wouldn't tell me what it was; but he said he was in a position to turn the whole city over to us, if we wanted it. He said if I was interested, he'd put me in touch with the right party. I told him I'd think it over and let him know. Here's his card."

Lownsdale reached in a drawer of his desk, and tossed a little bit of pasteboard over to Riordan. The detective sergeant took one glance at it, and then passed it back.

"Thank you, Mr. Lownsdale," he said. "I sure appreciate your stand. And any time you think you need any special agents, you just call on the police, and it won't cost you anything. That's what we're here for. I'll be going now."

"Glad to have helped you, sergeant. If you want me as a witness, just call me up. I don't approve of stuff like this at all."

"Thank you again, sir, but I don't think we'll need any witnesses. I wish you luck in your trackage fight, sir."

From Lownsdale's office Riordan went to the City Court, where he got a warrant charging "alteration of a building without a permit," without telling for whom he wanted it, persuading the clerk to leave the name blank, and then he drove to headquarters, and went up to the detective Bureau.

Captain Brady looked up in some surprise at his entrance.

"Hello, boy," he said, "what's wrong?"

"Nothing, chief. Just dropped in."

"Find that missing party you were fussing about last night?"

"Yeah. He's home now."

Captain Brady regarded his aide silently for several moments.

"I know perfectly well, boy, that you got a hen on," he said. "What you want me to do?"

"Got the dope on that City Hall thing yet, chief?"

"Not a smell of it."

"Want to clear it up quick?"

"So that's it, is it? Boy, how do you do this stuff? You're getting too fast for me. What do you want me to do?"

Captain Brady's question was pathetic, and Riordan sensed it.

"Listen, chief, it was just luck," he said. "I stumbled onto it. You would have done the same thing. And now I want you to finish it off. You know, chief, we always work together—it don't make any difference who gets the stuff."

"Yes, boy, I know. What you want me to do?"

Riordan's eyes twinkled. "Well, chief, I'd like to have you call up Mr. Saunderson, of the traction company, and ask him to be so kind as to come down here and bring the franchise with him. Tell him it's important; you can word it right. I'd do it myself, but you know him better than I do."

Brady looked sharply at his aide, then reached for his telephone, and spoke quietly into it at some length. Riordan walked across the room, and stood looking out of the window while he was speaking. Then he went over to his own desk and sat down.

8

IN AT THE FINISH

TEN MINUTES LATER Richard Launderson, plainly much excited, was ushered into the inner office of the detective bureau. He barely nodded to Riordan as he rushed to Brady's desk, and tossed a heavy envelope before the captain.

"There," he said, "is the envelope. Now where's the franchise?"

Brady picked the envelope up and drew out some neatly folded paper. Opening it, he found it entirely blank.

"Of course you know all about it, Brady, or you wouldn't have telephoned me as you did," said the traction chief. "Now, for Heaven's sake, do your stuff."

Captain Brady looked at his caller. "Mr. Saunderson," he said, "I want to make a deal with you. You've got a lot more drag with his honor the mayor than I have. I've been trying to get Riordan, here, made a lieutenant for a long time. His honor, he promises and promises, but that's all. Riordan will get you your franchise if you'll see what you can do toward getting him made—"

"Brady, listen. I'll get Riordan made chief of police if you'll clear this thing up. Do you know what it means? It means I've got a crook somewhere in my own office, and nothing my company has is safe. You get me the man who stole that franchise, and you and Riordan can have anything you want," interrupted Saunderson.

"Hear that, boy? Do your stuff," said Brady to his aide.

Saunderson turned to Riordan.

"I got to know something, sir, first," said the sergeant. "How many real copies of this franchise are there?"

"Two, Riordan. That is, two legal ones. The council and mayor, when they granted this, signed two copies. One was given to the company, and the other is on file in the city auditor's office. Beside that, of course, there are—what's the matter, Brady?"

Captain Brady had leaped to his feet, and was muttering weird and fiery curses.

Riordan spoke up quickly, to keep his chief from saying what he knew was on the tip of his tongue, waiting for a chance to get out.

"Don't mind him, Mr. Saunderson," he said. "He's just so mad at the fellow that pulled this deal that he can't control himself. You see, we've got to make a deal to get this franchise back, and the chief hates to do it. That's what makes him so wild."

"Go ahead and make your deal, but get me that franchise. I'll stand for anything." Saunderson was almost as excited as Captain Brady had been; for at Riordan's words the older man had pulled himself together, and resumed his chair.

"The deal is this, sir," continued Riordan. "The party that actually took that franchise from your office has got to be protected. The party wasn't a thief, sir. The party was asked to get the franchise out of your vault for reference, and did so. Then this envelope, with the blank paper in it, was given back. The party didn't know anything about it. You got to take my word for that."

Saunderson nodded. "All right, I'll agree to that. For the present, anyway. Now, get that franchise."

"Push the button, chief."

Captain Brady poked a finger savagely at one of the ivory disks on his desk. Two detectives entered from the outer room, Riordan took the John Doe warrant from his pocket, wrote something upon its face, and handed it to one of the sleuths.

"Hop over to the Empire Building, and get that guy," he said. "Make it snappy, and don't stand for any stalls. Bring him in here."

The detectives looked at the warrant, their eyes growing big.

"You heard him, didn't yuh?" roared Brady. "Snap to it."

The two saluted, and left the room.

Riordan reached for one of the telephones, and called a number. While he was waiting for it, he turned to Saunderson. "You're going to have a good deal of fixing to do in a few minutes," he said. "I've sent for a particular friend of yours."

The telephone clicked, and he spoke into it, while Brady and Saunderson listened intently.

"This Main 6729?... I want to speak to Mr. Ward... yes, Rufus Ward... Hello... Hello, Mr. Ward... Mr. Ward, this is Detective Sergeant Riordan at headquarters speaking.

"I've just sent a couple of men over with a warrant for you... Yes, sir... Yes, sir, the charge is specified, violation of section sixteen of the building code, making alterations on a building without a permit from the inspector's office…

"Yes, sir, opening a chimney, it was… Now listen, Mr. Ward, Captain Brady and Mr. Saunderson, of the traction company, are waiting here with me, and they want you to bring those papers with you when you come over… Yes, sir, both of the papers."

Riordan hung up the receiver and placed the instrument back on top of Brady's desk.

"He said he'd be right over," he announced, calmly.

Saunderson was the first to speak.

"What did the old fool intend to do with it?" he asked.

"Peddle it, sir. You see, he had both of them," answered Riordan. "He was going to peddle one to the Interurban Company if they'd buy it, and then hold the other himself, as an ace in the hole. If the Interurban tried to double cross him, he had a check on 'em.

"His idea was this: That with both the original franchises in his possession, his firm could make a legal case that the traction company couldn't show any valid right to operate cars in the city. He could claim that there was no proof the copies of the old papers were genuine. Then he could make you deal with the Interurban Company or with him any way he wanted."

Saunderson took out his handkerchief, and wiped his forehead.

"Then that was a real burglary at the city auditor's office after all? They got the other copy of the franchise there?"

"Yes, sir."

The traction chief considered it for a long time. "Well," he said at length, "I'm sure obliged to you and Captain

Brady for the way you've handled this thing. Not only have you got it all stopped, but there's been no hint about what it really was in the papers. And I sure appreciate that. Of course you'll let me take care of—of Rufe Ward."

Captain Brady locked up. "I don't know," he said. "It seems to me like Ward had about run out his string here. I think we'll cinch him this time. You or your company won't have to figure in it. We'll get him on the auditor's office job."

Saunderson shrugged his shoulders.

The three sat silently for many minutes, each considering the situation in the light in which it most closely affected him.

The door to the office opened, and one of the two detectives who had gone forth a few minutes before entered. He handed a long envelope to Riordan.

"Where's your man? Where's your partner?" snapped Brady.

"Olson's with him, sir, waiting for the coroner. He gave me this envelope for Sergeant Riordan when we went into his office, and then before Olson or I could get around his table to him he jerked his hand up and shot himself, sir."

Brady waved the man outside. Sergeant Riordan opened the envelope, and took out two sets of papers, which he passed to his chief. Brady spread them out; they were the two originals of the traction company's franchise, the paper stiff with age, and the signatures black and old. He handed one to Saunderson, folded the other, and replaced it in the envelope.

"I'll take this one up to Pangbourne," he said. "I guess

that 'll be all, Mr. Saunderson. And you won't forget to speak to the mayor about the young lad, here?"

"I'll go, see him right now, Brady. And then I'll come back and tell you how grateful I am, and let you tell me all about it. I want to hear it. You'll wait here for me?"

"I'll be here for some time, Mr. Saunderson."

When the traction chief had left the room, Brady turned to his aide.

"Charlie Turner?" he asked.

Riordan nodded his head. "Uh-huh! I shook hands with him last night. His hand was all calloused where he held that drill. What the girl said about his being excited over the franchise fight give me the line on it. You'd have thought of it, too, chief, if you hadn't been so riled at the time."

"I'd never have thought of it in a thousand years, boy. But now, of course, I see it all as plain as day. The old fossil just did what Rufe Ward told him to do. Ward probably got him that janitor's job just on purpose, and told him the combination of the vault. All he had to do was sneak up there when the other janitors was working downstairs, and drill till he got tired, and then go back to polishing brass.

"That was a stall, of course, to make it look like a mystery, boring that hole in the chimney. And to cover up finger-prints with soot.

"He was always one of Ward's yes-men. Sure, Ward told him all about it, what to do, and the combination and everything. Ward used to have that office when he was city clerk, you know, when he handled the auditor's busi-ness, too.

"Well, boy, you sure did a fine job, and you saved me a

lot of grief. And if Saunderson don't get you made a lieu-tenant, damn me, I'll quit, and they'll make you a captain. I owe it to you, boy, the way you covered me up."

"Forget it, chief. You'd have thought of it, too, only that girl got you all riled up last night."

THE HAUNTED STREET

*A Ghostly Figure Danced at Night, and
All the City Came to Watch, But Brady and
Riordan Were Not Baffled By Shadows*

1

SHADOWS ON THE WALL

SERGEANT RIORDAN AND Captain of Detectives Brady, swapping opinions in the neighborhood of four o'clock in the afternoon, when the former relieved the latter in command, were discussing the chances of the council passing the ordinance that would make Riordan a lieutenant, with an advance in salary, as a reward for certain things he had done in the line of duty, when the door to the inner office was opened and Willis, from the outer desk, put in a word.

"If you please, sir, captain," he said addressing Brady, "there's a minister outside who wants to see you. He wouldn't tell me what he had on his mind."

"I've gone off shift," answered Brady with a wink and a smile. "Put him on Riordan here "

The caller thus ushered in looked from one to the other of the officers, and noting that the sergeant was the most attentive, addressed himself to him.

"I'm Dr. Wiles, of the First Spiritist Church," he said. "I have a peculiar request to make. I wonder if you'd assign a man to act as a bodyguard for me while I make an' experiment?"

Captain Brady, who had been making much business

of closing his desk, and getting ready to depart, turned abruptly and stared at their visitor.

"What sort of an experiment, doctor?" asked Riordan, as if such requests were the commonest things in the world.

"As I said, I'm a spiritist," repeated the caller. "I want to spend a night at the tower end of Twelfth Street, and see if I can get *en rapport* with the spirit that is reported to be there."

"And why the bodyguard, doctor?"

"Why—it's rather a tough neighborhood, isn't it?"

"You'd better step up to the sixth floor and see the man in Room 601, sir," said Brady cutting in.

The visitor laughed. "No, captain," he answered, "I'm not crazy. You needn't send me to the emergency hospital. You see, I know what that room number signifies. I am in all seriousness."

"Tell us about it then," said Brady bluntly. "I didn't know we had a ghost in the city."

"Sit down, doctor, and make yourself at home," cut in Riordan, indicating a chair. "You've evidently got something we don't know about."

The visitor sat down.

"You must know about it, gentlemen," began the spiritist. "Why, it's all over town. There's some strange phenomenon to be noticed down on lower Twelfth Street at night—a shadow cast upon the wails, when there is nothing there to cast it, apparently. The people who have seen it, mostly somewhat uneducated people, call it a 'haunt' or ghost. As a spiritist I believe, the phenomenon is worth investigating."

Brady looked at Riordan, raising his eyebrows. In reply the detective sergeant shook his head, ever so slightly.

"There on wall was the shadow... and I shot under my arm"

"It's all news to me," he said. "What form did you hear this shadow, as you call it, takes?"

"I'm surprised you haven't heard about it, gentlemen. It has been reported to me from several sources. Not exactly by anybody who saw the phenomenon, but at least by people who have talked to those who have seen it. The shadow is rather threatening in aspect, some reports say it is running, others that it bears an uplifted hand, as if about to strike at something."

"Where about on Twelfth Street?" The question was Riordan's.

"At the lower end, sergeant; near the flats leading to the river. The shadow is seen on the wall of the Globe Warehouse."

Captain Brady reached for his telephone. "Tell whoever's on the night desk to step up here. Captain Brady speaking," he said.

"You wait a minute," he added, turning to his caller.

"We'll find out about this right now. Personally I'm inclined to think your friends have been spoofing you; the only spirits down there I know about are in occasional wandering drunks."

The door to the office opened presently and one of the uniformed men entered.

"Sergeant Fielding," said Brady "what's this about a ghost or something down at the Globe Warehouse, on lower Twelfth?"

"Why, captain, I don't know. Some hop-head yarn, I guess. There's been a lot of talk."

"Any of the boys seen it?" interrupted Brady.

"Well, captain, I wouldn't say. Wilson, now, who had that beat regular, asked to be transferred to reserve duty for awhile. Said he'd hurt his foot at home, and couldn't walk very good. Some of the boys say he said something about it."

"Is he down in the back room now?"

"Yes, sir."

"Send him up to me."

Sergeant Fielding departed, and shortly one of the uniformed policemen entered.

"What's this stuff about a ghost on your beat," demanded Brady.

The patrolman looked from Brady to Riordan, then to the caller, then back at the captain.

"Well, sir, I wouldn't say it was a ghost. But it's mighty strange, sir. It's a shadow on the wall of the warehouse, sir—and there's nothing there to make the shadow, sir."

"Tell us about it—all you know," cut in Riordan kindly.

"This gentleman here, Wilson, is a shadow expert, and he's interested. So are we. Tell us all about it."

The patrolman seemed relieved at the tone of Riordan's voice.

"Well, sergeant," he said, "it was like this. About a month ago, I guess it was, I was just turning into Twelfth Street off'n Taylor, when a citizen runs into me, just as I rounded the corner. I grabbed him an' asked him what was his hurry—thought I had something, maybe.

"He says he was coming up from past the warehouse and a man chased him. I says what kind of a man, and he says he don't know; that he happened to look over his shoulder, and he sees his shadow on the wall of the warehouse, right behind him, with one hand up in the air like he had a blackjack in it and was going to soak him one. I says to come on back with me and we'll look.

"We went back down there and there was nobody in sight. He says where this happened was right by the warehouse, about thirty feet south of the arc light that hangs in the street there. Well, I took a look around, and there wasn't nothing to be seen.

"Two or three nights later I was on Taylor Street, near Twelfth, when I heard yelling down on Twelfth. I run round and down Twelfth, and there was three men there. They'd been fishing down to the river, they said, and was coming back up Twelfth Street, when right by the warehouse they see a shadow of somebody jumping at them. They yelled and run.

"We went back down there, but there wasn't nobody in sight. I took a good look through them empty shacks opposite the warehouse, but there wasn't nobody there either, nor any sign of anybody being there lately. But all three of these fellers swore they'd seen this shadow jump at them, and only one of 'em had been drinking enough so you could smell his breath.

"Well, after that I went down past the warehouse every night, twice. Once on my first rounds, and then again about half past ten. And the night before I hurt my foot at home I seen it. I was coming up from the end of the street, where the pavement stops, and had just about got to the middle of the warehouse, when out of the corner of my eye I seen a shadow on the wall. I whipped out my gun and turned round, but there wasn't a soul there but me.

"I tell you, sergeant, it made me feel sort of weak. I looked at the wall, and there was that shadow, swaying a little, with one hand up in the air like it was going to hit something. Then it faded away. I was plumb scared, I admit it. Then I says to myself that it's my shadow, and felt better.

"But as I looked I see it couldn't be my shadow, for the arc light was casting my shadow flat on the sidewalk, and this was on the wall. So I didn't feel so good, and I come on up the street. Next morning at home I hit my foot with the ax when I was splitting a knot, and asked to be relieved from patrol for a week or so."

"Who took your beat?" asked Brady.

"Sherman, sir."

"He seen this thing?"

"Yes, sir. The second night he was on the beat, he tells me. He says it's no place for him and he ain't going down there any more. He can see the whole street from the corner, so it's no use to go down there."

"Fine kind of cop, he is," commented Brady. "Anybody else you know of seen this thing?"

"Yes, sir. There's Tony Miguel, who has his fish boat anchored down there in the river. He was going down one night an' seen it. He's moved his boat up to the public docks. And I hear quite a number of other folks has seen it, but I don't know their names."

"Did you make a report on it?"

"No, sir. Think I want them reporters to josh the life out of me in the papers?"

"That'll do. Report back downstairs."

When the door had closed behind the patrolman Dr. Wiles spoke up.

"You see, captain? There is something there. I do not say it is a spirit—but I think it worth investigating."

"I agree with you."

"Then you'll give me a bodyguard?"

"No. And listen to me. You keep out of that neighborhood. I'll do the investigating. With all respect to you, sir, and your calling, I don't think there's anything there. But if there is something there, I think it's something for the police to handle. That's a bad end of town for citizens to be prowling round in at night. You keep out of it."

"Very well, captain. But if, after you have investigated, you find the matter still puzzles you, will you let me know?"

"Yes, sir. If I can't locate this ghost, you'll be welcome to try. Good evening, sir."

Their caller gone, Brady turned to his chief aid. "I'm going to the show with the wife to-night, boy. After I take her home I'll tell her I got a little business to do, and I'll slope down there. Never mind you coming. I guess one real cop is about all that's needed to stop any monkeyshines down there."

"You got an idea, chief, what it is?"

"Sure I've got an idea. If it isn't all bunk, it's some bum on prowl who's hid himself out in one of them shacks. I wish they'd burn down. We've had enough trouble in them, taking it all and all. Well, you keep your ears open, I've got to be going."

2

A SHOT ON TWELFTH STREET

SERGEANT RIORDAN, PREPARING for his trip home at midnight, when his shift ended, was just putting on his street clothes when his telephone jingled.

"Yeah," he barked into the instrument.

"Sergeant Riordan? This is Fielding, downstairs, speaking. I'm sending the wagon out to Twelfth Street. There's been a shooting. Sherman just phoned in. I thought maybe you'd like—"

Riordan hung up the receiver, reached for his shoulder-holster with one hand and his mackinaw with the other, got them both on almost simultaneously, jammed his hat on his head, and catapulted through the outer office.

"Coupla you guys," he shouted, "come along."

Down in the police garage he clambered into his roadster and started the engine. As the machine rolled out of the doorway two of the detectives tumbled in beside him. Three blocks ahead of him he could see the tail-light of the patrol, and he took after it, passing the heavier vehicle as it rounded the corner into Twelfth Street.

Then, kicking his siren open, he stepped on the accelerator and his car fled down the deserted highway, a shrieking, quivering demon of speed, the clanging gong of the patrol growing fainter and fainter behind him.

He had gone nearly the full length of Twelfth Street when he saw two flash lights waving ahead of him, and he brought his car to a grinding stop at the corner of Taylor Street, where, at the intersection, Captain Brady and Patrolman Sherman were standing. He tumbled out and hurried up to his chief.

"You get 'im?"

"How many you got with you?" demanded Brady.

"Two," answered Riordan, pointing to the pair of sleuths who were climbing from his machine. "And the wagon's behind us, probably with four or five reserves and the interne."

"We'll wait for 'em," said Brady. Riordan asked no questions; he knew his chief too well. But he scanned the neighborhood for either a still or moving figure. But, aside from Brady and Sherman and the two men who had come with him, the street was deserted.

Then the patrol wagon dashed up and disgorged three of the reserves and the emergency hospital interne.

"You boys comb them shacks over there," snapped Brady. "Sherman, you stand here at the warehouse door. If the watchman or anybody comes out, you nail 'em and hold 'em for me. Doc, you'd better sit with the driver and keep him company for a bit. Boy, you come with me."

The detective captain led the way down to the end of the paving of Twelfth Street, the reserves fanning out across the pavement and plunging into a row of shacks on the opposite side. As Brady and Riordan stepped off the sidewalk into the lush grass that covered the river flat the captain leaned close to his side.

"Boy," he said, "I think I've made a blame fool out of you and the rest of 'em. But they mustn't know it, see? I'll tell you how it was. Like I said I was going to do, I took the wife home from the show and then I drove out to the end of Fourteenth Street. I left my car there and circled round over the flats till I come about here. Then I took a good long look. You know, that shadow stuff.

"But there was nothing stirring. So I walked up Twelfth Street, past the warehouse, thinking what a fool I was. And just before I got to the warehouse door I turned half-way round, to take a last look, and there on the wall was a shadow of some guy with his hand raised like he was going to sap me. I whipped my gun out and shot—under my arm. Then I turned the rest of the way around and there was nobody there—nobody.

"Boy, I sure had the willies for a minute. Then I ran back here and took a scout around. There was nobody on the flats. I was afraid by that time Sherman would have heard my shot and come up and take a drive for luck if he saw me, so I sneaked over to Fourteenth Street quick and got in my bus and drove up to the corner there.

"Just as I got there Sherman came running up and says he heard a shot. I told him I'd heard it too, and to call the wagon and we'd comb the flats. I didn't figure you'd show up. But I might have known you would. That's that."

"This shadow, chief, how near was it?"

"Right on top of me. I tell you I thought it was real. Of course I didn't stop to think the light was ahead of me, and that if a guy had been behind me his shadow would have been behind mine. It was so real and so threatening I knew it was time to shoot, and I didn't waste any movements. The minute I fired, of course, I knew I'd pulled a boner. But at that it won't do any harm to frisk those shacks and this neighborhood good."

Riordan looked about him through the darkness, then back at the arc light, under which the reserves were gathering as they came out of the tumble-down shacks. "Let's go back," he said.

The patrolmen reported the shacks all empty and showing no sign of recent occupancy.

"Take a look out over the flats, boys," said Brady. "Circle out, clear to the river with your flash lights. Somebody sure fired a gat here."

As the men moved off, the door of the warehouse creaked, and then they heard Sherman's voice. A moment later he and the watchman joined the group under the light.

"You hear a shot?" asked Brady, flashing his golden star.

"I thought I did, cap'n. I was up back on the top floor. I come down as soon as I could, but I had to ring two boxes on the way down. Then I looked out of the office window and see you and the bulls and I opened the door. Somebody was hit?"

"You heard any funny goings on around here lately?"

"No, sir; there's been no disturbance since them drunks in the shacks last summer, when the bulls come out and raided 'em."

"Heard anything about a ghost or something out here?"

The man snorted. "Lot o' old women's talk. Yes, I heard it. I don't take no stock in it, though."

"Ever seen anything?"

"Nothin' like that, sir. Once in awhile somebody goes through here late from the river, that's all."

"Well, go on back and tend to your boxes. We'll look after this."

"Very good, sir."

The patrolmen came back from the flats, reporting nothing to be seen. One of the men thought he had seen tracks leading off to the right, but didn't follow them.

"Well," said Brady, "guess it was somebody on the river took a shot at something. Sound travels far at night, you know. Better go on in. I'm going home, sergeant, you'd better take them dicks back with you. Never mind making a report on this. I'll look after it myself in the morning. Good night, men, and I want to say you made a good run out here. Shows you're on your toes. That's the stuff."

3

"THERE IT IS AGAIN"

WHEN SERGEANT RIORDAN reported for duty the next afternoon, Captain Brady almost immediately referred to the proceedings of the previous night, and the steps he had taken.

"I got a line on the ghost," he said, smiling contentedly. "I don't intend to let anything like that buffalo me. You got any ideas on it, boy?"

"You go ahead and tell me what you've done, chief. You said last night you'd look after it. Why should I butt into your case?"

Brady regarded his aid quizzically. "That means you haven't been altogether dumb, don't it? Well, I happen to know you haven't been working on any line that I've been working on, so I'll tell you what I did.

"In the first place, I had the reporters in here and told 'em all about it. They've made funny stories out of it. You'll see 'em in the evening papers. And I did that to balk this here ghost; for it's a cinch somebody has rigged that thing up to scare people out of that street so they can put something over on the quiet. And the best way I know to make that street popular is to tell it to the papers. I'll bet you to-night there'll be a mob out there, looking for this ghost. And I'll bet you the mob scares the ghost away."

"Uh-huh, I guess so."

"You guess so, do you, boy? Well, we'll see. You think that was a good idea, giving it to the papers?"

"Sure, it's better to give it to 'em before they find out about it. You told 'em you took a shot at it, did you?"

Brady winced. "No. I left that out. I said somebody maybe took a shot at it, and we went out there on a trouble call and saw this here shadow. I don't mind the papers kidding the ghost, but I don't want them to kid me none."

"Well, and then what, chief?"

"I'll tell you, boy. Figuring that somebody wanted to scare people off the lower end of Twelfth Street, I asks myself why would they want to do that? What's down there that's valuable? It certainly isn't the shacks, and the only other thing there is the warehouse. So I called up the manager of the Globe Company and asked him what he had in there that maybe somebody would want to swipe, if the street was lonely enough.

"He says he hasn't got anything to speak of now, aside from household goods and some groceries, but that next week there's a shipment of silk coming in. And then I had it, see?

"One of them silk gangs has framed that thing. They figured they'd make the street unpopular and that would leave 'em a clear get-away when they stage their raid. Well, by giving this to the papers I've roused public curiosity, and I betcha we'll have to put a traffic cop down there to handle the crowds."

"Silk, eh? Where from and for whom?"

"The Orient, boy. There's a silk cargo coming into Tacoma pretty soon, and while most of it is going through to the East by express, there's a sizable shipment coming here for the Gow Loon Company, down in Chinatown. When I found out about the silk I called up the Importers' Fidelity Company and they told me all about it.

"It seems every now and then one of these Chinese firms gets a big batch of silk sent over, and they warehouse it and then parcel it out to the Chinks in the different cities. One company wholesales it, you see, and jobs it out to the others. It's Gow Loon's turn this time, that's why it's coming here."

"How much silk?"

"The Importers' Fidelity didn't know. Said he hadn't got the papers yet. The stuff comes over in million dollar cargoes. He said he supposed this split here would be worth maybe fifteen or twenty thousand dollars. He'll get the papers on it when the cargo is unloaded at Tacoma. The Fidelity handles insurance on it, you know."

"Did you tell 'em about the ghost, too?"

"No, what's the use of scaring them? Now that we know what it is I reckon we can take care of any silk gang. I got a special report on those birds, with pictures. Here it is, throw it in your desk and take a look at it later on to-night."

Riordan reached for the report and pigeonholed it.

"That's fine, chief," he said. "And what makes the ghost?"

"I don't know yet, boy. But I'll betcha I know to-morrow. I'm having Halloran lay out in those shacks to-night, and if the crowd doesn't scare the ghost off, or if it shows up after the crowd goes, I'll bet you Halloran will find where it comes from.

"Being a shadow on the wall, the light that makes it must come from somewhere, and lying there and studying it, Halloran ought to be able to locate the beam that makes it. It's my idea somebody near there's got a little magic lantern hidden away, or something like that."

"Yeah, most likely it's something like that—throws the shadow on the wall, like a picture on a screen. That's what I call good deduction, chief," said Riordan.

"Good what?"

"Good deduction, like *Sherlock Holmes*—"

"You're kidding me, eh," interrupted Brady. "Well, what do you think it is, then?"

"I don't know, chief. I guess you've got the right dope on that silk, anyway. Listens good."

"Well, then, what are you pulling this Sherlock stuff about?"

"Nothing, chief. It *is* deduction, isn't it? And good, I claim, too."

Captain Brady made no reply. He jammed on his hat, closed his desk, and walked out, without saying good night. Riordan laughed silently a moment, and then turned to his routine reports.

When he had gone through them and attended to such details of the night's work as were most important, he took out the special report Captain Brady had prepared on the silk thieves and studied it carefully. He paid particular attention to the pictures of known "silk men" that were with it, and then went out to the Bertillon room and for some time pored over the record books there.

Later on the reporters came in and told him that there was a big crowd out on lower Twelfth Street looking for the ghost, but that nobody had seen it up to the time they had left. There was a jam of automobiles there, they said, and two traffic men had been sent out to keep things moving.

Riordan had nothing new to offer them in the way of ghost news, and presently they went away and wrote new and funnier stories about the weird wraith.

Returning from lunch about half past ten, Sergeant Riordan called in Nichols to take charge of things and, slipping off his uniform donned old trousers, a flannel shirt and his mackinaw, volunteered the information that he might be gone some time.

Then he went to the police garage and, climbing into his car, drove leisurely out to the lower end of Twelfth Street. He found a curious crowd still milling round, with a fair sprinkling of automobile parties, which one traffic cop was quite successfully keeping moving.

Parking his machine by the Globe Warehouse, Riordan mingled with the crowd awhile, enjoying the repartee that was being tossed about, and gradually working his way down toward the end of the pavement where the street ended in the river flats.

He had nearly reached this point when the noise of the crowd was suddenly hushed, and then two or three screams rang out from the women, followed by a general cry of: "There it is—see—on the wall, there." Wheeling about Riordan caught a glimpse of the threatening shadow, tremblingly poised on the blank wall of the warehouse. But even as he looked it blurred and vanished.

The crowd was all pushing down toward the corner, from where "the ghost" could be best seen, and Riordan let people shove past him and made his way unobserved out into the darkness on the flats. He stood there awhile, watching the milling crowd, and then circled slowly about until he was in the shadows behind the row of shacks opposite the Globe Warehouse.

Noiselessly he slipped through a broken out window of one of these and padded forward slowly. The partitions between the shacks had been broken out, so that one could make his way along the entire line of them, a distance of perhaps half a block. Outside, the crowd was to be heard, its noises muffled; within the dark buildings there was not a sound.

"Halloran," Riordan called softly. "It's Riordan; where are you?"

He listened, but received no reply. Slipping quietly ahead into the adjoining shack he called again. This time he got an answer:

"Up in the attic, second shack from the corner."

He moved forward toward the voice, testing every step in the dark, for much of the flooring was rotten. Finally a guttural whisper sounded above him.

"Careful, Mat, that floor's rotten. Around by the back it's better. There. Now reach up—there's a beam you can pull yourself up on and work over to the front. I'm sure glad to have company."

Riordan worked his way up and along until he was beside his fellow officer. Lying flat on his stomach he could look out through a rent in the roof, over the heads of the crowd, at the blank wall of the warehouse opposite.

"You seen it?" he asked.

"Three times, Mat. The crowd didn't see it the first two times; there was too many auto headlights down there to blind 'em. And there was a million people here then. Most of 'em have gone by now. But I'm free to say it give me hair a rise the first time I seen it. Now I'm used to it, almost. But I'm glad you're here."

"Where is it? Did it move any?"

"It waves back and forth, Mat. But it's always in about the same place—see where that mortar stain runs down over the brick? Well, just to the right of that, under the letter 'L' in the sign, 'Globe Warehouse.' It's right in there."

"I just got a glimpse of it last time, but I was way down toward the end of the pavement. How long did it last?"

"The first time it was just a flash. The second time, Mat, I should say it flickered there for maybe a minute. This last time, not so long. But I could see it plainer, there wasn't so many lights."

"Did it move, you say?"

"It just wavered, Mat. It was always at the same place, but trembled like. And sort of faded out. By gorry, it's a creepy thing."

"Creepy, maybe, but you know it's some sort of hokus pokus. You couldn't get an idea what cast that shadow, could you?"

"No. I ain't got enough used to it yet to try and fi— There it is again!"

4

A CHOP SUEY PARLOR

RIORDAN SAW IT this time, plainly. The shadow of a man, tall, maybe seven feet tall, he estimated, clearly outlined on the brick wall of the warehouse. One hand was raised overhead in a threatening gesture; the knees were slightly bent, as if the form was about to spring. The outline was at moments vividly distinct, then wavered and clouded. Even as Riordan looked the thing took on a sudden great cloudiness, seemed to bulge forward, and vanished utterly.

The crowd below appeared less enthusiastic, and began to thin out. Of course it was getting late, but the glamour of ghost hunting seemed to be palling on the public.

"We'll have it all to ourselves pretty soon," said Riordan. "I hope it comes again soon, so we can get a line on it."

"How long does the cap'n want me to lay up here?" asked Halloran.

"Not so very long. Just till we get a line on this thing. Tell you what you do—you know this dump better than I do. Take a prowl all round it. I'll stay here. Don't use your light, but use your head. If you see anybody in any of these shacks, come back and let me know and we'll go call on him."

Halloran crept off in the dark. Riordan heard a board

creak, then a more distant one, and then had the solitude of the place to himself. His estimation of Halloran rose at once; it was not the cheerfulest place in the world to lie and wait for supernatural visitors. The crowd below, apparently fed up on ghosts, and much more subdued in its behavior, was rapidly melting away.

Presently there was but a handful of people in the street, and the motorcycle man on duty got on his machine and chugged back toward the city. Every time the electric light on the corner flickered or sputtered as its arc broke momentarily, plunging the street in a second of darkness, more of the onlookers departed.

Suddenly the shadow leaped out again on the warehouse wall. As nearly as Riordan could judge, it was projected from immediately in front of him, so distinct were its outlines. Then it clouded and disappeared, leaving only the dimly illumined wall with its mortar stain shining dimly white like a curtain.

Halloran eased himself back into place beside Riordan.

"Not a soul but us two in the dump," he said. "I've been all over it. And nobody on the roof. I went out on the flats behind and took a look. The arc light shows the roof as plain as day. I doubt if the roof would hold anybody. Ugh! There's the danged thing again!"

This time the ghost seemed to be afflicted with some dance of hate. It jigged up and down and back and forth on the bricks, its upheld arm shaking as with dire threat. Then as suddenly it vanished.

"Come on, let's go," said Riordan. Halloran was willing.

They slipped out through the rear of the shacks, and under Riordan's leadership circled back over the flats, keeping well out of the light that streamed from the last arc on Twelfth Street.

"I don't know when I've enjoyed a job less than to-night," Halloran finally ventured. "Not that I was scared, you know—but them shacks is too dirty to lie out in. I was sure glad when you come, sergeant; though I did wonder a bit if you'd go away and leave me there."

"You can tell the captain to-morrow that I ordered you to quit. There's no use lying there all night and watching that thing."

"You've an idea what it is then?"

"Yes, I've an idea. All I've got to do now is to find out if my idea's any good. Let's go over and have a look at the back of the warehouse—when we get in the shadow of the building it'll be all right to throw your light."

Halloran's flash light, however, revealed nothing unusual at the rear of the Globe Warehouse. The lush grass of the flats grew up to within a few feet of the wall, and next the building itself were piles of waste, blown there by the eddying winds.

Here and there piles of charred wood and old tin cans showed where hoboes, boys, or fishermen had made brief camp in the shelter of the dead walls of the big building; but if Riordan had expected to see the ground disturbed anywhere, he was disappointed. However, he kept his own counsel. At the end of their inspection he said:

"I got my car parked up at the corner; come on and I'll give you a lift down town. I'll have to drop you on Broadway, that's as far as I'm going."

As they swung into Twelfth Street they found it deserted. The crowd that had come for a thrill had dwindled away as the hour waxed late, and they had the block to themselves. Moving along the warehouse, they inspected the bricks closely, paused for a moment or two under the white mortar stain, but were not treated to an appearance of the ghostly and threatening shadow. They climbed into Riordan's car, and soon were gliding back toward the heart of the city.

"Something makes that shadow, Mat," Halloran finally hazarded. "But what gets me is where the light is that casts it. There's nothing opposite but those shacks, and we know the light didn't come from there. And there isn't anything on the flats, either."

"You don't go much on the ghost theory then?"

"I might have at first, Mat. But after seeing it so often, I got to admit it was less terrifying. No, I wouldn't say as I thought it was a ghost; though the first time it sure made my hair rise. Do you think it might be something in the wall of the warehouse?"

"I'm aiming to go through the inside of that place pretty thoroughly to-morrow. But I don't think I'll find anything."

Which was as far as Riordan would go. He dropped Halloran at Broadway, turned his car down that thoroughfare for several blocks, and then turning again, drove into that part of the city known as Chinatown. Leaving his roadster he entered one of the less pretentious chop suey "parlors," and taking a seat at a table in the rear, ordered a pot of tea, rice, and chow mein. For the next half hour there was little to distinguish the detective sergeant from the other patrons of the place, save that, perhaps, he appeared rougher than they, due to his clothes, his scowl, and his big frame.

As he finished his repast, and tipped back in his chair while he reached in his pockets, as if looking for something to smoke, one of several Chinese seated at a corner table rose and came over to him, extending a cigar in foil.

"Hello, sarge," he said. "You smoke him."

Riordan took the cigar and lighted it. "Takes you boys to remember faces, eh?" he bandied. "Chinaman never forget, eh?"

The Celestial smiled slightly and shook his head. "No forget Sarge Rio'dan. Wha's mattee, sarge, you down here like these clothes?"

"Oh, been bummin' around. Look-see, you know. This place all right."

"Yes, this place all light," the Chinese agreed. "All China place, all light now. No more bad."

Riordan laughed. "That's good. No more hop, eh? No more fan-tan? What you boys do, eh?"

The Chinese again smiled. "You wan' hop, sarge? Or fan-tan? Or mark lot-ley slip? You all light—I take you, if you want."

The detective sergeant laughed and shook his head. "No, I don't want any. Just hungry; come in for chow. Pay now and go. Good night."

"No pay, sarge. You all light. All same clien', no pay. Good night."

Riordan shrugged his shoulders and made his way out to his car. He had scored a blank, and it nettled him. The Chinese had recognized him, probably from the first; and while he could not place the Celestial at all, he realized that no matter how long he had sat in the place he would not have been permitted to see what he had gone there to observe.

And that was if any patrons of the place left by way of the kitchen instead of the front door; for the suey parlor was known to be the entrance to a resort of far less innocent character, a place where the initiated could get either excitement or forgetfulness.

Balked for the time being in his pursuit, Riordan determined to call it a day; and swinging his car about, drove home without returning to police headquarters. He tumbled into bed at once, setting his alarm clock, however, for seven in the morning. What he could not find out at night, perhaps he could discover the next day, he said to himself. And then he laughed as his head touched the pillow—of course, the Chinese knew him; he had parked his car in front of the place, and it bore, beneath its license plate, the mark of officialdom, while the huge siren mounted on the front also told all beholders it was not a private machine. He had forgotten, for the moment.

5

KELLY MAKES A CALL

THE NEXT AFTERNOON, when he came on duty, he found Captain Brady far from cheery in his greeting. However, he had expected that.

"Boy," said the senior officer, "how comes it that when I assign Halloran to certain work, you take him off it?"

"Halloran had done all he could, chief. Staying there the rest of the night wouldn't have helped him any. Anyhow, you didn't tell me how long you wanted him to stay there."

"I told you I was going to put him there to locate the beam of light that cast that shadow. He didn't do it."

He could have laid there all night and not locate it. There isn't any beam."

Brady opened his mouth as if to make a quick reply, and then held it open for some time. At last he said:

"Boy, you got to forgive me for being harsh with you. I didn't mean anything by it. You sort of rubbed me the wrong way, jerking Halloran off that job—but you're right; I didn't tell you how long I wanted him there. And you know a whole lot more than he does. And if you say there isn't any beam of light casting that shadow, I reckon you must know what you're talking about. But this thing's getting my goat. Did you see this morning's papers?"

"No, chief—it happens I didn't. I— er, I was up early and running around, and didn't get a chance to read 'em. What did they say?"

"They said all sorts of things. The most charitable thing they said was that it all was some sort of a publicity or advertising stunt. And they give the police a good razz, too. Said we were either in on it or else a bunch of simpletons. You see, I broke the story to 'em in the first place, and now that they've decided it's advertising something, they're sore at me for steering 'em onto it. And, of course, I can't alibi, either."

"Well, chief, don't you care—maybe we can show 'em something yet. You got any more dope on your silk gang?"

Brady tipped back in his chair and scratched his head. "I'm not so keen on that silk gang stuff to-day as I was," he admitted. "Suppose you tell me what you got. I know you been working on this all day, for I couldn't get you at your house. You say that shadow isn't made by a beam of light; what does make it then?"

"Oh, light makes it, all right, chief," answered Riordan. "What I meant was that there wasn't any sort of a beam like you sent Halloran out to hunt for. Of course, it's a shadow, and a shadow's got to be cast by light—but there isn't any special beam for this job; no magic lantern stuff, or anything like that. That's why I pulled Halloran off post. I knew he wouldn't find anything if he stayed there all night."

"Do you know what makes that shadow?"

"I got a pretty good idea, but I haven't proved it yet."

"Well, let's go and prove it right now. I'm fed up on this thing."

Riordan shook his head. "Nope. Not right now. Leave

the ghost be awhile, chief. If we tip our hands now we may lose something that's going to be pretty good, I think. This silk shipment's coming in next Monday night, and we got to leave that ghost alone and unmolested till after that. If we move the ghost before then, why, certain parties that made the ghost possible will know we're wise, and they'll blow. And—"

"Then it is silk thieves," interrupted Brady, hope struggling to show in his voice, though he was trying not to hide it.

"Listen, chief, I hate to do this. But it isn't my case. It isn't your case. I stumbled onto what it was to-day, in my digging around, and I got a promise we get in on it if we're good; that's the best I could do. After this silk gets here, you'll get all the action and glory you want."

Brady leaned forward and looked closely at his aid for several moments. Then he abruptly swung round, closed his desk with a bang, and got up.

"I'm goin' to quit," he said savagely. "That's all; I'm through. I'm getting too old. I'm going to quit before they find out about me and throw me out. Boy, you'd better put somebody on to-night, and come down to-morrow morning and sit in. I'm through."

Riordan smiled, got between his chief and the door, and then laughed.

"Listen, chief," he said, "don't talk that way, even in kidding. Why, you know more in ten minutes than anybody else round here knows in a month. You doped this here ghost thing right from the very start. You figured it was a plant to scare people, and then you found out something valuable was coming to the Globe Warehouse.

"And you lined up a bunch of reports on guys who'd be likely to try and get this stuff. You got all that while I was lying home asleep. See? And you give it to me.

"Then, banking on what you'd doped out, I did a little gum-shoeing, and just naturally stumbled onto something—why, a blind man would have stumbled onto it. But I had your dope to start on, see? And when I walked into this thing, after you give me the start—"

"You mean you and me has walked into a federal case," interrupted Captain Brady.

"I told you that you knew more'n anybody else, didn't I?" replied Riordan.

Captain Brady sat down again, and drew a deep breath. "Maybe I'm not so dumb, after all," he said smiling. "And they're going to let us in on it?"

"They're goin' to hand it to you, chief, on a silver platter. You'll get the reward, and everything—and you can tell the papers where to head in, too, when you get ready to break it. When I told them how you'd figured this thing out, they said you'd put your finger on the very thing that was puzzling them, and that they sure wanted you in on it."

Captain Brady's good humor returned all at once. He laughed loudly and long.

"Boy," he finally said, "you're good. But you're a rotten liar. I know them federals. They never give up anything, and never ask for help. Why should they? They've got the best men in the world. They might want us to make a little pinch, small fry, to clean up some angle of the case. But the whole works—never."

One of the men from the outer office knocked and then came in.

"Mr. Kelly, captain," he said, and stepping back, ushered in a tall, sinewy man, whom it was quite evident he respected highly. Then he withdrew, closing the door quickly.

Both Brady and Riordan rose to greet the caller, who nodded pleasantly to the sergeant and gripped Brady's extended hand. Then he dragged a chair forward and sat down.

"Cap," he said, "I want to tell you something. You got one real man working for you here."

He pointed at Riordan.

"He's pretty good, Mike," admitted Brady. "But he's a poor liar. I was just trying to impress that on him when you came in. What's on your mind? I didn't know you were in town."

Kelly turned to Sergeant Riordan. "I thought you said you'd see to it that the captain was here," he said smiling.

"Well, he's here, isn't he?" answered Riordan. "I hadn't had a chance yet to tell him you were coming."

Kelly laughed, then turned back to Brady. "Cap," he said, "this young bucko of yours walked right in on one of my cases to-day, hooked up the loose ends for me, and then told me he'd spoil the whole works if I didn't let you and him in on it. I'm going to see if the government won't take him off your hands—he's wasting a lot of time for himself as a plain cop."

Brady shot a wicked glance at his aid, who was grinning sheepishly; but to Kelly he answered:

"I'm sure obliged to you for the compliment, Mike. Riordan is pretty good, sometimes. Yes, he uses his head."

"Yes, and I can see your training in all he does, cap. You're some, fox yourself. I've often wished you'd taken me up, years ago, when I wanted you to join our service."

Brady shook his head slightly. "No, Mike, it's not for me. You move round too much. Me, I'm a home body. Like to stay in one place. But it's good of you to say that, just the same. Riordan, here, you ought to have—he's young yet, and good. And he's got no wife to hold him in one spot. Still lives with his mother."

"Couldn't live with anybody better. Probably his mother give him some of her brains, too. Well, cap, this thing looks now as if it might come off Monday night, or if not then, Tuesday. Can we rely on you to have some men ready? I don't think we'll have any trouble, but it may turn out to be rough stuff. You got men that are plenty hard? Of course, I'll be there, too, and some of the boys."

"I've got the hardest gang you ever saw, Mike, when it comes to that. And we'll all be ready Monday."

"That's good. I'm glad you understand—well, I just dropped in to tell you personally, so you'd know it was all right. I'll see you Monday, about eleven o'clock. Got to run now. Good-by."

6

QUIET AT HEADQUARTERS

AFTER THEIR CALLER had thus abruptly departed, Brady turned again to his aid.

"Boy, I take it all back," he said. "Everything. But if Mike Kelly himself hadn't told me, I'd never have believed it. Why, he even thinks I know what it's all about. You're a good liar, boy, to have fooled him. For Mike Kelly is just about the best that Uncle Sam has got. You know what he is, don't you?"

"You told me once before, that he was a Treasury detective, who most of the time was detached on special duty."

"Uh-huh. Now, suppose you tell me as much about this thing as you think I ought to know, so Monday night I can be of some use. Tell me easy, so I can get it through my head."

Riordan showed signs of being uncomfortable again. Captain Brady produced two cigars, and handing one to the younger man, lighted his own, and puffed meditatively. His aid smoked quietly for several minutes, and then gave a short cough to clear his throat.

"Remember, chief," he said, "you started this thing. That's what I told Kelly. How you'd doped out about the silk thieves and this thing being a plant, and had put Halloran up there in the shacks to figure the thing out.

"Well, last night I went up there, as you know, and took a look around. There wasn't any place from which a beam could be thrown to cast a direct shadow on that warehouse wall except from those shacks, or from an airplane. I combed the shacks, and Halloran combed them, and there wasn't anybody there but us. And there wasn't any airplane.

"The only other light was the arc at the corner. Any shadows that threw on the sidewalk were flat and at an angle: But a shadow which that arc might have thrown on the wall wouldn't necessarily be distorted that way. Rather, if somebody who knew about projection took the distortion into consideration, he could make the arc throw any sort of a shadow on the wall he wanted to. So I figured that the shadow really came from the arc."

"Simple as pie, now that you tell me. But I'd never have thought of that in a thousand years, boy."

"Oh, yes, you would, chief. It's only that you hadn't got round to that yet. You see, I got to figuring that way because you'd done all the preliminary work. Well, once I got that through my head, I watched the arc and let Halloran watch the wall. You know how those street arcs sputter every now and then, when the carbons burn off a bit and then drop down together again?

"Well, every time that shadow showed on the warehouse wall, it was just after the arc had done a particularly violent bit of sputtering. A little sputter didn't bring on the ghost, but a good violent sputter did. So it was reasonable to conclude, wasn't it, that the shadow came from the arc—just when the carbons were in a certain position?"

"Simple as shooting, boy. But I'd never have noticed it. I'd be watching the shadow, and not something a quarter of a block away."

"Well, after I found out that the arc and the ghost seemed to be hooked up, I figured it wasn't any use leaving Halloran lying there any more, so I told him to beat it home."

Captain Brady nodded his head. "You did just right, boy; and I'm sorry I barked at you when you came in."

The telephone on Captain Brady's desk jingled imperatively. He reached for it, expostulated into it violently, then hung up with a bang.

"It's the missus," he said, turning to Riordan. "We got company for dinner to-night, and she wants me home. Won't listen to reason—says I'm late now. I got to go. You can tell me the rest later. In the meantime I'll think about it. With the lead you've given me, and knowing Kelly is on the case, I ought to be able to dope it out. I'll be back about ten if I can get away. Lucky you're not married."

THE NEWSPAPERS HAVING intimated broadly that the ghost at the Globe Warehouse was some sort of an advertising or publicity scheme, the public very quickly got enough of it. The second night, it is true, there was a fair sized crowd out to view the phenomenon; but the third night there was but a handful of curious.

By Sunday night lower Twelfth Street had returned to its usual neglected condition, as far as the public was concerned, and only the occasional appearance of Patrolman Sherman on the corner, and the passage of two belated fishermen broke its desolateness. The fishermen hurried past the warehouse, and Sherman did not dally, but turned the corner away from it and continued on his beat. He had orders, in fact, to be particular to show no interest in the strange shadow.

The silk cargo arrived at Tacoma Monday afternoon. The Importers' Fidelity notified Captain Brady that the shipment for the Gow Loon Company would arrive Tuesday morning. Somewhat more than they had expected, in fact, nearly a carload, and worth two hundred thousand dollars. It would be trucked to the warehouse from the freight yards, and the Fidelity people would have special guards on hand.

If Captain Brady cared to assign a couple of his men, as well, they would be welcome. Captain Brady assigned Halloran and Ebbits to watch the silk in transit, and also informed the reporters of the arrival of the valuable shipment. The unusual commerce coming to the city was well advertised.

Monday night was noted as an exceptionally quiet night about police headquarters. Reporters remarked that seldom had there been so little doing. The back room downstairs was cluttered with reserves, and the detective bureau looked more like a sports club than anything else, practically all of the men sitting round and playing cards throughout the evening until time to go off shift.

In fact, their games appeared to be so interesting that many of them remained playing long after the hour of relief, but by one o'clock Tuesday morning they seemed to tire of this and departed, almost as if somebody had signaled them.

7

NOSE FOR NEWS

TUESDAY EVENING BEGAN very much the same way. There seemed to be no business to take either reserves or detectives out upon the street. One of the reporters, with a better nose for news than the rest, finally noted that Captain of Detectives Brady was also in the office, though Sergeant Riordan was on duty and in charge.

"Don't you ever go home, cap?" he asked casually enough.

"What would I go home for, son?" replied the captain. "The missus is host to the Ladies' Aid to-night, house full of old hens. I'm more comfortable curled up here."

The reporter was a married man himself, and the explanation satisfied him, so he went down to the pressroom and sat in the poker game, which had already started, due to the dull outlook. Along about nine o'clock the same reporter, sensing something, dropped out of the game for a few hands, saying he was going to have a look around.

He went downstairs to the main lobby and found everything as usual. The sergeant on duty reported everything was quiet.

Swinging around, the reporter started for the elevator to ascend to the detective bureau. He was startled to note, as he passed the door of the back room, that the chamber was utterly devoid of reserves. Yet two hours previously it had been crowded with bluecoats.

He was a good reporter. He gave no sign of what he had seen. Entering the elevator he rode to the second floor, stepped out, and paused in the hallway to light a cigarette. As he did so he listened intently, and heard absolutely nothing.

When he had been on that floor before there had been enough noise coming from the detective bureau to imitate a political convention. He pushed open the door leading to the main office, and entered. MacIntyre was sitting at the desk, none else was in sight. He pushed into the picture-book room, and it, too, was empty.

"Where's everybody, Mac?" he asked nonchalantly.

"Out to lunch, I guess."

The reporter turned around and sauntered out; and then sped swiftly downstairs, through an inner passageway, and into the garage. Aside from the two police patrols, the place was devoid of cars. He crossed over to the drivers' room, and found but one of them.

"Where's Bill?" he asked.

"Out to lunch, I guess."

"He is like fun! Can that stuff. Quit stalling me. Everybody's out of this place but one sergeant and two deskmen and you. All the cars are out. I ain't dumb—what's doing?"

"That so," replied the driver, apparently not much interested.

The reporter moved to the telephone and called his office.

"Gimme the city editor," he said. "That you, boss? This is Cole, down at headquarters. There's something doing—

everybody out all at once. Know of anything in the wind? Heard anything from the sheriff's office?"

He listened to his superior's reply, then hung up and moved quickly out into the night. A block up the street he hailed a wandering taxi and showed his star to the bandit at the wheel.

"I'm on the *Chronicle*," he said. "Had much extra business to-night?"

The driver stuck his tongue in his cheek. "Supposin' I have," he parleyed.

"Take me to the same place and there's five dollars in it."

The taxi bandit opened the door of his vehicle and the reporter climbed in. Presently the machine was speeding out toward Twelfth Street. Two blocks from the warehouse it halted abruptly, and the driver reached a paw through the front window. "Gimme the five," he said.

The exchange being made, he drove on again, slowly. In the middle of the block he stopped again. Both doors of the taxi were jerked open simultaneously, and a man looked in from either side.

"Where you aiming to go, young feller?" one of them asked.

"What's it to you?"

The man moved back his coat. "I'm a deputy United States marshal," he said.

"Well, I'm a reporter on the *Chronicle*," replied the passenger, showing his press star.

The deputy grinned. "Tough luck," he commented, sagely. "You're a long ways from the *Chronicle* building. You'd better turn around and drive back. No visitors allowed at this end of town. Now be nice about it, this is

Uncle Sam talking. Turn her around, driver, and go back at least two blocks, and stay back. Then you won't get into any trouble."

The two doors slammed, the taxi gears grated into mesh, and the vehicle lurched about as it turned. Two blocks back it turned a corner and the reporter hopped out and bade it adieu. He had the craft of his kind. He made no direct effort to return toward the warehouse.

He held his course till he reached Fifteenth Street, then turned toward the river. Unmolested he reached the end of the pavement, hesitated a moment, then stepped out upon the dark, lush grass of the flats. Two steps forward he took and then he was grasped by strong hands and jerked down flat.

"One peep out of you," said a gruff voice, "and it's all off."

He was dragged into a little depression in the flats, and a beam from a shielded flash light blinded him. Then darkness again.

"It's one of them plaguey reporters," said the voice. "Better call the sergeant."

The scribe was much relieved, and he waited in silence while a form moved away through the murk. Presently two forms slipped back.

"How many of the boys came out with you, son?" asked a new voice, which he recognized.

"None of 'em, Riordan. I slipped away. Had a hunch."

"How'd you find out we were here?"

"Bribed a taxi bandit to take me where he took the last bunch. He brought me out Twelfth Street. Deputy marshal stopped me. So I circled round. What's doing?"

"You're Jimmy Cole, of the *Chronicle,* aren't you?"

"Guessed it in the dark, sarge."

"Well, this is doing. You give me your word to stick by me, and not to prowl around none, and you can stay. Otherwise I'll have to send you down to the harbor patrol launch on the river and keep you there. If you're down there you won't know anything at all; if you be good and stick with me you may get a story."

"I'll stick to you, sarge. Honor bright."

"All right. Now listen, you stick right close to me and keep your mouth shut. If you go to prowling round, somebody's liable to clout you one for luck, and ask questions afterward."

"I'll stick, sarge."

Riordan took his hand and led him off through the shadows that covered the flats like black velvet. Finally he halted in a clump of bushes and, sinking onto a box that was there, pulled the reporter down beside him.

"We're waiting for a party, son," he explained. "Maybe it won't come off. But we're goin' to wait. You sit right still and don't talk."

Cole was impressed. He knew Riordan fairly well, and found him unusually serious. And he appreciated greatly the chance of being "in" on a story—a big story—that the detective sergeant had given him. So he settled himself comfortably on the box and waited.

As his eyes became more accustomed to the dark he made out his location, approximately. They were almost immediately behind the warehouse, but a little to one side, and perhaps a hundred feet from the building. The bushes about them concealed them perfectly. Across the flats, before him, there was nothing to be seen, save a faint mist rising wraithlike from the ground.

In the distance was a reflection, wavering back and forth, which he knew was some light upon the river. Behind him the warehouse loomed a black cube, outlined against the glare of lights from the city beyond, There was no sound at all.

8

SEVEN OUT OF THE EARTH

HOW LONG HE sat there, listening and straining his eyes to see something, Cole could not tell. He was beginning to feel drowsy when Riordan nudged him sharply. Instantly alert, he strained his eyes again. The mist rising from the flats was now more noticeable as it turned into night fog.

But aside from its rising, shifting clouds he could see nothing. Then he saw something dark in the fog, moving staggeringly forward. It was a man, he made out, following some zig-zag path over the flats. Behind it appeared another dark object, also wavering in the mist, then another and another.

Seven, in all, of the figures came into view, moving slowly but determinedly forward, evidently feeling their way along one of the many paths that led crisscross through the grass. The figures passed within twenty feet of the clump of bushes, then disappeared in the darker shadow of the warehouse.

Cole was about to ask a question when he felt Riordan's hand press softly upon his lips. He remained silent and listened. Presently through the night air came soft, thudding noises; then sharper sounds, as of hard objects striking still harder ones. Then there was a creak as of a rending board, followed by instant silence.

A moment later the noises began again, then lessened, seeming to sink into the ground. Then everything became quiet once more. The reporter leaned close to Riordan.

"That the party?" he whispered inquiringly.

"Part of it—pretty soon now, I reckon. Mind you, stick right beside me. Right beside me, mind you."

They sat silent again for some minutes and then with startling suddenness the whole place was bathed in seemingly blinding white light.

"Come on, let's go," snapped Riordan, rising from his place and starting toward the warehouse.

Cole, following at his side, looked up. The top of the warehouse was lined with flood-lights, all pointing down and illuminating the flats like a giant stage. Across this lighted area a mass of men were converging, like an army in open formation, toward a pile of fresh earth near the base of the blank brick wall of the rear of the warehouse. In the van the reporter recognized Captain Brady and a handful of his detectives, each with his revolver in hand.

And then there erupted forth from behind the pile of fresh earth a group of men—seven of them—who paused startled as they scrambled into the brightly lighted area. Just a moment they hesitated, and then Cole saw their hands reach for hidden weapons.

"Stick 'em up," barked Brady. "Way up, quick!"

There was an instant of hesitation, then seven pairs of hands reached toward the flood lights above. Brady and his sleuths kept them covered, while others of the advancing men, infiltrating between them, snapped handcuffs on the uplifted wrists.

"Good," said Brady. "That's us. Now you, boy, go ahead."

Part of the men surrounded Brady and his prisoners, and started marching back toward the river. The others gathered about the freshly turned earth and looked at Riordan. He watched the backs of the retreating party for a moment, then moved ahead.

The upturned earth revealed a roughly timbered tunnel leading toward the warehouse. Into this Riordan plunged, followed by Cole and a handful of the men. The others, evidently by prearrangement, stood about the opening or patrolled the flat near by. Even as Cole noted this the flood lights were switched off, plunging the whole place into darkness.

Riordan produced a flash light and led the way down the tunnel. It sloped sharply, then leveled and rose, and in a few steps they came out in the basement of the great building that towered at the end of Twelfth Street. Here the party gradually dwindled, as one by one its members dropped out and took up position behind the great columns that rose from the foundations to support the weighted floors above. Riordan, Cole, and three others went ahead, ascended a flight of stairs, and came out in a great chamber filled with tightly corded bales.

"Silk, son," said Riordan, waving his hand. "Two hundred thousand dollars' worth, maybe."

"And those men that came in over the flats were going to steal it? Pretty clever trap, sarge. How'd you get onto it?" asked Cole.

"Stick around awhile, you ain't seen nothin' yet,"

answered the detective sergeant with a smile. "Here, sit on about two thousand dollars' worth of silk, and take it easy."

Cole lounged on a bale, and the others did likewise. But presently the sound of distant voices came to them, and their attitudes stiffened slightly. The voices grew louder and nearer, and a group came down a stairway into the huge chamber. At its head, was a tall, sinewy man; beside him walked a Chinese in modern dress; behind came several other Celestials, all in American clothes, and in the rear a group of less carefully garbed men, among whom Cole recognized a number of deputy sheriffs and other local officers.

"This your stuff, Mr. Loon?" asked the tall man, pointing to the bales. "Better look it over and see if it's all here. They might have got away with some before we surprised them."

The leading Chinese looked about, then said something to one of his companions, and the Celestials scattered about the chamber, checking the bales. Two officers moved about with each man.

Gathering about their leader again there was a subdued chattering for a moment, and then the Chinese first addressed nodded his head.

"It is all right, thank you," he said. "Would it be permitted to see the persons who attempted to steal it?"

"Presently," answered the tall man in authority. "First I'd like to have you sign this paper, saying the stuff is all here."

He passed over a document, which the Chinese read carefully. Then he reached in his pocket, drew forth a fountain pen, and slowly signed.

"Now, Mr. Loon," said the tall man, pocketing the paper,

"I want you to see something. My name is Kelly, sir; I'm a government agent. Watch closely."

He bent over the nearest bale, slit the seam of the covering with his pocketknife, rolled it back, and then pulled sharply at the folds of silk within. They came away easily, revealing a row of small tins.

The Chinese started forward, but restrained themselves at a scarcely perceptible sign from their leader as the officers moved in on them. Kelly took one of the tins, pried it open, and held it forth.

"Queer silk, isn't it?" he snapped.

Gow Loon waved his hands, but said nothing.

"You'll notice, Mr. Loon, that there are quite a number of us here," Kelly said, with an unpleasant smile. "So it won't pay to start anything. You're all under arrest, just now it's possession of opium. You have signed this paper, saying these bales are your property. Later on we'll be more particular in the charges, maybe; this will hold you for to-night. You and your men go along peaceable with the boys now and everything will be nice."

Gow Loon again waved his hands. "My attorney? Would it be permitted—"

"All in good time. You go along now."

Slowly the party filed from the chamber, and then Kelly came over to where Riordan was, looking at Cole inquiringly as he did so.

"He's a friend of mine," explained the detective sergeant. "One of the reporters. He smelled this out and came in after we were planted. I had to keep him with me to keep him quiet."

Kelly grinned. "Well, we'll keep him with us some more.

Come on down to headquarters. Brady will want to hear all about it. And I want to get a good look at that friend of yours there, too. Got your car near here?"

"On the next block," answered Riordan. "Let's go out through the tunnel. It'll be quicker, and we'll dodge that gang going out the door."

9

OPIUM HI-JACKER

COLE WAS TAKEN into Captain Brady's office with them. On the drive back to the heart of the city Riordan and Kelly had sketched in for him the main facts of the seizure, so he could get his "story," but they insisted on his staying for the rest of it. The reporter was willing enough, for he realized he was going to get something his rivals would not be able to gather from the mere blotter reports.

Captain Brady was waiting with ill-concealed curiosity, and he had chairs all placed and cigars handy.

"I want to hear about this as much as you do, Brady," said Kelly. "Of course I know what happened, but I want to hear how this sergeant of yours got his end. It was all new stuff when he put it up to me. All we were concerned in was getting Gow Loon and his gang. We've been trailing this silk ever since it started, but we never expected to get two gangs. Spill it, Riordan, it's getting late."

"There isn't much to tell," began the detective sergeant. "You see, Captain Brady here gave me the start on it. He dug up about there being silk coming to the warehouse—after we got this ghost thing pinned on to us. He had it doped that the ghost was rigged to scare people away from the warehouse, so the thieves would have a better chance.

"Well, the more I got to thinking about it the more I figured he was right—only in a way he hadn't mentioned to me. So I went out and hid out with one of the boys he had watching this ghost, and discovered that there was some kind of a connection between the ghost and the flickering and sputtering of that arc light—in short, that the arc cast the shadow that made the ghost.

"By that time the captain here had told the newspapers about the ghost and there was a big crowd out there looking at it. And the idea occurred to me that maybe whoever had framed this ghost had figured it as a sort of drawing card to *that* side of the warehouse, as well as a stunt to scare people out of the locality at night.

"And, thinking that over, the idea came to me that it was a fool plan, at best, and one that no sane man would figure up. And then it came to me that it was just the sort of a stunt a 'hop-head' would pull. You know, them guys are sometimes awful clever, but their reasoning's twisted.

"Well, when I got as far as that I decided to slip down to 'Dopey' Louie's place and see if there were any new 'hop-heads' hanging round—and there was where my luck came in. 'Cause after I'd been there awhile there was a Chinaman came over and began talking to me, and he talked different from any low-brow Chink I ever heard before.

"Half the time he sounded the letter 'r' in words just like we do, and the rest of the time he sounded it like it was 'l.' And I never see no common Chink that could roll an 'r,' no sir, only them high-class, educated ones like Gow Loon. And there was nothing high-class about this Chink that was rollin' out 'r' at me, an' calling me 'sarge.'

"What's more, this Chink wanted to pay my bill down there, and offered me something besides. Now your Chink is a fine friend and all that, and a nice enough fellow to meet; but he has his peculiarities. An' among them is these: he don't stand treat except on ceremonial occasions, and in a ceremonious way; and when he offers graft it's in a business way and downright bold and open—no hinting round."

"I'll say," interrupted Kelly to Captain Brady, "you got a right smart and observing lad with you, cap. He ought to be in the government service."

"He's a good boy," said Brady. "Go on, boy, I want to get the rest of it."

Riordan blew a cloud of smoke at the ceiling. "After that," he continued, "it was just like falling into it. I went up to the immigration office and asked Barney Winters up there what he knew about white folks who made up as Chinks so good you couldn't hardly tell 'em apart. 'Not so often,' says Barney. 'In fact outside of a dope smuggler named Shank Spink I don't know of any.'

"I asked him did he have any record of this guy Spink, and he throws a whole book at me. Spink, it seems, is well known on the Atlantic coast, and has done a couple of stretches. Kelly can tell about him, chief.

"Well, this stuff Barney had about Spink was a dead-ringer for the funny Chink that got friendly with me in Dopey Louie's place, and I told Barney so. And he told me to see Kelly, that he was in town on another case and likely would be interested. So I did, but before I went to see him I mosied out to the warehouse and had a good look around.

"Inside there wasn't anything in particular; but around

back of it, it seemed to me, there was one of those paths through the grass on the flats worn down altogether too much for a path that didn't lead anywhere.

"I didn't want to spoil anything by doing any snooping then, so I went home, got into my fishing clothes and went back to the flats and fished a bit. Then I come up to the lee of the warehouse and built me a little fire, like a lot of them fishermen do, and ate some lunch and had a good look.

"And you know, chief, I'm a sort of familiar with what they called camouflage in the late muss across the water— and that there ground had sure been camouflaged good. Too good, in fact.

"It showed where somebody'd dug a square hole, and then laid a line of old boxes and cans and busted tree limbs and driftwood and other junk to keep you from walking on a line between where the hole had been dug and the warehouse wall. It showed there was a tunnel there, and nothing else but.

"So I was all hunky-dory then, and almost ready to see Kelly; but first I had to get a look at that arc light. So I went home and got into citizen's clothes, like I was some kind of a power company wimpus, and then I got one of the trouble shooters to go with me and lower that arc so we could have a look at it.

"While we were looking at it I had a notebook out and made believe copy the numbers on it, and that sort of stuff, so if anybody was looking we'd seem harmless enough— and on the post that holds the bottom carbon-carrier was a funny little bunch of metal just opposite where the two carbons meet.

"It had been soldered on. It didn't seem to have any

particular shape, but I knew the sort of a shadow it would cast on the warehouse wall when the carbons were in just the right position.

"Then I went down to the power company and had a look at the records, and I find the arc-tender on the lower Twelfth Street circuit is one Nathan Bartholomew. And, checking on him, I find he's a graduate of a technical school, worked for awhile in China, but lost his job because he got to using dope, and he came over here and went on the bum, and finally the Salvation Army gets hold of him and tries to straighten him up, and gets him a job as arc tender with the power company."

"You'd better send out and get him," interrupted Brady.

"Don't worry, chief, I got him. Got him this afternoon. He's upstairs now. Well, after I'd got that stuff I went and saw Kelly, here. He did the rest of the works."

Kelly laughed quietly. "Yes, sir, captain," he said, "the lad is what you might say good. I'll get him away from you, yet. But right now I want to try just one thing more—get this Bartholomew fellow down here, will you, and after he's in here have the Spink lad brought in. I want to see 'em when they first meet."

Captain Brady reached for his telephone and called the jail.

"Summers? This is Captain Brady speaking. I want you to send down that man Bartholomew, that Riordan booked this afternoon; and then, about two minutes later, send down that make-believe Chink I brought in with the bunch from the river flats. Yes, that's it."

A turnkey presently led in Bartholomew. The arc-tender was highly nervous, and seemed to be expecting trouble.

"You're all right," spoke up Kelly. "Just sit down here with us for a minute, man. Nobody's going to hurt you. There, sit down here by me and take life easy. That's it. I think maybe you'll get out of this all right; provided you use your head and come clean. I think maybe we can use you."

Bartholomew's worried expression vanished, and he was smiling at Kelly when the door opened again and two uniformed men entered, with a man between them who at first glance looked like a Chinese. He was handcuffed to each officer. On being shoved into the room he looked quickly about and then his eyes focused on Bartholomew with a malignant and unmistakable hatred.

"You dirty stool pigeon," he blurted out. "I'll get you for this; I'll cut your heart out, if I have to wait a thousand years!"

Kelly smiled happily and turned to Cole, the reporter.

"That there," he said, "is something you won't often see. That's Shank Spink, the only hi-jacker of opium in captivity in the United States. That's what your Sergeant Riordan found, while Uncle Sam's men were just working on an ordinary smuggling case. Yes, I'll say that with Riordan's help we've made a very pretty and complete haul."

FOR A POINT OF HONOR

*Evolving Around a Shot in the Night That
Struck Nowhere, Riordan's Case Unearthed
the Trickery of the Hidden Power*

1

TWO WOMEN SCREAM

DETECTIVE SERGEANT RIORDAN closed his desk, rose from his chair, yawned, took off his office coat, and slipped into street wear, passed into the outer office and waved a hand at Griggs, the second night relief man, and went down to the garage. Getting into his car he drove to the Central Garage and ordered his tank filled with gas.

"What's the matter, sarge, city all out of fuel?" asked the service boy.

"No, buddy, but I'm going joy riding, and I don't use the city's gas except when I'm on business. Maybe some of the boys do, but not me. I get enough to buy my own gas."

The tank filled, he paid the amount due, climbed in and drove leisurely away. The night was warm with the approaching summer, the sky clear and moonlit, and the highways mainly deserted. After doing his trick from four in the afternoon until midnight the sergeant felt the need of fresh air, and this night in particular, closing the first real warm day of the season, he craved the open country.

He drove out through the park, thence along the river road and out into the orchard country, enjoying the soft scents of the night and the cool quiet, which was broken only by the steady hum of his motor. For an hour and a half

"My hands are busy holding each other," said Riordan—

he urged his car on through the night, and then, swinging over to another main highway, turned back toward the city and his own home.

It was three o'clock by the distant city hall chimes as he turned into the residence section known as Riverdale Park, which he must traverse to get to his house, and he was comfortably looking forward to tumbling into bed, when his professional senses were aroused by a sharp yet smothered report.

He shut off his motor instantly, turned out the lights of his car, and let the big machine roll along dark and noiselessly while he listened. A lesser, yet sharper crash came to his ears, apparently from ahead and around the corner of the block to the right; then he heard the shrieking of a window being raised, and immediately after the still of the night was broken by a woman's voice, screaming:

"Help! Help! Police! Help!"

Turning on his engine and lights with one brush of his hand across the instrument board, he stepped on the accelerator and his big roadster leaped ahead and then swerved

—*"The door opens when you turn the knob"*

sharply around the corner, veritably on two wheels. As it did so, he heard another window shriek open, and another female voice joined the first in a terrified chorus of screams.

Jerking his spotlight upward and to the right, and sweeping the dwellings with it. Riordan almost instantly focused its beam upon one of two double houses that stood midway down the block, from the second story of which a woman was leaning and shouting, while from the floor above appeared the ludicrous figure of a negro maid, outdoing her mistress in shrieks of alarm.

Even as Riordan brought his car to a halt in front of the house and sprang out, a window in the adjoining house was thrown up and a man stuck a night-capped head out, while across the street other windows were raised as alarmed householders were awakened by the uproar. Throwing open his coat so that his golden detective sergeant's star could be plainly seen, Riordan leaped down and ran up on the lawn of the double house.

"What's the matter, madam?" he shouted. "I'm a policeman."

Though the negress on the third floor still continued to scream hysterically, the woman on the second floor ceased her calls.

"Oh, I'm so glad you got here," she said, "there's some-body in the house."

"Don't worry, madam, we'll get him," answered Riordan. "You just slip on something and run down and let me in."

"No, no," exclaimed the woman, "I'll not leave this room. I've got the door locked, and I'll not open it—not till you're inside. You'll have to kick in the door, or something."

Riordan ran up the steps of the house and threw his full weight against the front door, but the heavy oak held and he made not the slightest impression on it. He dashed down to the basement, but an iron gate, locked on the inside, barred that entrance. Coming up to the lawn again, he hailed the man leaning from the window of the house next door.

"You got a gun? Get it, and keep your head out the window. I'm going round to the back of the house, if anybody shows, coming out of the front while I'm gone, shoot him and ask questions afterward."

The neighbor disappeared from the window for a moment, then reappeared, a brightly-nickeled revolver in his hand.

"Remember, shoot if you seen anybody," said Riordan, and he raced across the lawn and through the shrubbery, vaulted a low fence and approached the back of the house. There he moved with more caution, scanning the grass of the rear yard for footprints.

Seeing none he moved to the rear windows, and tried each one, but all were bolted. Then he tried the back door, which he saw opened inward, but it would not budge; nor did hurling his weight against it do more than make it creak. It was evidently barred on the inside.

He circled on about the house, and again came out on the lawn. The negress, leaning from her window on the top floor was still shouting lustily, and paid no attention to Riordan's calls. The woman on the second floor refused to leave her room. The detective sergeant looked up at the neighbor, still leaning from his window, gun in hand.

"You'll have to come down and let me in your house," he said. "Maybe you've got a ladder and I can find a window that isn't latched, or something."

The man disappeared, and Riordan mounted the steps leading to his front door. This was swung back presently, and the householder admitted him.

"Tell you what, officer," he said. "Best thing for you to do is to come up to the roof. I'll open my skylight, and you can cross over to Randall's roof and kick a pane out of theirs and so let yourself in."

"All right, let's go. After you let me out on the roof, you run down and tell that woman how I'm going to get in, so she won't have a fit when she hears me in the house. Then you telephone police headquarters and tell 'em Sergeant Riordan said to send a squad of men out here."

In a minute he was through the skylight and on the roof. Before stepping over on to the adjoining roof he took a survey of the ground below him, looking for some moving figure. But the back and front yards were deserted, as far as he could see.

Then he whipped out his knife, gouged the putty from one of the frames in the skylight of the locked-up house, removed the pane, reached a hand in and found the catch, and opening it, lifted the glass covering.

Peering in he saw no ladder beneath. The skylight opened into what was evidently a storeroom. Lowering himself through the opening, he dropped to the floor, pawed his way over some trunks and found the door. It was locked from the other side, but a well-aimed kick at the cheap lock broke it open, and he found himself in a hallway.

Striking a match—he had left his flash light in his automobile—he located a light button and flooded the hall with brilliance. Then he made his way down the stairs, turning on the lights as he went to the main floor.

There he pulled out his revolver, and made a quick tour of the rooms, flooding each one with light as he entered it. There was nobody to be seen, nor any sign of a disturbance.

Down to the basement he went next, and after examining that, opened the cellar door and investigated everything in that chamber, from the coal pile to the furnace. Not only was there nobody anywhere in the house, aside from the two women, but there was no sign of anything having been rifled or disturbed.

As Riordan mounted to the main floor again he heard the distant wail of sirens, and he opened the front door as two motorcycle men swept up the street. Leaving their machines leaning against his car, they ran up the steps.

"You two boys take a scout round the neighborhood," he ordered. "If you see anybody, stop him. If you don't see anybody, take a hunt through all the shrubbery in these yards. Anybody come aside from you?"

"Yes, sergeant," answered one of the men, as he moved off, "the wagon's on the way out with some of the boys."

Riordan sat down on the steps. The negress on the top floor was still screaming. The next door neighbor had donned his trousers and a sweater and come out, and seeing Riordan, stepped to his side.

"That nigger's sure got a good voice," he said.

Riordan nodded and smiled. "Tell me," he said, "did you hear anything before the screaming began?"

"I don't know, officer. I was wakened from my sleep, and I had a feeling I'd heard something. Then I heard a door slam. Thought it was in my house. I was debating whether to get up and investigate, when a window was thrown up and I heard Mrs. Randall calling for help. Then that darned nigger started. I got up to see what it was all about, and looking out of the window, saw your car pull up. Lucky you were so near. I guess the women screaming frightened off whoever it was."

"You didn't hear a shot, did you?"

"I don't know. Something wakened me, but what it was I couldn't say."

"What you know about these people?"

"The Randalls? Why, not very much. Young couple. They only moved in here a little while ago. I understand he's some kind of a contractor or something. Away a good deal. His wife seems to be a nice woman, rather quiet."

2

TALES OF THE TWO

THERE WAS THE sound of another siren, and the patrol wagon rumbled up and disgorged two uniformed men and one in plain clothes, who came running up the steps.

"You two harnessed bulls take a scout round," said Riordan. "There's a coupla motorcycle men prowling the neighborhood, so don't shoot at shadows. One of you tell the driver to keep his eye on the door here. You, Willis, come with me."

The policemen moved away, and the plainclothes man entered the house with Riordan. As they did so the negress, apparently satisfied that protection was at hand, stopped her screaming.

"Thank goodness that concert's over, Willis. That woman has been yelling for fifteen minutes without any let-up. Listen now; I want you to go over this floor and the basement like you'd lost a penny somewhere and thought maybe it had rolled under the piano. Don't touch anything, but use your eyes. Make a lot of noise as you move, too. When you get through, come back here. I'm going upstairs and have a talk with the madam."

"What's it all about, sarge?"

"I don't know. And while you're at it, look for a bullet hole."

Willis set to his work and Riordan mounted to the second floor. Going to a door at the front of the hall, he knocked.

"Sergeant Riordan, madam. I'd like to talk with you. I've got one officer in the house and five outside, looking round."

The key turned in the lock, the door opened, and an exceptionally pretty brunette, with a dressing sacque thrown over her and blue slippers peeking beneath, stepped out.

"Oh, sergeant, I was never so frightened in my life. I don't know what I'd have done if you hadn't come so promptly."

"I was very glad to be in the neighborhood, madam. I heard your calls, and got here as soon as I could. Now will you tell me what happened, please?"

"Why, I was sound asleep, and suddenly I was wakened. There was a man in the room. I screamed. He ran out. I leaped out of bed, shut and locked the door, and then threw open the window and called for help."

"What sort of a man, madam?"

"I don't know. I was so frightened."

"Did he have a hat on?"

"Yes—no, it was a cap, I think. Gray cap."

"A mask?"

"No."

"Did he have whiskers or a mustache?"

"A beard, I think."

"What kind of a face?"

"Oh, a terrible one."

"What was he doing when you saw him?"

"Standing right here, in the doorway."

"Was your door locked when you went to bed?"

"No, I had left it open, it was so warm."

"Was the man armed, did he carry a gun, I mean?"

"I—I don't know."

"Will you call your maid down, please? I want to talk to her."

"Oh, sergeant, she's all right. She had nothing to do with it. Why, Virginia has been with me for—oh, ever so long."

Sergeant Riordan smiled. "I'm sure she's all right, madam. But I'd like to talk to her. Maybe she heard something. She was awake, too, you know."

"Yes, I heard her screaming."

"Will you call her, please?"

The woman hesitated a moment, then stepped out into the hall.

"Virginia! Virginia!" she called. "Put on your clothes and come down, the policeman wants to talk to you."

"Yas, Mis' Randall, I'se comin'."

Riordan reached in a pocket and pulled out a pad and pencil.

"Just as a matter of form, madam, will you give me your name?"

"Mrs. Elizabeth Randall."

"Your husband's name?"

"John Randall."

"His business, please?"

"He's with the State Contracting Company."

"And he's away to-night?"

"Yes, he had to go out of town. I expect him back on the Owl train—it's due at seven, I think."

"And your maid's name?"

"Virginia Thompson."

"Thank you. Now, Mrs. Randall, would you mind stepping downstairs and looking over your silverware and such things, and see if anything has been taken? One of my men, Willis is his name, is down there looking around. But I told him not to touch anything. We want to know if anything was stolen."

"Very well, sergeant. But if you don't mind, I'll slip on a dress first. I'll be right down."

Riordan bowed, and she stepped back in her room and closed the door. The detective sergeant walked back down the hall and sat down on the stairs. Presently he heard a door on the floor above open, and then shuffling feet. He turned to see the negro maid coming down.

"Hello, Virginia," he said, rising; "quite a lot of excitement for one night, eh? Come on downstairs, I want to talk to you."

He went down to the main floor, followed by the negress, whom he led into a rear room.

"Now you tell me just what you heard," he said pleasantly.

"Well, boss, I cain't tell you so much. It was like this. I was woke up by voices. I thought maybe Marse Randall come home. I heard Mis' Randall talking excited like to somebody, and then I know it warn't Marse Randall. She say: 'Don' you do it,' an' then I hear a great big bang like a firecracker goin' off, and then a door slam and I hear Mis' Randall begin to yell, an' I opens my winder and yells, too."

Riordan stepped to the doorway and called: "Oh, Willis, come here!" The plainclothes man hurried up from the basement.

"Willis, this is Virginia Thompson, the maid here. You take her out in the kitchen and talk to her. And maybe she'll make you a cup of coffee, or something. You go on with Mr. Willis, Virginia, you'll find he's a right nice cop."

Leaving them, Riordan went to the front door. The two motorcycle men were there, waiting. At his appearance one of them spoke up:

"Not a thing in sight, sarge. And nobody in the neighborhood saw anything. That nigger woke 'em all up, I guess. One party thought he heard a shot, but wasn't sure. No marks on any of the windows in the back of the house, nor the front, either, as far as we could see. And the doors all look fast."

"All right. You boys had better go on in. Tell one of them harnessed bulls to stay around, let the wagon and the other one go in. Willis will stay here with me. Tell the bull who stays to find the man on this beat and get what he can about these folks. Have him wait for me, I'll take him in with me in my bus. You made a quick run out here, boys, and I want to compliment you on it."

The two saluted and moved off. Riordan turned back and sat down in the parlor, in plain sight of the stairway. He had been there but a moment when Mrs. Randall came down.

"Did you talk to Virginia, sergeant?"

"She just came down a minute ago, Mrs. Randall. I turned her over to Detective Willis; they're in the kitchen now. I had to step outside to talk to the boys who came out."

"I'd like to hear what she says to the detective."

Riordan laughed. "She probably won't be able to tell him much. She seemed scared white. I told him to jolly her along and get her in a good humor."

"I suppose she was terribly frightened."

"Well, it's all over now. The men who were outside have just reported to me that they can't find anything. Whoever it was got away, without leaving any trace. Now, Mrs. Randall, would you mind having a look around, and seeing if anything is missing?"

"Not at all, sergeant. Let's go in the dining room first."

Together they went all over the ground floor of the house. She examined all the silverware, and found it intact. The bookcases in the library showed no signs of having been tampered with. Mr. Randall's desk in his den was open, but undisturbed, and Mrs. Randall said none of his papers appeared to have been dislodged. Before coming downstairs, she said, she had looked through the dresser drawers upstairs, and none of her jewelry had been molested.

"I must have frightened the man away," she concluded, as they returned to the parlor, "before he had got to work."

"That was very fortunate," said Riordan, sitting down on the sofa and settling comfortably. Mrs. Randall remained standing a few moments, then dropped into an armchair.

"Now that I think of it," she said, "the man's beard was red."

"And he wore a dark cap, you said?" queried Riordan.

"Yes, I think that was it. Sort of an indistinct color."

"Would you say he was a big man, or a little one?"

"Fairly large, sergeant. Perhaps it was because he was fat."

"About how old would you say he was?"

"Oh, I don't know—thirty or forty. I didn't get a very good look at him."

"Did you notice the color of his eyes?"

"They were blue, I think."

"Did he wear a coat, or overcoat?"

"I think he had on overalls."

"And you were awake when he entered your room?"

"No—I wakened suddenly, and he was standing in the doorway."

"Across the room from your bed?"

"Yes."

"Mrs. Randall, doesn't it seem strange to you that you could wake from a sound sleep in a dark room, and notice that the man had a gray cap and blue eyes?"

"That is the impression I got, sergeant," she answered levelly.

3

LOOK FOR A DARK-HAIRED FELLOW

"BUT A MOMENT ago you agreed with me that he wore a dark cap."

"An indistinct color, I said, sergeant. It was dark, you know. Gray looks dark in the half light."

"And do eyes look blue in the dark, too?"

"There was moonlight in the room, sergeant. You can see for yourself that it is very light outside."

"One of the neighbors thought he heard a shot."

"That must have been what wakened me."

Sergeant Riordan looked at her silently, but her eyes never wavered.

"Or maybe it was the back-firing of an automobile," she added a moment later. "Something wakened me—and he was standing in the door of my room."

"Mrs. Randall, did you lock the house up when you retired, or did the maid?"

"I locked it up, sergeant. You see, my husband was away, and I was particular."

"When did he go away?"

"Yesterday afternoon."

"And you expect him back early this morning?"

"Yes, he just went down to Mountainview to see about a contract. There was to be a council meeting, and his firm was bidding for some work. He expected to be through in time to get the Owl train as it came through there this morning. He ought to be on the way home now."

"Your husband makes pretty good money? I mean by that, Mrs. Randall, would a burglar be apt to visit your house—is your husband known as well-to-do?"

"This is a rather good neighborhood, isn't it, sergeant? Mr. Randall has an interest in the State Contract Company."

"Have you any idea, Mrs. Randall, what this intruder might have been after? I mean by that, was there anything special in the house that he might have known about?"

She looked at him as if she did not comprehend. Then gathering her wits, she answered.

"Why, I suppose he was just a burglar."

"Did it impress you as strange—or rather, does it now impress you as strange, that the man went directly to your room, without disturbing anything downstairs?"

Again she regarded him with a puzzled look, and then replied slowly: "No, I do not know that it does, sergeant. I suppose he was looking for jewels that might be in the bedroom. Possibly he had planned to start at the top and work down."

"And you didn't hear anything like a pistol shot?"

"Something wakened me—I do not know what it was. I cannot imagine why he should fire a pistol and make a noise. Then, sergeant, there would be a bullet hole somewhere would there not, if he had fired a revolver?"

"Not necessarily, Mrs. Randall: he might have used blank cartridges, just to frighten you."

She appeared to consider this. After some moments of quiet, she said:

"I was so terrified when I saw him I do not know clearly exactly what he did. Possibly, if he had used blank cartridges, he might have fired a revolver. Why do you ask about the shot?"

"Because two of the neighbors have said they thought they heard a shot, before you screamed."

"Possibly that was the banging of a door, when he ran from the house."

"Possibly. Well, Mrs. Randall, I will not keep you up any longer. Would you care to have me detail a policeman to remain in or about the house until your husband comes home?"

"No, thank you, sergeant. I am sure we will not be disturbed any further tonight—or this morning—it is morning, isn't it?"

"Very well then. I'll go down into the kitchen and get my assistant, and we'll leave you. But I wish you'd bear this in mind, Mrs. Randall. To-morrow, or the next day, or any time, after you've thought this experience over, and you recall some incident that perhaps you haven't told me, I wish you'd either come down to the detective bureau and tell me about it, or call me up on the telephone. Sergeant Riordan, you'll remember the name?"

"Yes, sergeant. Thank you very much for your interest, and for your promptness in getting here. I shall tell my husband all about it when he returns, and he will probably see you and express his gratitude personally. You'll send Virginia up from downstairs as you leave, will you?"

Riordan bowed and descended to the lower floor. Willis was drinking coffee and eating a sandwich, and the negro maid seemed to be thoroughly over her alarm and enjoying playing hostess.

"Virginia, would you like to have ten dollars?" asked the sergeant bluntly.

Her teeth showed in an ivory smile. "Does a duck swim, boss?" she answered.

Riordan reached in a pocket and drew forth a ten-dollar bill, and deliberately tore it in half. One piece he pushed toward her, and the other he returned to his pocket.

"You come down to the detective bureau in the evening, in two days, Virginia," he said, "and I'll give you the other half of the bill. Understand? In two days."

"Yas, sir."

"But you've got to earn it, Virginia. Until you get the other half of that bill, I want you to keep your mouth shut about what you told me a little while ago. If Mrs. Randall or anybody else asks you what you told the detective here, you say you told him that Mrs. Randall's screams woke you up, and that after that you just yelled yourself and don't remember anything else till she called you to come down and talk to me. Get that?"

"Yas, sir."

"All right. I'll know whether you keep your word. If you do that for two days, you can have the other half of this ten-dollar bill. If you talk your fool head off, you can keep the half you've got, and it won't do you any good at all. Remember now. Two days."

"Yas, boss, I'll remembah. You leab it to me."

"All right. Come on, Willis, let's beat it."

Riordan and the plainclothes man ascended to the main floor again, bowed to Mrs. Randall, who was waiting in the hallway, and passed out the front door. On the lawn they were joined by the uniformed patrolman, and all climbed into Riordan's car, which promptly moved down the street and around the corner.

There he slowed down almost to a stop, and then suddenly changing his mind, stepped on the accelerator and sped away to headquarters. He dismissed the uniformed man, and beckoned Willis to follow him upstairs to the detective bureau.

"Ring up three of the boys, Griggs," he said, to the man at the outer desk, "and have 'em down here right away. As soon as they come in spread 'em out round the hotels and lodging houses. I want a young fellow, either very tall or very short, with dark hair, brown eyes, smooth-shaven, who got a room, probably a room and bath at a hotel, soon after three this morning.

"Tell 'em to rouse up any parties answering that description and make 'em give an account of themselves. I want their names if they sound good. If they can't give a satisfactory account, I want 'em brought in to me. I'll be in the office here till Captain Brady comes on. Tell 'em to work the better class hotels first."

"Yes, sergeant," answered Griggs, and he turned to the telephone. Riordan led Willis into the inner office. There he tossed off his coat, unbuttoned his vest, and tilted back in his office chair.

"Make yourself comfortable, Willis—and here's a cigar. Now, what'd you get out of that nigger?"

The plainclothes man settled into a chair, lighted his cigar and blew two or three smoke rings at the ceiling.

"Not a whole lot, sarge. That is, not a lot that was worth much. The Randalls been married about three years. She's been with 'em all the time. She was in Mrs. Randall's family before she was married. Says the young wife has a mind of her own, but she and her husband get along as well as most folks.

"No special trouble. Got enough money to be comfortable on, but don't go much. He's full of business and tired at night or else away at some meeting somewhere, like to-night; and she's a great reader, and plays the piano a lot.

"Coming down to to-night, the maid said she went to bed about ten o'clock and Mrs. Randall was downstairs playing the piano. The girl didn't know anything was wrong till she was wakened up by voices. Said she thought Randall had come home, but pretty soon she realized it wasn't Randall, but somebody else, arguing with the wife.

"She couldn't hear what it was about. She thought it was kind o' funny, and was just about to get up and open the door of her room to get an earful, when she heard Mrs. Randall raise her voice and say 'don't do that.'

"Then she heard what she guessed was a shot, and a door slam, and then heard Mrs. Randall scream. She thought there'd been bloody murder done, and she began to yell herself. She didn't recognize the other voice, hasn't the slightest idea who it was.

"I asked her was there a triangle in the house, you know, some other man hanging 'round, but she said there was nothing like that in the family, not at all. I drilled her pretty hard on that, but she wouldn't crack, a bit.

"She stuck to it that there wasn't any other man with Mrs. Randall than her husband, and that he wasn't fussing with any other woman. They were both in love of the old-fashioned kind, she was sure. And that was all I could get out of her."

"What'd you make out of the house?"

"Sarge, aside from the front door, which you opened, I never seen a tighter house in my life. Everything was shut and locked and bolted and fastened on the first two floors where I was, I mean the main floor and the basement.

"Everything but the back basement door. The lock on that was broke, but there was a lawn mower jammed across it like a bar, and the wood was worn where it had rested. This maid, she said the lock had been broke a long time, and that they used the lawn mower to keep the door shut with.

"The door opens inward, and there was no sign that it had been tampered with. I had to give the lawn mower handle a sharp blow up with my hand to dislodge it when I examined the door, it was jammed down in place that solid."

Well, what do you think about it?"

"If there was anybody in that house, sarge, he was a climber, a second-story man. But I don't think there was any crook there at all. I think Mrs. Randall had some caller, and had a fuss with him. Maybe he tried to get funny with her, because her husband was away. As to the shooting, I think she did the gun play herself."

Riordan stuck his tongue in his cheek. "I hadn't thought

of that," he said slowly. "She would be the kind to do it, at that. Cool as a cucumber she was when she got hold of herself. And she's covering something up too. She might have taken a shot at this guy, at that—that would account for there being no bullet holes in the house; he might have carried it with him.

"Step outside and have Griggs call the hospitals for a shooting case. If a guy was drilled good enough to carry a bullet away with him, most any doc would send him to a hospital."

4

A GRIM TABLEAU

WILLIS ROSE AND left the inner office, and Riordan closed his eyes and tilted farther back in his chair. He was lounging that way when the plain clothes man returned.

"Nothing doing at the hospitals, sarge. We left word for 'em to call in if there was any cases like that."

"That's good headwork, telling 'em to call. You ain't half bad, Willis. Griggs routed out some of the boys, has he?"

"Yes, sarge, he's got Halloran. Wright, and Ebbits drilling the hotels. Where'd you get the description of that guy? Mrs. Randall give it to you?"

Riordan blew a puff of smoke at the ceiling. "Yeah," he replied. "That description was as near as I could come to just the opposite of what she told me. She said the man wore overalls, a gray cap, had a red beard, and blue eyes. Lot to see in the dark, I'll say."

He turned and reached for his telephone. "Gimme downstairs—this is Sergeant Riordan speaking. Them motor cycle men that went out on that burglary call, did they make out any reports?—Yes, send 'em up to me."

Presently a uniformed man opened the door and passed in a couple of sheets of paper. Willis took them.

"Read 'em to me," said Riordan.

Willis held the report sheets to the light. "All right, here goes: 'At 3:15 this A.M. we were sent out on a call to Riverdale Park to answer a call for burglars. We found Sergeant Riordan there, and, at his orders, investigated the premises at 916 Forest Avenue. There were no marks of entry on any of the doors or windows, nor were we able to see any tracks on the lawn.

" 'Investigation of the neighborhood showed no suspicious persons. Inquiring among the neighbors showed that Mr. Richard Gale, 215 Margate Terrace, had heard a shot, followed by a woman's scream. Mr. Joseph Taylor, next door, at 914 Forest Avenue, also had heard a shot. Neither of these witnesses saw anybody leave the premises, nor any suspicious characters in the neighborhood.

" 'After we had investigated, Sergeant Riordan ordered us to report back to the station, saying he would take care of the case. Respectfully submitted, Holmes and Sinclair, Second Night Relief.' That's all there is to it, sarge, and I'll say that's good, short, concise, and to the point."

"Yeah; lay it on my desk."

The telephone tinkled, and Riordan swung around and reached for the receiver.

"Detective Bureau, Police Headquarters," he said, speaking into the instrument. "Yes, this is Riordan—who?—oh, yes, Halloran. What you got?—uh-huh—he did, eh? Well, you listen: you pick out a nice comfortable chair in the lobby and camp there. If the bird gets up before he's called, tell him to wait, that I'm coming up and want to see him. I'll be there myself at eight. Yeah, you got it. Good-by!"

He hung up and sank down in his chair again. Willis leaned forward eagerly.

"Got something, sarge?"

"I dunno. Find out after awhile. Fellow at the Belmont Grand sort of answers that description, and checked in about the right time. Halloran's going to wait for him. Meanwhile you'd better report off and go home. You've done first rate. When you go out, tell Griggs to wake me up at half past seven sharp; I'm going to take a snooze right here till then. Good night to you."

A FEW MINUTES after eight o'clock in the morning Detective Sergeant Riordan entered the gilded lobby of the Belmont Grand and he was not a whit less glorious than that highly decorated place.

He wore his dress uniform, his gold braid equaled, if it did not outshine, the gold that decorated the marble pillars and fancy chairs of the hotel; and his star gleamed upon the breast of his blue uniform like a searchlight. Taking a quick glance around, he saw Halloran and a well-dressed man sitting on one of the lounges, and went to them at once.

"This is the night clerk, sarge," spoke up Halloran, indicating his companion with a gesture of his thumb. "I thought maybe you'd want to see him."

Riordan nodded to the hotel employee, and sat down beside him.

"Tell me about this guest," he said.

"Well, sergeant, he came in this morning about four o'clock—a little before that, maybe ten minutes to four. He was kind of nervous, but dressed swell. Said he'd been at a party and lost his friends, and wanted a room and bath and to be called at eight.

"Registered as James Tipton, St. Louis, Missouri, and paid with a five dollar bill. The room and bath were four dollars. As I gave him the extra dollar back he pulled a long envelope from his pocket and asked me to lock it up in the safe and give him a receipt for it.

"I was making out one of our regular receipts we give in cases like that, and asked him what was the contents, and he said ten thousand dollars. I told him that was pretty steep, and we'd have to count it. He laughs, says he's here on a business deal, opens the envelope, and there was more money than I'd ever seen in my life.

"Three one thousand dollar bills, eight five hundred dollar ones, and the rest in hundred dollar notes and fifties. She was ten thousand, all right. We put it back in the envelope, sealed it up, and I gave him the receipt, which he put in a wallet, and I put the money in the safe.

"He was a tall man, well dressed in a dark suit, high hat, light overcoat, muffler round his neck. He was smooth shaven, sharp featured, pretty high class, I should say, dark hair and snappy brown eyes. He seemed to have plenty of money besides this envelope, for when he started to pay for his room he pulled out quite a good-sized roll. Gertie, on the switchboard, called him just as I went off shift."

"You tell Moffat, the manager, about the ten thousand?" asked Riordan.

"Yes, sir, and that you were coming down. Mr. Moffat and the house detective are in the office now."

"Good. I'll step over and see 'em. You stick here, Halloran, and if this bird comes down, flag him."

Riordan crossed the lobby and made his way around behind the desk to Mr. Moffat's office. As he entered, "Deacon" Hennessey, the house detective, stepped forward to shake hands with him, and then introduced him to the manager.

"I've heard of you, Riordan," said Moffat, "but I guess this is the first time I've actually met you. What's wrong with this man with all the money?"

"I wouldn't say anything was wrong, sir. And I wouldn't say it was right, either. I'm looking for a fellow like him, and I want your help with this bird. If you don't mind, I'd like to wait in here till he comes down and puts in a claim for that money. I'd like to have you tell the clerk to stall him—say the money is locked in the safe and they'll have to get you to open it, or something like that.

"Send a bell-hop for you, see? And then you and I and the Deacon, here, will all go out together and act like we're closing in on him. If he's all right he won't notice the play; but if he's the man I want, well, chances are he'll start something."

"All right, sergeant, I'll arrange it." Moffat stepped out to give instructions to the clerk, and Riordan turned to Hennessy. "You breeze out to where Halloran's sitting, Deacon," he said, "and tell him about the play. Tell him when we come out to surround this guy for him to rush up, like he was expecting the fellow to make a break. But tell him not to touch the guy, no matter what happens. I'll do all the touchin' that's necessary."

"All right, Matt. I'll be right back."

Riordan dropped into a chair and picked up the morning paper. Presently Moffat returned and reported that everything had been arranged. He chatted with Riordan a few minutes, and then turned to his morning mail. The

Deacon came in presently and sat down quietly to wait developments.

It was almost half an hour later when a bell-hop thrust his head in the office:

"Beg pardon, sir," he said, "but the clerk says to please step around and open the safe, sir."

The three men rose from their chairs, paused a minute, and then filed out into the lobby. As they approached the desk they made rather an imposing spectacle. The manager in the lead, looking serious; the Deacon sidling along with his beady eyes fixed upon a tall young man who was leaning over the counter, tapping nervously on the register pad; and Sergeant Riordan, a deep scowl on his face, striding menacingly forward and shifting his eyes back and forth between the guest and the street door, swinging slightly away from the others as if he wanted to be in a position to block any attempt at escape the guest of the house might make.

The young man did not miss the tableau, either. He jerked erect, looked at the three men, then behind him. And as his eyes turned in that direction he beheld the burly form of Halloran apparently rushing in lumbering fashion right at him. And Halloran's right hand was behind his right hip, as if he was reaching for a pistol.

Mr. Moffat stepped up to the guest of the house. "You wanted to see me?" he asked.

"Yes—yes, oh, yes," responded the guest. "But there's no hurry. I left some money with the clerk to-night—last night, I mean; and he says you've locked it in the safe. I want it, please. But there's no hurry—er—I think I'll go get breakfast first. You'll have it when I come back?"

"Why, certainly—"

But Moffat could say no more, for the guest suddenly turned and hurried away, dodging between the scowling Riordan and the threatening Halloran, and almost running as he swept through the revolving doors that led to the street.

"Well, I declare," exclaimed Moffat. "That was odd."

Riordan laughed. "It worked pretty good," he said. "I knew I'd find a use for this dress uniform some time, aside from parades. Let's have a look at that envelope, if you don't mind."

Moffat signaled to the clerk on duty, and that worthy produced a long, bulging packet from the sphere safe under the counter, and passed it to the manager, who, in turn, gave it to Riordan. The envelope, save for certain cabalistic notations put on by the night clerk, was blank; but in its upper left-hand corner was printed:

If not called for in five days
RETURN TO STATE CONTRACT CO.

Riordan smiled and handed it back. "Lock it up in your big safe," he said. "If the bird comes back, give it to him."

"Excuse me, sir," cut in the day clerk, reaching over the counter and tapping the manager on the shoulder, "but the gentleman left his claim receipt here."

He passed the pink slip of paper to Moffat.

5

WARRANT FOR ROBBERY

"WELL, OF ALL things!" said the hotel manager. "He not only ran off and left ten thousand dollars here, but left his claim slip as well. Why didn't you grab him, sergeant?"

"I got nothing against him, sir," answered the detective. "And he'll be back. But now, since he's left his claim slip behind, don't you give him that money till he proves who he is, and that he's got a right to it. If he comes back, maybe you'd better telephone me or Captain Brady, and let one or the other of us listen to his explanation. You can claim you want to protect yourself."

"Certainly, sergeant, I'll be glad to do that. In fact, I'm convinced there's something crooked about this."

Riordan laughed. "Maybe there is. Well, much obliged to you. I'll be going now. Come along, Halloran, let's leave the deacon to keep an eye on things."

Outside the hotel Halloran turned to his superior.

"You know who that guy was?" he asked.

"No."

"That's young Billy Chase, son of the president of the State Contract Company. Wild young blood, he is."

"That so?" replied Riordan, but seemed not interested. A moment later he said: "Well, you go on down and tell the captain I'm going home to bed, and if he wants me to call up. There's nothing on this case to worry about." And turning abruptly, he left Halloran trudging on his way toward headquarters.

When Riordan reported for duty at four that afternoon Captain Brady greeted him with a smile.

"Got a trade-last for you, boy," he said. "Party named John Randall was in here this morning and said he wanted to thank you and me and the whole department for the prompt and efficient work last night out at his house."

"That's nice, chief."

"I'll say it's nice. Nice for me, it was. I didn't know a thing about it, and I had to stall him along. And after he went out, pleased as could be at himself and us, I had a heck of a time finding out what it was all about. I finally found Holmes and Sinclair's report on your desk, and that give me a lead, and then I dug 'round a bit more and got a vague idea on it. Why didn't you leave me a report?"

"You know what it's all about, don't you?"

"I do now."

"Fine, then you write a report and let me read it. I don't know what it is myself yet."

Captain Brady snorted. "Trying to be funny, eh? I wouldn't take it from anybody but you. Why, the woman had a bad dream, or something. Her husband said she was given to nervous spells, and must have had one while he was away."

"Yeah, she's got a nervous temperament, just like I have. Didn't Halloran tell you anything?"

"Halloran? Sure, he said you had him on some case, but

threw him off it, and said for him to tell me you'd gone home to bed, that it wasn't important, anyway."

"He didn't say anything about ten thousand dollars?"

"No."

"Well, I'll be jiggered! I knew that bird was close-mouthed, but I thought he'd got a thrill this morning."

"What's this about ten thous—"

The door to the office opened and one of the men from the outer office poked in his head. "Lady to see Sergeant Riordan, sir; says it's important."

"Fan her in."

The head disappeared, and almost immediately there entered the mistress of the house at 916 Forest Avenue, whom Riordan had met before the dawn of the day then drawing to a close. He pushed a chair forward for her.

"This is Mrs. John Randall, chief," he said. "Mrs. Randall, this is Captain Brady, in charge of the bureau. Something gone wrong?"

She acknowledged the introduction with a nod. "I wanted to see you sergeant. I telephoned a little while ago, but they said you wouldn't be on duty till four. So I came down."

"Anything I can do, Mrs. Randall, I'll be only too glad to do. What is it?"

"Could I see you alone?"

"Not while the captain's here, madam. You see, he's in charge daytimes. But you can feel perfectly free to talk to him, just as you did to me."

She bit her lip and hesitated.

"Sergeant Riordan and I work together, ma'am," said Captain Brady. "We never have any secrets from each other.

Your husband was in to see me this morning, ma'am, and spoke to me about—about the matter out at your house. It's about that?"

She flashed him a look of doubt, then, noting Riordan's nod of confirmation, smiled quickly.

"It's about my husband," she said.

"They're trying to arrest him."

"They? Who?" The words snapped from Captain Brady's mouth.

"The Protective Association. A man who said his name was Partridge was at the house."

"Oh, yes, Partridge. I know him," said Captain Brady. He looked at Riordan, then turned back to their visitor. "And what's Partridge want Mr. Randall for, ma'am?"

She seemed much relieved as she noted the enmity toward Partridge in Captain Brady's tone. She did not know that they were not only professional enemies, but personal ones as well; but she sensed that she was talking to a man who did not think much of the head of the Protective Association.

"Something about robbery, I believe, captain."

"And you were surprised when this man Partridge came to your home?" asked Sergeant Riordan, entering the conversation again.

Mrs. Randall turned in her chair and faced him, and looked at him steadily for several moments.

"You notice what I told you, chief," said Riordan. "She's got that nervous temperament."

Brady smiled grimly. "Your husband, Mrs. Randall," he said, "was in here this morning. He said he wanted to thank Sergeant Riordan here for what he'd done last night. Said you were alone in the house and nervous and had been frightened at something. The sergeant doesn't think you're the nervous kind."

"I don't think I'm very nervous," she said, without taking her eyes from Riordan's. "If I was, I'd be nervous now. This man Partridge followed me down here. I suppose he thinks I don't know it."

Riordan walked over to the window and glanced out.

"That's right," he said. "Pat's over across the street in a doorway. Regular sleuth, he is. We'll have to take you out through another door when you leave, or Pat'll wear himself out following you. But what's the idea, Mrs. Randall?"

She waited until the detective sergeant had resumed his seat, and then, turning to Captain Brady, she began to talk.

"My husband, you know, has an interest in the State Contract Company. After he returned this morning—he was out of town on business last night, you know—I told him about the occurrence at our house last night. Then he went down town to his office.

"He must have stopped to see you on his way, captain. Well, after he'd been at the office awhile he telephoned me that he'd had a disagreement with Mr. Chase, he's the president of the company, you know, and that there might be some trouble, but for me not to worry.

"A little later he telephoned me that he was—that he was at a certain place, and that he wanted me to come and see him. Just as I was going out to meet him this man Partridge came. He was very unpleasant; quite impudent, in fact.

"He said my husband had committed a robbery and that he was going to arrest him. I told him Mr. Randall wasn't at home. He wanted to search the house, but as he hadn't any warrant, none that he'd show, at least, I wouldn't let him. Finally he went away.

"I waited a little while and then I started out to meet my husband; and found this man Partridge following me. I tried to get rid of him, but couldn't. So I went into a drug store and called my husband on the telephone—using the automatic instrument, so Partridge couldn't trace the number and so discover where my husband was.

"I told John, my husband, all about it; and he said he'd wait where he was until I saw him—until I found a way to see him. Then I went down town and tried to give this man Partridge the slip in the department stores; but he came right up and stayed beside me. So I went home again.

"Later this afternoon I tried to go to my husband again, but there was a man began to follow me. It wasn't Partridge, but I suppose it was one of his men. So I went home and telephoned, trying to reach Sergeant Riordan. Now I'm here—and when I left the house this man Partridge was around again, and followed me. I want to know if you can't get rid of Partridge for me?"

6

PARTRIDGE EXPLAINS
HIS TACTICS

CAPTAIN BRADY SHOOK his head. "Unless Partridge does something that's against the law, I'm afraid we can't help you, Mrs. Randall. You see, as an authorized private detective. Partridge has certain privileges."

"Can he follow me around like that?"

"Apparently he can, madam."

"Can't you go out and detain him on some pretext for five minutes, and let me get out another door and take a taxicab?"

"That might be done. But we might be compounding a felony, if we did that. If Partridge wants to arrest your husband, he must have some reason. He's not an utter fool, and he knows his legal limits. In a way he's pretty clever. If you've talked to your husband you must know about this charge that he's hiding from—what was it you said it was, robbery?"

She turned to Sergeant Riordan. "Can't *you* do something, sergeant?"

Riordan smiled. "I'm afraid not, Mrs. Randall. That is, not blind. You're not playing fair with us, so you can't expect us to play fair with you."

"Not fair, what do you mean, sergeant?"

"Well, you're keeping too much back. Just as you did this morning, Mrs. Randall, when I was at your house."

"Why! I told you everything this morning, sergeant."

Riordan shook his head. "Mrs. Randall, you remember I asked you about a revolver this morning? Did you tell me everything about that?"

"I told you I was so excited I didn't recall anything definite. There might have been a revolver fired."

"And why would this man in your house fire a revolver?"

"I'm sure I don't know—perhaps to frighten me; that is, if he did fire one. The neighbors, you know, might have been mistaken. They might have been confused—it might have been a door slamming, or the backfire of an automobile."

"Quite true, Mrs. Randall. Now I'm going to tell you something. I'm going to tell you what brought me to your house so soon. I was driving by, a block away, when I heard a revolver shot. I am a policeman, Mrs. Randall, and I know what pistol shots sound like. And after I heard the shot I heard a door slam.

"And then I heard you scream for help, and then your maid took up the screaming. That's why I got there so quickly. It was just an accident that I happened to be driving in the neighborhood; but I know what I heard. Now if you expect us to do anything for you, you've got to tell us about that revolver shot."

"I've told you I was so startled when the man came into my room—"

"Listen, Mrs. Randall," interrupted Riordan. "There are just two possibilities. Either you, yourself, fired that shot at the intruder, and hit him, for there were no bullet marks in the walls of your house, or else he fired the shot, using a blank cartridge.

"I say there is no other possibility, for it is evident that he didn't fire a bullet and strike you. If you had fired a blank cartridge to frighten the man away, you would have told me about it.

"The only reason you would not tell me would be if you had fired the shot and knew you had hit the man and he had carried the bullet from the house in his body, and might be found wounded or dead outside. You might, in that case, prefer to deny that you had done any shooting."

"How keenly you reason, sergeant," she said with a smile. But for several minutes she said no more. Finally she changed the subject abruptly.

"Partridge said my husband had stolen some money from the firm. My husband told me over the telephone they were trying to frame him. That was why he wanted to see me."

"How much money?" asked Captain Brady.

"Ten thousand dollars."

Brady, in spite of himself, gave a start and looked at Riordan, who was gazing at the ceiling, apparently studying the cracks that ran across it in jagged black lines. There was silence in the office for several minutes, broken at last by Riordan.

"Come on," he said. "You tell me about the gunplay, and I'll agree to get Partridge off the scent."

"I haven't the faintest recollection of any gunplay, sergeant."

Mrs. Randall made the statement in a firm and level

voice, and looked Riordan straight in the eye as she answered.

The detective sergeant shrugged his shoulders, got up, and opened the office door, beckoning to somebody outside. In a moment Detective Halloran entered the room.

"Halloran, this is Mrs. John Randall, of Forest Avenue," he said. "She needs an escort. Go with her. Mrs. Randall, Halloran will take you out the rear of the building. I'm going down and talk to Partridge for five minutes."

If Captain Brady had expected their caller to show gratitude he was disappointed.

"Thank you, sergeant," she said. "But I don't require an escort. I should very much appreciate being shown the way to the rear door of this building, however. But once outside I would prefer to—to be unescorted."

"All right, Mrs. Randall, we'll try something else. Halloran, go downstairs. Across the street, opposite the garage, you'll see Partridge standing in a doorway. Bring him up here."

"Bring him up, sergeant?" Halloran's face expressed mild enjoyment and anticipation.

"Yeah, *bring* him up," snapped Captain Brady.

Halloran moved with surprising quickness for a man of his large frame. And a few moments later he was back again, with Mr. Partridge, slightly ruffled and fussing with his necktie, by his side.

"That'll do Halloran," said the captain. And as the detective left the office he turned to Partridge.

"What's the matter, Pat?" he asked. "This lady here says you've been annoying her."

"I haven't meant to annoy her, captain."

"She says you've been following her. Pushed along by her side in a department store and acted very obnoxious. We can't stand for that, you know."

"I tried to be polite, captain. The truth of the matter is I want her husband, and I was following her because I think she's going to meet him. She says he isn't at their home."

"What you want him for?"

"Embezzlement or robbery, captain."

"Why don't you get a warrant?"

"Maybe I will, captain. I was instructed by my client to keep the case quiet, if possible. If she'd rather have a warrant and stuff in the newspapers, she's sure following the right tactics."

"Embezzlement's a felony. That's police business. What's the case?"

"Well, captain, Mr. Chase, president of the State Contract Company, gave her husband ten thousand dollars for a certain purpose. He didn't use it for that purpose, and he says it was stolen from him. And he's disappeared. It looks to me like he stole it, all right, or knows who did."

Captain Brady rubbed his chin. "You step outside for a few minutes, Partridge. You can watch the door. I'll call you back pretty soon. I want to talk to Mrs. Randall confidentially a minute."

7

INKLINGS LEAK OUT

THE HEAD OF the Protective Association looked at the rear and seldom used door to Captain Brady's office, then shrugged his shoulders, rose, and stepped to the general room without, where he sat down and made pretense of ignoring the unfriendly looks cast in his direction by the sleuths who happened to be in the office. As the door closed behind him Captain Brady turned to Mrs. Randall and said, severely:

"Madam, I don't know what your game is. If you're trying to shield your husband that's your business, and I don't suppose you're to be blamed. But it's reasonable to suppose that old man Chase isn't making charges like that for fun, and laying himself open to suit by putting Partridge on your husband's trail.

"Now my advice to you is to come clean in this matter and quit stalling. You seem to think we can help you. We're policemen here, and we don't help criminals, and we don't like mysteries. If we can help the honest public it's our business to do it; but it is also our business to catch crooks. Now make up your mind quick what you're going to do,"

"My husband is not a thief. I am not a thief. This man

Partridge is interfering with my seeing my husband. I want your protection from Partridge so I may see my husband."

The answer was firm; a dispassionate statement of fact. Captain Brady was impressed. He pursed his lips, then asked:

"Did your husband have ten thousand dollars, as Partridge says?"

"Yes."

"Was it stolen from him?"

"No."

"Has he got it with him now?"

"No."

Captain Brady threw up his hands. "I give up; it's too much for me!" he said. "Madam, I think you'd better—"

"Pardon me a minute, chief," cut in Sergeant Riordan. "I'm just beginning to get the drift of all this. I think Mrs. Randall has come to the right place, chief. Let me ask her something:

"Mrs. Randall, I want to outline a situation to you. And then I want you to tell me if I am correct. Last night, or yesterday afternoon, your husband returned from his office and told you he was going away for the night—up to Mountainview. He told you what he was going there for.

"You and he had a—well, let us say a disagreement. Some argument. As usual in such cases the wife won— you had your way. Mr. Randall made his trip to Mountainview. During his absence something you had not foreseen occurred, at the end of which I happened to be passing your neighborhood and was attracted to your house by your screams.

"And because you did not wish to reveal to me the matter

about which you and your husband disagreed, you did not tell me all that occurred—all that made you scream. Since then other unforeseen things have occurred, and now you wish to tell me more of what happened in your house. Only you haven't been sure that I'd understand. Is that correct?"

Mrs. Randall, whose calm throughout the entire visit to the office had disconcerted Captain Brady, suddenly dashed her handkerchief to her face, and, hiding her eyes in it, choked with unrestrained sobs. For several minutes she shook in her chair, and then, almost as suddenly as she had given away to her feelings, she regained her self-control and looked up.

"Sergeant, you—you are a very nice man," she said, smiling through her tears. "More than that, you understand—a great deal. Let me tell you: last night Mr. Randall brought home ten thousand dollars to—for a certain purpose.

"He told me about it, and I told him it—the purpose was wrong. I finally convinced him that it was wrong. He left the money in the house and went to Mountainview. The man who was in our house last night must have stolen it, for it was gone when I looked—after you left.

"This morning when my husband returned I told him about it, and he said not to worry, that everything would be all right anyway. It seemed it would be. Then this thing occurred. You can see now why I've got to see my husband, without Partridge finding out where he is."

Riordan nodded his head, and closing his eyes, thought deeply. Captain Brady, however, did not appear to be in the same frame of mind.

"You mean to tell me you told your husband his ten thousand dollars were stolen, madam, and then he came down here to me and thanked me for what we'd done at your house last night? I don't believe it! The more you say the less straight this whole thing looks to me. I'm going to find out what's at the bottom of it, and find out right now."

"You're right, chief," said Riordan, opening his eyes and rising from his chair. "We'll find it all out, pronto." He moved to the door and opened it.

"Come in here, Pat," he said, closing the door again after the private detective's entry. "Pat, can you get hold of Chase on the telephone right now?"

"Sure—that is, I guess he's home."

"All right, call him up and tell him to come down here at once; that is, if he wants that ten thousand dollars. Do you think he wants the money, or Randall, the most?"

Partridge grinned. "I guess he wants the money, sergeant."

"All right, try it on him. There's the telephone."

Partridge went to the instrument and called the Chase residence, and conversed in low tones for a few minutes. Then he hung up and moved back to the center of the room.

"He'll be down in ten minutes."

"Good. Now, Pat, we don't want Mrs. Randall present when he gets here. You'll see why later. I'm going to have her go upstairs and wait with the matron till this little play is over; is that all right with you?"

"Sure, I've got no orders to get Mrs. Randall. I was just following her because I knew sooner or later she'd lead me to her husband."

Riordan pressed a button on Captain Brady's desk, and

presently one of the police matrons from the jail on the top floor entered the room.

"Mrs. Colvin," said Riordan, "this is Mrs. Randall. She wants to wait upstairs with you for a little while. Mrs. Randall, you'll find Mrs. Colvin has a very comfortable office, and some books for you to read. You'll wait there till I send for you—it may be three-quarters of an hour?"

"Certainly, sergeant."

She followed the matron from the room. Partridge sat down and lighted a cigarette. Captain Brady reached into his desk and found two cigars, one of which he passed to Riordan, and they both lighted up and smoked.

"You got to show me, boy," he said, addressing his aide. "You may be right, but the way it looks now I'm inclined to think Partridge here is on the right track, for once in his life."

"All right, chief. He may be. We'll soon know. But you let me do the talking, will you?"

"Sure, boy. It's your case—what there is of it. I'm frank to admit I don't know what it is all about yet."

They smoked in silence then until the door was opened and Mr. Chase was announced. He came in brusquely, nodded to the two police officers, and then turned on Partridge with a snarl.

"Who in time asked you to drag this thing up to the police?" he asked. "You told me you could handle it without that. Maybe I'm not ready to have this man pinched yet."

"Partridge didn't drag this thing in here, Mr. Chase," spoke up Riordan. "It was quite the opposite. One of my men dragged Partridge in here—by the coat collar, if I read the signs right."

8

CHASE FRAMES A DEAL

CHASE DROPPED INTO a chair, but sat straight, leaning forward.

"Well, what's it all about? Partridge said over the telephone that you had the money."

"Partridge didn't say anything of the kind. I heard him telephone you. He said if you wanted the money to come down here and get it."

Chase growled. "Well, it amounts to the same thing, doesn't it?"

"Not at all, Mr. Chase. There's this difference—do you want that ten thousand dollars, or do you want to throw your man Randall into jail?"

"I want the money first. What I do to Randall for trying to steal it is my business."

Riordan blew a cloud of smoke at the ceiling. "I don't get that view of it at all, Mr. Chase," he said. "If Randall stole that money, he committed grand larceny, at least. And if he did that it's a felony, and it's our business to arrest people who commit felonies and present a case against them so they'll be punished.

"Now if you want to punish Randall, the best thing you can do is to go down to the district attorney's office and swear out a warrant, and it will be turned over to us and we'll go out and get Randall. It's a case for us, if you want to look at it that way.

"On the other hand, if you just want the money, and don't want Randall, you ought to have employed a collection agency and not Partridge here. As it is now, you're liable to prosecution for conspiracy, intimidation, blackmail, and disorderly conduct; and, beside all that, Randall can sue you for defamation of character and probably get a good deal more than the ten thousand dollars. Partridge here has told too many people about his business, and made himself too obnoxious, for you to have the ghost of a chance to beat such a suit."

Chase flashed a glance at Partridge that made the head of the Protective Association squirm. Then he snapped at Riordan:

"What are you trying to do? Fix this?"

"Yeah, you might call it that. Only not the way you think. What do you want, the ten thousand dollars or do you want Randall?"

There was that texture of tone in Riordan's words that made Chase stop and think. He was accustomed to dealing with men of all sorts, city officials as well as others. He looked Riordan in the eye, and then pulled a cigar from his pocket and carefully cut the end from it with a goldhandled pocket knife. Putting it in his mouth he chewed it without lighting it. And, after a considerable pause, he said quietly:

"I guess I want the ten thousand dollars."

Riordan rose. "All right, let's go and get it. I've got my car in the garage. Chief, you'll come, and bring Pat with you?"

The other three rose at once, and they all went down to

the police garage and climbed into Riordan's auto. In less than five minutes they were at the Belmont Grand hotel, and Riordan led the way into Moffat's office. The manager greeted Chase warmly, for he was one of the best patrons of the house.

"Moffat, you got that envelope James Tipton, of St. Louis, left with you last night?"

"Why, yes, sergeant."

"Bring it in, will you—and the claim check for it, too?"

The hotel manager stepped out a side door, and returned in a minute, handing the bulky envelope and the claim slip to Riordan. The detective sergeant turned to the head of the contract company.

"I suppose you took down the numbers of the bills you gave to that party, didn't you?" he asked.

Chase flushed, hesitated, then nodded his head. "Why, yes, I did. How'd you guess it? I have them here in a notebook."

"Well, get your notebook out, and we'll check," said Riordan, ripping open the envelope.

He took the top bill, a thousand dollar one, and read off the number. "Got that one on your list? You have, eh! Let Moffat look over your shoulder at that list, and check the numbers with you as I call them."

Then, as Chase and Moffat watched the numbers, Riordan went through the entire packet of currency. Each number he read was on Chase's list.

"Looks like it was your money, doesn't it?" he said at the end.

Chase and Moffat both nodded their heads.

"Now I'm going to show you something," went on Riordan. "Here's the claim slip the man who stole that money signed. He signed the name James Tipton, and put down an address supposed to be in St. Louis. I want you to take a good look at the handwriting."

Holding the slip in both his hands, he thrust it before Chase's vision.

The president of the State Contract Company gazed at the writing, and the blood slowly left his face. Finally he leaned back in his chair and closed his eyes.

Riordan slipped the currency back into the envelope and put the claim slip on Moffat's desk.

"Moffat, I wish you'd make out a receipt," he said, "stating that you've given this ten thousand dollars to Ronald B. Chase, of the State Contract Company, it having been proved to you that Mr. Chase was entitled to the money. You keep the receipt, and if James Tipton, of St. Louis, ever calls for the money, you'll have Chase's receipt to protect you. You keep the claim slip, too."

The hotel manager stepped to his desk and wrote on a sheet of paper. Chase opened his eyes and sat up straight, looking at Riordan sharply.

"There, Mr. Chase," said the detective sergeant, "you sign this receipt and I'll give you the money. The receipt will protect Mr. Moffat in case Mr. Tipton ever calls for what he left. Moffat can then send him to you.

"There, that's it! Now we're all satisfied. Here's the ten thousand dollars. And, if you don't mind, Moffat will excuse us, and we'll go back to the detective bureau, there's something more I would like to tell you."

The ride back to police headquarters was a silent one.

The silence lasted till they were all seated again in Captain Brady's office.

"Now," said Riordan, "you listen to me. You gave that money to Randall and sent him up to Mountainview to see that the city council there awarded your firm a certain contract. It was a big contract, and you were willing to pay a big price for it. But you didn't intend to do your own dirty work, you wanted Randall to do it for you, so if anybody squealed and there was a stink you could pass the buck.

"Yet, for your own protection, you took down the numbers on those bills that were to be passed out, and you'd have had one of your yes-men up there check on where those bills showed up, so you would have something on the grafters.

"Well, for reasons of his own, Randall didn't take the money to Mountainview. Somebody in your confidence, who knew all about the deal, tipped off this James Tipton of St. Louis party, and he went to Randall's house and stole that money.

"And then, this morning, somebody in your confidence tipped you off to the fact that Randall hadn't bribed the council at Mountainview for you, and that he'd say he was robbed—the idea being to get Randall in dutch. And you, you just swallowed it all and hired Partridge here to get you in a whole lot of trouble.

"As it happens, Tipton's plans went wrong, just a little bit. And I happened to get in on the case. And, as you said here awhile back, I'm trying to 'fix it.' Well, is it fixed?"

Chase wheeled suddenly to Partridge. "Get to hell out of here," he roared. "Send me your bill. And if you ever

open your yap about this thing to anybody I'll kill you, if
I swing for it."

Partridge didn't even pause to say good evening. He
departed so quickly that the opening and closing of the
door seemed to make but one noise, instead of several
squeaks and a slam.

"That's that!" commented Riordan. Then he added,
pleasantly:

"Would you like me to have one of the police cars take
you home, Mr. Chase?"

The big contractor blinked. Then he rose. "No, thanks,
sergeant. I can get a taxi. But I can't understand why you've
done this thing."

"I didn't suppose you would understand. I didn't do it
for you, that's a cinch."

"But you've done me a very great favor. I'd like to shake
your hand."

"My hands are busy right now, holding each other,"
Riordan answered, putting both arms behind his back.
"The door opens when you turn the knob."

Chase flushed and turned to Captain Brady. "Any time,
captain, I can be of service to you or the young man here,
just let me know. Good evening, gentlemen."

Captain Brady grunted, and Chase left the office. Riordan dropped into the chair by his desk.

"Guess you might as well go, chief," he said. "I'll send
for Mrs. Randall in a minute."

"Boy, I'm going. I don't know how you did it, and I don't
know yet what it's all about. But I reckon I'd better not
know. What I don't know won't hurt me. Good night,

boy—and God bless you for a white, upstanding man! Boy, I'm proud of you!"

Left alone, Sergeant Riordan opened the windows and let some of the smoke in the room drift out. Then he reached for the telephone.

9

FIXED UP AN ALIBI

"**GIMME THE MATRON,** up in the jail," he said. "Uh-huh. Hello, Mrs. Colvin? This is Sergeant Riordan. Ask Mrs. Randall to find her way down here, will you? Thanks."

He opened the door into the outer office, and then closed the windows and sat down again.

Mrs. Randall came in and closed the door behind her. Her face bore signs of having been recently bathed, her hair was exactly and neatly arranged, and she looked much refreshed. She dropped into the big chair at Captain Brady's desk.

"Before you go, Mrs. Randall," said Riordan, "there's one thing I'd like to have you tell me. How do you suppose the intruder got out of your house last night?"

"Through the back door—the basement door, sergeant."

Riordan looked at the floor, and slowly tapped his foot on the worn carpet.

"It's all right," he said at length. "Chase has got his money. The whole ten thousand. Partridge won't bother you any more. And I'd advise your husband, if I were you, to go back to his business to-morrow morning, just as if nothing had happened."

He swung around to his desk and busied himself with some papers. Mrs. Randall did not move.

"You can go, when you want to," he said over his shoulder.

She got up, walked over to his desk, and stood leaning on it.

"Sergeant, I want to thank you. You don't know how much you have done for me. I don't know why you've protected me so. I appreciate it more than I can express. And I don't want you to think—"

"I don't think anything, Mrs. Randall," he interrupted.

"I don't want you to think what you're thinking, sergeant," she went on, heedless of his interruption. "Perhaps it will prove to you how much I appreciate what you have done if I tell you that several years ago young Billy Chase and I were—were engaged to be married. Then I found out something, and broke the engagement.

"Before that, through Billy, I had met John Randall, who was then a clerk in Mr. Chase's office. After—after the engagement was broken—John and I—well, we got married. He was very successful, and he rose rapidly, Mr. Chase finally taking him into the firm—giving him a small interest in the business.

"Yesterday Mr. Chase gave him that money to take to Mountainview—for a certain purpose. John didn't like the idea—he doesn't believe in doing business that way, but he said he supposed he'd have to. I advised him not to—as you said some time ago we had an argument about it. He went away without the money.

"Last night Billy telephoned me. He knew about the money, and he said John had gotten into trouble and he wanted to see me. I was suspicious when he telephoned because it was so late—but—well, I thought John might have gotten into some difficulty, so I told him—Billy, I mean—to come out to the house.

"Virginia had gone to bed, and I let him in myself. He told me he knew John hadn't taken the money: said somebody at Mountainview had telephoned him, and that the deal would be all off unless I'd give it to him and let him telegraph it up there.

"I refused to admit I had it, and he said he'd search the house for it. I knew then he was lying, that he wanted the money himself. I didn't dream then that his plan was to get John in trouble; I thought he just wanted it for some of his—his escapades.

"I threatened to call Virginia, and he laughed and drew a revolver from his pocket and said he was going to be a regular burglar. I pleaded with him, but it didn't do any good. He searched and searched and searched—and finally found it. I begged him not to take it. But he only laughed, and started to go out the front door. It was then I realized what time it was.

"Sergeant, my husband and I have been perfectly happy. There has never been anything between us, no cloud, nothing. But in a flash I saw that if Billy went out the front door of my home at three o'clock in the morning, when my husband was away, and any of the neighbors saw him, you know how it would seem. And if John should hear of it, it would break his heart. So I begged Billy to think of me—told him if he'd ever loved me, long ago, he'd realize how it was—

"And, sergeant, he has some spark of manhood left, even

if he has—if he has done queer things. 'Bless you, Elizabeth,' he said, 'I'm not utterly a rotter. I'll give you a real
alibi.' And with that he turned and ran down the basement
stairs and opened the back door—you saw it wasn't locked,
but that that old lawn mower acted as a bar to it.

"Then he fired a shot from his revolver through the
doorway, dashed out, and slammed the door behind him.
I heard the lawn mower fall back into place, and I ran
upstairs to my room, locked myself in and, throwing off
my dress, leaned out the window and began to scream."

Sergeant Riordan got up and held out his hand. "I knew
I was right about you, Mrs. Randall," he said. "Thank you
for telling me, though. Now forget it. Nobody knows. And
don't tell your husband, either—that's my advice. Let him
think it was just a burglar."

She took his hand and pressed it warmly, then turned
toward the door.

"I want to give you one more bit of advice, Mrs. Randall,"
he said. "Next time you have money in the house, if you
haven't a wall safe, don't hide it in the refrigerator. The
best place, really, is to stuff it behind the picture molding,
between the molding and the wall."

She laughed, a bit hysterically. "Why, sergeant, how did
you know it was in the refrigerator?"

"Because that was the one place you didn't look when
you and I went over the house to see if anything was missing. You looked in all the fool places in the world but that—
in your sewing basket, in the bread box in the pantry, under
the davenport cushions, in the flower vases, behind the
gas logs in the fireplace in the library—all the fool places.

But you steered away from the refrigerator every time you found yourself getting near it."

"Sergeant, I begin to think I made a mistake in not taking you completely into my confidence at first."

"You did that, Mrs. Randall. It is always a mistake not to trust the police. That's what they're for, ma'am, to be trusted. And you'll find the more you trust them the more worthy they are of being trusted. Good night, ma'am—and any time you need one of the boys you just call up.

"By the way, will you do something for me? Give this to your maid, Virginia, when you get home, please?"

And he thrust half of a ten dollar bill into her hand.

QUICK WORK

Sergeant Riordan Is Not Deceived by the
Neatest of Yarns, and He Turns This One
Inside Out With Incredible Ingenuity

1

"GENT OUTSIDE WANTS to see yuh, sergeant, and he's got a de-teck-a-tuff with him," said the doorman, leering as he thrust his face into the inner room, which was the office by day of Captain Brady and by night of his aid, Sergeant Riordan.

"What's he want?"

"Wants yuh to arrest a guy."

"Tell him to go downstairs to the desk, where they handle that sort of work. I've got troubles of my own."

"I did, sergeant. I know my onion! But this de-teck-a-tuff guy he's got with him, he says it's a case for the captain. I told him to come round to-morrow, that the skipper was at home; he says it won't wait and he'll have to see whoever's in charge."

"Oh, very well; fan them in."

Sergeant Riordan placed great reliance on the doorman. He could tell from his manner much about approaching visitors, and he was not a whit excited about the pair just announced. The doorman had been in the police business far longer than Riordan, and if he had not received advancement, he, at least, had piled up a great deal of experience.

The pair that he ushered in were commonplace enough. One of them was very evidently an unprogressive business

Mr. Gordon and Lacey rose to go, but—

man, set in his ways and distrustful of new methods. The other, whom the doorman had designated as a "de-teck-a-tuff," was a shifty-eyed individual, large and tall, but more given to fat than to muscle. He was snappily dressed, however, and his face showed cunning, if not wit.

"Very good of you to see us so promptly, sergeant," he said. "We had some difficulty in making the man outside realize that our business could not wait. This is Mr. Gordon, you probably know him—Angus K. Gordon, of the Gordon Exporting Company. I am Mr. Lacey."

Riordan nodded in acknowledgment and motioned toward two chairs that stood against the farther wall. Lacey brought them forward; Gordon sat in one and immediately moved forward till he was balanced on the edge of it, while his companion lounged into the other.

"Fact of the matter is, sergeant," Lacey said, "we have called to report a robbery, and to ask your co-operation in arresting the culprit. The man—"

—Riordan sharply ordered them back

"The doorman said you were a detective," interrupted Riordan, with a rising inflection.

"Er—yes, sergeant—I told him that. I have investigated this case from the start, gathered the evidence that points directly to the culprit—"

"And, as a detective," interrupted Riordan again, "you know that your first duty in a felony is to report it to the police. Have you done so?"

"Why, I'm doing that now, sergeant."

"When was this robbery committed?"

"A week ago Saturday, in the evening."

"That's twelve days ago. Do you call that immediately reporting it to the police? What office are you working out of anyway?"

"I'm not working out of any office. I'm a psychological investigator."

"Oh—you have a city license, of course?"

"No, I haven't. But I didn't come here to discuss my status."

Sergeant Riordan leaned forward in his chair and pointed a gunlike finger at his caller. "You listen to me," he said. "I'm trying to find out what kind of a man I'm talking to. You've come here to report a felony, and from what the doorman tells me, you've come here to get the police detective bureau to take hold of a case you'd worked up, and make an arrest for you.

"Now, before we go any farther, I've got to know your individual responsibility—if you have any. There's a million cranks and nuts a day wander in here and want to get somebody pinched. We usually find out, by asking them a few questions, whether they really know what they're doing. Arresting a man is a serious business.

"If you get him wrong you're open to heavy damages. The only reason I've talked to you as long as I have is because you sent in word that you were a detective. Now you try to tell me where to head in and I'll tell you what to do.

"You get out of here and take your case to the district attorney and get a warrant. Then, if he gives you one, you go downstairs and turn the warrant in at the desk, and the police will serve it for you. Or, if you don't like the police, take it to the constable's office or the sheriff's."

"He's right, Jed," said the older of the two callers. "You've got no license to get huffy at him; he's doing his duty, like a good officer. He's got to know, Jed, that we're all right."

Then, turning to Riordan, he continued: "Sergeant, I appreciate your position. But I guess my position as a business man in this city is guarantee that we're not cranks. As to going to the district attorney, we don't want to wait till to-morrow. The man who robbed my place will be in town to-night, and we, at least, want him detained. To-morrow, when the district attorney's office is open, may be too late.

"Lacey here is my man, and I'll be responsible for him. He isn't a regular detective, but he's a good investigator; and you'll admit that when he puts all his case before you. He's a little sensitive, that's all, and these questions you were firing at him sort of got his goat. You'll acccpt my guarantee, I guess. Now let's get down to brass tacks."

Sergeant Riordan shifted his attention to the business man.

"Who did you say you were?"

"I'm Angus K. Gordon, Gordon Exporting Company, 201-203 Center Street. I live at 5567 Courtney Avenue, own my own house, and am a taxpayer."

"Got anything on you to prove it?"

Mr. Gordon flushed, hesitated a moment, then reached in his coat pocket.

"Here's some letters. Here's my passbook at the bank. Here's my driver's license and my automobile license receipt. Here's my lodge card."

Riordan looked at the proffered papers and passed them back.

"All right, Mr. Gordon. Now, first off I want you to answer me this: Why didn't you report this robbery to the police when it happened; say a week ago Monday, anyway, when you probably discovered it?"

"There were reasons, sergeant."

"Well, what were they?"

"We weren't sure, at that time, as to whether it was a robbery or not. In fact we didn't discover it till later in the week. Then, even, I didn't want to be unjust to—to a certain party—so I had Lacey here investigate it."

"Lacey works for you, does he?"

"Yes, he's my confidential clerk."

"Been with you long?"

"About eight years—he's all right. I'll vouch for him."

"All right, Mr. Gordon, now tell me your story."

"I'd rather have Jed, here, tell you. Go ahead, Jed."

"On Tuesday, the fifteenth of the month," began Lacey, somewhat as a schoolboy recites a lesson, "Mr. Gordon called me into his office and told me some of the firm's funds were missing, and asked me to investigate the matter quietly. Mr. Gordon's office is on the second floor of the warehouse building that the Gordon Exporting Company occupies, situated in the rear of the premises.

"Opening from his office is a storeroom, in which we keep the firm's records and also holding a safe in which we always keep a considerable sum of money to use in emergencies such as often arise in our business.

"This storeroom has no other door save that which leads from Mr. Gordon's office. There is a hallway passes along in front of Mr. Gordon's office, leading to the stairway, and between this hallway and the rear of the building are the other offices of the firm.

"The rooms are arranged as follows, from the rear wall: first, this storeroom I have mentioned, then Mr. Gordon's office, then an anteroom in which I have my desk, and then the general offices where the several clerks have their desks. The rest of the building is given over entirely to warehouse purposes.

"All these rooms have inter-connecting doors, and all of

them, except the storeroom, also have doors opening onto the hallway, which runs the full width of the building. The rear of the building abuts on the alley between Center and Commerce Streets and there is a fire escape on the rear wall, opposite the general offices.

"The stairway is at the south end of the building, and leads down to a hallway on the street floor that has doors both on Center Street and on the alley. There is also a freight door opening on the alley on the ground floor; and at the north end of the building there is a hydraulic freight lift that runs from the basement to the third floor. That will give you, I think, the layout of the premises. I have a rough sketch of the second floor here."

He placed the paper on Riordan's desk, and hitching his chair forward, went on with his recital.

"After calling me into his office and telling me that some funds were missing, Mr. Gordon asked me to check over the books and see just how much money ought to be on hand in the safe, and then to check over the currency and coin in the safe and see if his suspicions were correct. This I did, and the books showed there ought to be nine thousand and twelve dollars in the safe.

"Checking over the money in the safe, I found there was only one thousand, five hundred and twelve dollars there, showing a shortage of exactly seven thousand, five hundred dollars.

"I so reported to Mr. Gordon, and he said my figures agreed with his, substantiating his suspicion. He then told me to investigate the matter further, but to be very sure of my ground before I reached any decision, as he said he did not want to accuse, unjustly, any of the clerks."

"What made you think one of the clerks had taken this money? Why not a burglar?" asked Riordan.

"I am coming to that, sergeant. Every morning when I come down to work, at eight o'clock, I go carefully over the building. Up to the time Mr. Gordon told me of his discovery and suspicion I had noted nothing irregular about the windows or doors. The warehouse is also protected by district telegraph wires, and there had been no report of the burglar alarm going off at any time.

"Also nothing had been disturbed anywhere about the premises, so it was evident that the robbery had been committed by somebody who was familiar with the interior arrangements, and by somebody who had keys with which to enter the building. In other words, it was evidently what you would call an 'inside job.'

"This very much simplified my investigations. Mr. Gordon employs ten clerks besides myself. Only two of them have keys to the building, and only one of them carries a key to the safe. And very probably only two of them knew there was any considerable amount of money in the safe."

2

"YOU GOT A key to the safe, too?" interrupted Riordan.

"Yes, sergeant."

"A key all you need to get into the safe? What kind of a box is it, anyway?"

"It is an old safe, very old. It has a combination-knob for the outer doors, and a key for the inner doors. The combination was working properly, so it was evident that whoever had taken the money knew the combination, as well as had a key to the inner doors. Aside from Mr. Gordon and myself, the only man in the firm's employ who knows the combination and who has a key is the cashier. Therefore my suspicions were naturally immediately directed to him."

"You think it's wise to keep nine thousand dollars odd in a can like that?" asked Riordan.

Mr. Gordon laughed testily. "It's been safe all these years. Nobody outside my confidential employees knows we have any special amount of money there; we do most of our business by check. And I've always prided myself that I had honest employees."

"Many a man is honest up to five thousand dollars," commented Riordan. "When you get over that sum you want to watch it; take it from me. Go on: you suspected the cashier, and I suppose you laid over him?"

"I investigated his movements thoroughly, sergeant," resumed Lacey. "I could not, as you say, 'lay over him,' because he was out of the city. But I looked closely into his affairs, and I found—"

"Say," exploded Riordan, "what are you trying to give me? Your cashier blows town and you miss seven thousand, five hundred, and all you do for ten or twelve days is look closely into his affairs? And you say you can't wait till to-morrow to get action on this case! Come on, tell me the rest of the joke."

"I don't like your manner, sergeant. If you will restrain yourself I will tell you the facts; but I must tell them in my own way. The facts of the matter are these: our cashier, Abner Wallace, was married on the evening of Saturday, the twelfth of the month. Both Mr. Gordon and I were at the wedding.

"Following the ceremony Wallace and his bride left on their honeymoon, and we bade them good-by at the door of his home, supposing they would take the nine o'clock train for Clear Lake, where they were planning to spend the next ten days.

"Mr. Gordon had closed and locked the safe Saturday afternoon, and the money was intact in it then, as far as he knows. This would seem, therefore, to preclude the possibility that the cashier had anything to do with the robbery."

"What makes him think the money was there Saturday afternoon?"

"Because he took from the inner compartment of the safe a wedding present for the bride. He had the present in the money compartment, and he says the compartment was full, apparently, at that time. Wallace had quit work at noon that day, to prepare for the ceremony, and had particularly insisted on checking his accounts that morning, before he went away."

"He checked them with you?" asked Riordan.

"Yes, we went over the books and money together. He checked them with me, because I was going to assume his duties while he was absent."

"Uh-huh—go on."

"Well, sergeant, as I was saying, I investigated his movements thoroughly. There appeared to be nothing suspicious until I discovered that he and his bride did not take the nine o'clock train, but went to a hotel instead, and did not leave for Clear Lake until Sunday morning. While I was loth to suspect him of this crime, that seemed to me to be a curious circumstance, and so I looked further into his affairs.

"On Thursday, the seventeenth, there was deposited in the Merchants & Traders Bank the sum of seven thousand, five hundred dollars to the account of A. Wallace.

"Discovering this, I felt it my duty, as an investigator, to look further and closer into Wallace's private affairs; for in the meantime my investigation of the other employees of the firm had shown conclusively that none of them could be in the slightest way concerned in the robbery.

"On Saturday of last week, therefore, I went to Mr. Wallace's home, Number 24 St. Mark's Place, and told his parents that he had telegraphed me to get some of his shirts and express them to him, and so obtained access to his room. While rummaging about I found a pair of tennis shoes, on the soles of which were traces of red paint.

"Wrapping up these shoes with his shirts I took them

down to my office in the Export Trading Company building and considered the possible significance of the red
paint. It was this: the fire escape on the rear of the building
had been recently repainted, first with a coating of red-lead
paint and then with black.

"By consulting my books I was able to discover that the
fire escape was given its first coat on Friday, the day before
Wallace was married, and that the second, or black, coat
was put on on Monday. Therefore if the red-lead paint had
not dried thoroughly by Saturday night, and if Wallace
had entered the building via the fire escape Saturday night,
the shoes he wore would be apt to bear traces of this paint.

"Also it seemed plausible to me that if he had gotten
paint on his shoes coming into the building that way, there
might be tracks in red paint still discernible upon the floors
or window casing.

"I therefore used a magnifying glass and went over
the floors of the offices thoroughly, and was rewarded by
finding a fairly distinct trail of red paint marks from the
window in the general offices opening onto the fire escape,
through the general office to Wallace's desk, then through
my office, and in the storeroom over to and in front of the
safe.

"There were no marks in Mr. Gordon's office, because
there is a carpet on that floor. This seemed a promising
development, so after marking the red paint traces on the
floor with chalked rings, I went to Mr. Gordon's house and
told him, and he came down to the warehouse and verified
my discoveries.

"Sunday morning we both of us called at the Wallace
home, and there managed to learn, by adroitly framing

the conversation, that Wallace had surprised his people by an early morning visit Sunday, saying he had forgotten his fishing rod the night before and wanted to take it with him. He went to his room to get it, and then hurried away to catch the morning train to Clear Lake.

"He was due to return to work last Tuesday, but Monday morning we received a telegram from him from Clear Lake saying Mrs. Wallace was ill, and that he would not be home until Thursday night, and would be at work Friday morning. Thursday is to-night, and the train is due at half past ten.

"That is why we have called on you—we want you to send an officer with us, and we will point him out to you, and you will arrest him and hold him to-night. To-morrow we will apply to the district attorney's office for a formal warrant. Those dots, there on that sketch plan of the offices you have, indicate the spots where I found the red paint trail."

Riordan looked again at the drawing and nodded his head.

"You happen to have the incriminating shoes with you, too?" he asked.

"I have."

Lacey reached into the pockets of his coat and drew out two worn tennis shoes, with rubber soles, which he passed to Riordan. The detective sergeant looked at them closely, and placed them on his desk, on top of the sketch of the offices.

"Tell me some more about this fellow Wallace," he said.

Lacey drew out his wallet and took from it a small photograph, and handed that over.

"There's a rather good picture of him," he said. "He is twenty-five years old now. He has been with Mr. Gordon for four years, since he was twenty-one. His uncle, his father's brother, was a former partner of Mr. Gordon's, and he wanted the young man to enter the same business. Mr. Gordon feels this defection of his keenly."

Sergeant Riordan swung slowly round in his chair and reached for his desk phone. Taking the receiver from the hook he said:

"Gimme Central—hello—hello! Main, seven-six-nine-two, please—yes—hello—this is Riordan talking; put on your street clothes an' come down here, I got a job for you—yes—good-by."

He hung up, and swung back to face his callers.

"I'll have a man here pretty soon for you," he said. "He'll go down to the train and see if this Wallace party's on board. You think he'll come back, do you? Don't think he'll try and run out on you? Looks to me like this sick wife telegram might be a stall."

"No, I think he'll be back. You see, I don't think he suspects that we have the slightest idea he committed this robbery. I think, from my investigations, that he believes he has done something very clever, and that this seven thousand five hundred dollars is safely hidden away."

"It's funny, a young fellow, just gettin' married, would take a fool chance like that," said Riordan. "He might know he'd be caught."

Mr. Gordon wagged his head. "I can't understand it, sergeant. I was going to take him into the firm, later on, too. It was a great shock to me. But the evidence Lacey has found seems conclusive, doesn't it?"

"Well, sir, I wouldn't go so far as to say that. But it's pretty good. Take my advice, however, and don't have your office floor washed for awhile. You may want a jury to see those paint spots."

"I've instructed the clerks not to walk where the chalk marks were," said Gordon. "Told them we were figuring on some electrical work, and the marks were for the estimators. But the clerks could corroborate their locations, if that was necessary."

The telephone jingled, and Riordan reached for it.

"Hello! Yes, this is Sergeant Riordan. Oh, yes, chief— yes. Yes, that's right—yes—all right!"

Putting the instrument down, he made a notation on a pad upon his desk, and then turned back to his callers.

"You say you don't think the evidence is conclusive?" asked Lacey. "Why not, may I ask?"

Riordan smiled. "I'm not a psychologist," he answered. "I'm just a police officer. I'm not saying you haven't done a thorough job of investigating, though I wouldn't have done it just that way. And I'm not saying you haven't hooked up a pretty plausible account of what may have happened.

"Maybe you could get by with a jury, if you had a good prosecutor, and if the prisoner didn't have too good a lawyer. But as far as I can see, yet, you haven't hooked up this fellow Wallace with actual possession of the money. At the bank now, where you discovered he had an account, do you reckon the teller could identify him?"

"He gave me a pretty good description of him. I didn't tell him why I wanted to know, just asked about the account."

"How'd you happen to light on the Merchants & Traders?"

"I tried all the banks, systematically."

"You did, eh? That was good work. How'd you go about it, whom did you ask, I mean? Go to the 'W' window in each case?"

"No, sergeant. I went to one of the officers. Told them I was from Mr. Gordon, and was looking for a new account, recently opened, of approximately seven thousand dollars. I gave the impression I was trying to check on a client's financial standing."

"Any of the banks suggest you go to Dunn or Bradstreet?"

"They made that suggestion at some of them, yes. At the one where I found the account, they told me about it."

"What gave you the idea the man would bank the money?"

"From observing him, I got the impression he would work that way, if he ever turned crooked."

"You never got the impression, though, beforehand, that he might turn crook?"

"No, I can't say that I did."

3

THE DOOR TO the office opened and Captain of Detectives Brady entered. There was nothing about his appearance to suggest he was the head of the department. He had received Riordan's telephone message to put on his street clothes and come on down—given in an unusual manner.

He had almost immediately called back and asked his aid if there was some reason for his request, and if there was also a reason why he should conceal his identity; to which Riordan had answered in affirmative monosyllables. So on entering the room, he stood at a somewhat slouchy attendance, as detectives were in the habit of doing when summoned for instructions.

Riordan nodded to him, passed him the photograph of Wallace and said:

"Take this picture and go down to the depot and get this guy. He'll likely be on the ten thirty train from the high line. Probably have a woman with him, and a fishing outfit. Bring him and the woman up here."

"Yes, sergeant."

"Don't be rough with him. Give him a song and dance; tell him who you are, and say you want him here to explain a little matter. I'll be here."

"Yes, sergeant," answered Brady, turning toward the door.

Mr. Gordon and Lacey rose, the former saying:

"Much obliged, sergeant. We'll go with the officer and point out the man to him."

"You sit down where you were," rasped Riordan. "I want to talk some more to you."

Mr. Gordon, somewhat surprised, sank back in his chair. Lacey kept moving toward the door.

"I'd better go, anyway," he said. "The officer might miss him in the crowd from the train."

"Don't you worry none, Lacey," snapped Riordan. "If the man you want is on that train, my man'll bring him in. You sit down here."

Captain Brady stood by the door, his face blank. Lacey looked at him, then shrugged his shoulders and turned back to his chair. After he had seated himself, Brady walked from the room.

"Your proceeding strikes me as rather peculiar, sergeant, at least," said Lacey, giving evidence of being somewhat ill at ease.

"We police work differently from you investigators," answered Riordan. "You turned this case over to me, didn't you? Wanted me to get your man? Well, I'm going to get him—maybe sooner than you think, too."

Lacey and Gordon exchanged uncomfortable glances, and then gave their undivided and silent attention to the detective sergeant.

"You said you were planning on taking this fellow Wallace into the firm; tell me about that," Riordan requested.

"Why, he—why, he seemed to be a promising young man," said Gordon. "I'm getting old, and the business needs a partner if it's to be carried on. Wallace—Wallace impressed me favorably."

"This man of yours here"—pointing to Lacey—"said Wallace was the nephew of your former partner. Where's your partner now?"

"He's dead. Died four years ago."

"Leave a will?"

"Why, certainly."

"What did he do with the interest he had in your firm—who'd he leave it to? You?"

"No."

"Well?"

"His will directed that the partnership should continue, and that his share of the earnings be paid to his widow. His stock in the company—he held fifty per cent of it—he directed should be held in trust for his nephew, who was to receive it when he married."

"Then, as a matter of legal fact, this man Wallace is your partner now, eh?"

"We haven't turned the stock over to him yet."

"But as a matter of fact, the minute he married, that stock became his property, didn't it?"

"I suppose so."

"How much is the stock worth?"

"Twenty-five thousand dollars, on its face. Probably its actual value is more."

"Well, then, as a matter of fact, if he took this money as Lacey here has figured it out, after he was married, he was your partner and had a perfect license to take it, didn't he?"

Mr. Gordon's face lost its gathering frowns, and the

increasing anxiety that had been growing in his eyes vanished. He even smiled slightly and cast a look at Lacey.

"Oh, I see what you are trying to get at now, sergeant," he said. "I didn't understand the reason of your questions before. Yes, I suppose he had a legal right to take the money—that is, to take it openly. That might be made a point in his favor in his trial, anyway. But you must remember he did not take it openly.

"He entered the place by stealth, in the nighttime, as a burglar, and he stole the money as a thief steals, and then endeavored to sequester it to his own credit in a bank where he was not known. You must remember, sergeant, that it is not only what a man does that counts, but the manner in which he does it.

"For example, if you and I were standing close together and I struck at a mosquito, and in swinging my arm, also struck you, that would be an accident. But if I deliberately struck you, intentionally, and merely claimed to have been striking at a mosquito, that would be assault. You see the difference?

"In this case this man stole that money secretly, entering the premises like a thief. Besides, he has not yet been given his stock. I was going to attend to that after he came back from his honeymoon—if this thing had not occurred."

"You've got the stock then?"

"It is in my safety deposit box, at my bank."

"Yet the will provided he was to get it when he married?"

"The will didn't say he was to get it at the ceremony."

"You think the fact that Wallace didn't leave town on the night train, after his wedding, but went to a hotel with his bride, is strange, do you?"

"I think it is incriminating evidence, in connection with the rest of the evidence Lacey's investigations have produced. It shows an intent to deceive as to his movements. It shows he had planned this thing out."

"When did you find out about the hotel?"

"Sunday morning, when we called at his home."

"Did you check on the hotel, to see if he left his rooms that night?"

"That would be hard to do," spoke up Lacey. "He probably left his wife in the room. In that case he wouldn't have turned his key in to the clerk. Or perhaps he took his key with him."

"Did you, in your investigations, try to find out that very important point?"

"No, sergeant, and I don't consider it important. It is very unlikely that the clerk would know of his movements—of the movements of any of the guests of the house."

Riordan snorted. "You don't know much about hotels, do you? Specially about newly-married couples in hotels. And you didn't think it was important to see if you could produce evidence that this man was out of the hotel at the time of the robbery; yet you thought it important enough to go buzz all the banks in town to see if he'd opened an account in them. Supposing he did open this account, how do you know he didn't have seven thousand five hundred dollars? Maybe somebody gave it to him for a wedding present."

"That would be a very strange coincidence, sergeant. However, as to the matter of the night clerk possibly noticing whether he left the hotel or not, I will check on that to-morrow. I see you think it important; possibly the district attorney will think it important, too."

Riordan laughed. "You ask him," he said. "You ask him whether he wants to issue a warrant for a man who may have a perfect alibi."

"But he could only have his wife to testify to a possible alibi, sergeant," interjected Gordon. "And her testimony would have no weight."

"So you and Lacey talked that over, did you?"

Mr. Gordon started to reply, then closed his mouth. Lacey frowned, and said hurriedly:

"Mr. Gordon and I have discussed every bit of evidence I have obtained, sergeant. He has weighed it all very carefully, for he was loth to take action in this matter until he was sure of his ground. The point you have raised, about Wallace being, perhaps, in effect, his actual legal partner, has, you see—"

4

THE DOOR OPENED, interrupting conversation, and Captain Brady entered, followed by a handsome young woman and a tall, smiling, pleasant looking young man.

"Mr. and Mrs. Wallace," said Brady. "This, ma'am, is Sergeant Riordan, my chief aid. You'll like him, and so will your husband. Boy, this is Mr. Wallace."

Riordan rose, bowed to the bride, and extended a hand to the young man, while Captain Brady dragged forward a couple of chairs. Lacey and Mr. Gordon made no move to greet the new arrivals.

"Mr. Wallace," said Riordan, "I had to have the chief, here, ask you to come up, for I've got a case on that I think you'll be interested in, and I had to act quick. I trust the captain explained?"

"He was very nice about it, sergeant. What seems to be the matter?"

"You know these two birds?"

For the first time Wallace took a look at the two men who were sitting almost out of his direct vision as he entered the door.

"Why, yes," he laughed. "Ought to. I've worked with Mr. Gordon for four years. I'm going to be his partner. The other is Lacey, his clerk."

He walked over to Gordon and held out his hand,

nodding at the same time to Lacey. Gordon did not take the proffered grip, however, and made no reply to Wallace's greeting.

"This is no family reunion, Wallace," said Lacey sternly.

"Now, let's all sit down and talk a little, folks," said Riordan. "You let me have my way in this, and we'll get it over quick."

As soon as Wallace had settled in his chair, his face reflecting his bewilderment, Sergeant Riordan turned to the bride, who evidently thought the gathering some kind of a joke.

"Mrs. Wallace," he asked, "after you and your husband went to the hotel the night you were married, did Mr. Wallace leave you for a little while—to go out and do an errand? I want you to answer me truthfully, please."

"Why, no, sir. No, no; he didn't leave me."

"Not until the next morning?"

"No—not until the next morning. He'd forgotten his fishing rod, and took a taxi home to get it, just before train time. Why?"

"Thank you, Mrs. Wallace."

Riordan turned round to his desk and picked up the tennis shoes with the red paint on the soles.

"Ever see these shoes before, Wallace?" he asked.

The young man bent forward and looked at them.

"Yes, sergeant. They are mine," he answered promptly.

"When do you recall seeing them last?"

"I can't just say, sergeant. They were in my closet at home. I don't recollect having used them since last fall."

"I guess that's right—there's dust a mile deep in them."

Mr. Gordon drew in his breath with a hissing sound. Lacey looked at the door.

"The door's no good, Lacey," said Riordan. "Room outside is full of dicks—not psychologists, either. If they saw you running they wouldn't be able to read your motives, they'd just take a shot at you. Window's no good, either— Cap'n Brady, here, would get in your way."

Wallace looked bewilderedly from Lacey to Gordon, then back at Riordan.

"Has—has Lacey done something?" he asked.

"I'm inclined to think he has, Mr. Wallace. Truth of the matter is, young man, your firm has been robbed of a little matter of seven thousand, five hundred dollars, as near as I can judge. Maybe Mr. Gordon here can give you the exact figures. But I think maybe we can get the money back. Don't you think so, Lacey?"

"If you're trying to fix this thing up—out of some mistaken motives of soft heartedness," said Lacey, savagely, "you'll find you can't do it. I demand that you arrest that man, Abner Wallace."

"*You* don't demand anything, not *you!*" snapped Riordan. "If that's the way you want it, I'll do a little demanding. Chief"—turning to Captain Brady—"these two birds blew in here to-night with as neat a frame as you'd see in a thousand years. You see, this young man here, Mr. Wallace, he inherits a half interest in Mr. Gordon's company when he gets married. Gets it from his uncle's will—uncle is Gordon's, former partner, who's dead, now.

"Gordon doesn't want to give up half the business, so he and this other man, Lacey, they get their heads together and try to frame a robbery so it would look like Wallace had done it. If they can prove Wallace is a crook, maybe they can gerrymander him out of the half interest; at least make him pay up to save his face, and so get some of his fifty per cent of stock away from him, so Gordon can control the firm.

"But they brought in too much evidence, and some of it wasn't any good. They had it all down pat, including footprints, and where the money was hid. This fellow Lacey is a psychologist, and he knows just how people act, he does. So he finds all the evidence he needs.

"Some of the evidence is these shoes—see that red paint on the bottom of 'em? Well, he says Wallace wore the shoes when he burglarized the place, and left a trail of footprints all over—like the dots on this here map of the place he drew. Says the prints didn't show on the carpet in Gordon's office. Look at the shoes."

Captain Brady held out his hands, and Riordan tossed the shoes to him. He held them up to the light, examining them, and slowly a grin spread over his face.

"Where's the red paint supposed to have come from?" he asked.

"Fire escape, painted six hours before, anyway; maybe longer."

Brady tossed the shoes to his aid.

"He doesn't know much about paint, does he? Nor about rubber soled shoes with corrugations in 'em; and what carpet does to paint in the valleys between the high spots," he commented.

"No," continued Riordan, "his psychology sort of slipped up on the paint. Lacey, sometime—when you're doing a stretch in prison, you step in some paint and then walk round and see what kind of footprints you leave—and how many of 'em—and how much paint will stay on your shoes. You'll be surprised at what you learn.

"Besides that, chief, he tells me how he went to all the banks in town and buzzed 'em till he found one where Wallace had deposited this seven thousand, five hundred dollars he stole. Being a psychologist, he can get information out of banks, he can. And he and Gordon, they talked over the alibi Mrs. Wallace might possibly give, too.

"They sure had a nice case. Personally. I think they figured on blackmailing the lad, here, out of his stock; but at that they might have been fools enough to think they could shove it over on the D.A. and get an indictment. You can never tell about these psychology chaps—they know so darned much; or think they do."

"Damn you!" shouted Gordon, suddenly turning on Lacey.

Captain Brady yanked him back into his chair.

"None of that!" he ordered.

Riordan turned to Wallace.

"Well, sir," he said, "it's up to you. I'm going to lock this man Lacey up for investigation. I can hold him for forty eight hours on that. And if you say so, sir, I'll lock up Gordon, too. But this money they've made believe steal, is on deposit at the Merchants and Traders bank, in the name of 'A. Wallace.' Lacey, he looks more or less like you, in a general way, and he probably had his hat pulled down over his face when he put it in there. I reckon you and Mr. Gordon can get it out.

"My advice to you, sir, would be to buy Mr. Gordon out and take over the business. He'll probably sell to you real reasonable if you coax him. I don't think you could get anywhere trying to prosecute him, but you might, at that. As for Lacey, I think we can take care of him for you—we can get rid of him, anyway, if Mr. Gordon and you don't care to file charges against him. What do you want me to do with Mr. Gordon—hold him, or let him out, so you and he can talk matters over at the office to-morrow?"

Wallace looked at his wife. She nodded her head.

"I guess you'd better let him go, sergeant," answered the younger man. "He never did like me—I could see that—but I didn't realize until now that the reason was that he didn't want to share the company with me. I guess, as you say, he'll be willing to make some sort of a deal with me.

"As for Lacey, we'll see. I'm very much obliged to you, sergeant, for defending me this way—why, I didn't even know I was in jeopardy till the captain, here, met me at the train. I think it's quite wonderful work."

"Just police work, sir. That's what we're here for—to catch crooks and protect honest folks. I'll call one of the police cars, sir, and send you and the missus home in it—don't be afraid, there'll be no signs on it. Later on I'll let Mr. Gordon go; I want to talk to him first about Lacey here."

"If you squeal on me," shouted Lacey, shaking his knotted fist furiously at Gordon, "I'll—"

But that was all of it, for Captain Brady grabbed him and bundled him out of the room.

www.ingramcontent.com/pod-product-compliance
Lightning Source LLC
Chambersburg PA
CBHW031155020726
47499CB00002B/377